AGAINST EVERY EXPECTATION

A PRIDE & PREJUDICE VARIATION

PAIGE BADGETT

Quills & Quartos
PUBLISHING

Edited by Jennifer Altman and Jo Abbott

Cover by Carpe Librum Book Design

ISBN 978-1-956613-14-8 (ebook) and 978-1-956613-15-5 (paperback)

For my Nani, Pinky—
the finest (albeit, most embellishing) storyteller I know

PROLOGUE

"You were cut at the assembly last night?" Lady Catherine asked, though it seemed a statement rather than a question to Charlotte Collins.

Unthinkingly, Charlotte bounced on the balls of her feet —which caused Lady Catherine to scowl at her with even greater fury—while her mind frantically chastised her body to keep its peace. It would not do to upset her husband or his patroness further. How was she to know what she had done to upset the woman? She had only lived in Kent for seven weeks and had not yet had the honour of making the acquaintance of the neighbourhood beyond their parish. While it was certainly a higher society than that around Meryton, she had believed being the wife of the parson would grant her some acceptance. But if the assembly was any indication, it seemed it did not.

Charlotte nodded in response to the grand woman, hoping that Lady Catherine would not force her to voice acceptance of the blame. She had no reply to satisfy the lady's enquiries. She kept her eyes trained on her disobedient feet, praying that Lady Catherine would be satisfied with the scolding and not require her to articulate her contrition.

She knew well enough that the social assault of which she had been a victim had likely more to do with her husband or Lady Catherine herself. When could she have had time enough to fashion herself an enemy? She had never even been introduced to Mrs Sykes! Never before had she been the recipient of wagging tongues and whispers at a social event. She might not have had the charms and graces of her Bennet friends, but she had always been well liked.

Charlotte's husband, the Mr William Collins, had been to the Sykes's home many times in the previous month, sitting at the bedside of the lady's mother-in-law as she nearly succumbed to an infection of the lungs. Should not Lady Catherine be addressing him? Charlotte glanced over at her husband, who nodded along and kept his obedient eyes trained on her ladyship's feet. He would surely know far better than she what might have upset Mrs Sykes. Why would he not speak up?

"Mrs Collins!" Lady Catherine thundered, and Charlotte's head snapped up.

"Pardon me, your ladyship; I was not attending," she responded rather more meekly than was her wont, attempting to keep her own counsel. When had she become such a ninny? Wool-gathering and fidgeting? She was never so inattentive, nor had she been taken to task in this way since she was a young child. Her mother and father were lackadaisical when it came to parenting, but on the whole, she had required no correction. She always did what was expected of her, consistently making rational choices—

including the marriage she found herself in. *Though of late that has not seemed so very rational at all!*

"As I was saying," Lady Catherine's voice cut through her thoughts once more. "I have given Mr Collins clear instructions about his role in this neighbourhood. As a clergyman and the recipient of the living in Hunsford, his actions—and by association yours, as his wife—reflect too on Rosings Park. It is not to be borne!"

Charlotte nodded once again.

"I advised Mr Collins to journey to Hertfordshire and bring home a wife—a gentlewoman—to set the example of marriage for the parish. Why he should bring home the daughter of a shopkeeper, I shall never know! But I shall endeavour to make the best of what he has procured."

Charlotte winced. She lifted only her eyes—eager to see if her husband would at the very least defend her social position—only to see him continue to nod in agreement. She looked back to her feet. Her father, Sir William Lucas, had been knighted during her childhood. Their years of trade had faded into a memory after her family's long acceptance into gentle society in Hertfordshire.

Lady Catherine was staring at her expectantly. Was she to nod again? Perhaps that was best. She should keep her mouth closed and accept the penance for whatever had brought her to this shameful moment in her life.

Nay, she knew what had brought her so low—her husband.

She was usually content to smile and nod while Mr Collins profusely thanked her ladyship for all her condescension, but she was approaching the limit of what she could tolerate. Before their marriage, she had assumed her husband would be quite malleable and easily guided by her, but Charlotte was not long in Kent before she recognised he was already ruled by one lady and would not be shifting his allegiance any time soon.

Her husband interrupted her thoughts to add in his own measure of reprimand. "Lady Catherine was quite clear, Mrs Collins. The wife of the Hunsford parson, even one of your humble standing, has an important and vital position in the parish. Our role is to set an example. Not only are we a connexion to our Heavenly Father, but I flatter myself, we can also help those in need of her ladyship's guidance."

Charlotte hoped he had finished, but he continued. "Just the other day I was able to provide a service to the Smith family in regard to their field that keeps taking water after each rain. It was brought to my attention that a dam had been built upriver to divert the water for a reflecting pool. It was Lady Catherine who took that information and identified that when the rain breaches the dam, it then comes pouring through other properties at unnatural speed. If it were not for my employment in service to our community and her infinite wisdom, I would not have been able to provide this important information to the Smith family, to explain to them why their property continues to flood."

Charlotte almost stomped her booted foot down on the marble floor. A childlike tantrum was building inside her and was going to pour out of every inch of her being at any moment. Suddenly it all made more sense. This type of interference that Lady Catherine enjoyed—silencing people's complaints and scolding them into harmony— surely engendered a vast amount of displeasure in the nearby villages and estates. This was likely why she had been cut at the assembly, for, having married Mr Collins, they all presumed to think her part of the problem. Charlotte was tired of being a sensible woman. She wanted to run down the lane back to the parsonage and rage about her home until everyone in her wake was as miserable as she.

Still, she held her tongue.

Lady Catherine sniffed and pressed on, "I take no pleasure in bringing my neighbours to task. But it is only right that I discovered what that Thomas Sykes was doing to my tenants. Why he should have need for a pretty pool of water in front of that dilapidated manor, I shall never know. Could he not have planted a rose garden for the enjoyment of his wife instead?"

In the end, Charlotte did not run all the way down the lane, but she did outpace her husband. She hoped dearly that he would give up the chase, but he huffed and puffed behind her, attempting to converse through his heavy breathing.

"My dear—" she heard between breaths. "Mrs Collins, please—"

His efforts only pushed her feet faster. She felt compelled to move quickly—the heat building in her cheeks was welcome on a blustery afternoon.

Charlotte threw open her front door and bypassed their startled maid as she flew up the stairs. She needed to think—merely a moment would do.

Charlotte walked with purpose into her room, eager to release the breath she was holding. As soon as the door was closed behind her, she fell back against it, panting. Hands on her hips, she bent at the waist and closed her eyes. *Calm yourself.*

The room seemed to tilt as she regained her composure. A few more deep breaths, and she was willing to part with the support of the door. As she stepped further into her chamber, her eyes went immediately to the lumpy fraying chair settled by the fireplace. What was it doing there? She had requested its removal weeks ago.

A deep breath did nothing to soothe her anger. She gritted her teeth and clenched her fists, preparing for a battle with her servants—or rather, Lady Catherine's appointed servants. She had little time to calm herself after she rang for her lady's maid, Hayes. The maid arrived moments later; she was attentive, Charlotte had to admit that.

"Hayes, can you please tell me where the settee and chair I selected for my chamber have gone?"

"Oh, yes ma'am. They were removed to the morning room just this afternoon at the master's request."

"And he asked you to move this chair back into my chamber as well?"

"Yes, ma'am."

She was careful not to show any emotion in response to that news, well aware that as agreeable as Hayes was, she no doubt reported directly to Lady Catherine. "That will be all. Thank you," Charlotte mumbled.

Yes, it appeared that would be all. Lady Catherine and her edicts were weaved into each thread of her marriage. It was, after all, kind that she had condescended to help decorate and prepare the parsonage ahead of Charlotte's arrival, but it did not follow that the lady of the house should not be allowed to make changes as she saw fit.

Lady Catherine beckoned Mr Collins to her estate nearly every day to provide a vast supply of recommendations varying from the way one should run their household, to reviewing each of his sermons, and even the ideal manner in which one might beget an heir—*detestable woman!*

The indignity of moving her furnishings about was nothing to when Lady Catherine had dismissed Charlotte's maid. Charlotte had gone to some effort to persuade her mother to part with Sarah and arrange her position and her travel—after all, it was rather customary for a woman to bring some dear servant with her when she married.

Unfortunately for Charlotte (and Sarah), Lady Catherine took one look at the maid and promptly had her removed from the household. She went as far as instructing Mr Collins not to pay that week's wage or to offer Sarah a sum to take the post coach back to Hertfordshire. Fortunately, Charlotte had enough in her reticule to provide the needed funds, for surely Sarah did not. Fury had made her hands shake as she handed her the money, and she could not meet Sarah's eye as she stammered out an apology.

That moment had been the first time Charlotte had seen what unkindness was possible in Mr Collins. He was more concerned with his appearance than his obligation to humanity, as should be the priority of a parson, should it not?

Her husband's patroness insinuated herself into their lives to a point where Charlotte felt she could not even breathe without Lady Catherine's authority. She should not have been shocked when her husband began a routine of only visiting her bed on Tuesdays and Thursdays, at the direction of her ladyship. The true surprise was that Mr Collins saw nothing amiss in allowing his patroness to insert herself into his marriage bed.

But this indignity—rearranging her furnishings without her knowledge—she could not bear in complaisance. Surely she had some say in the running of her own household. Charlotte descended the stairs and approached her husband's study. She paused to settle her breathing, then lifted her chin and ordered herself to behave with a modicum of dignity as she knocked on his door.

"Come," she heard from within.

He was still red in the face from his efforts to catch her on their walk home and did not look pleased to see her.

"My dear." He did not stand but instead nodded at the seat in front of his desk.

"I have come to speak to you about the recent changes to the furnishings in my chamber."

"Oh yes, that." He flicked his hand in the air, dismissing any cause for concern. "Lady Catherine believes those two pieces were shown to a greater advantage in the morning room. I do believe she is right. Should she deign to visit our humble abode, I am certain she will be pleased to see the room restored to her original scheme."

"I see."

"She did tell me before I left for Hertfordshire that if I brought home a wife to Kent, she would condescend to visit her, and I do flatter myself that she has visited weekly since your arrival." He smiled contentedly. "You are most fortunate to receive her guidance."

"Yes, she has visited with regularity. I do wonder, however," she began carefully, "if you might allow me to select the furniture for my own bedchamber in the future."

"Oh, my dear, of course. Should her ladyship consider it necessary to make additional changes to our home, I would be pleased for you to participate. I cannot boast a great aptitude for furnishings and frippery and all those accomplishments of a young lady, so I will leave it to you."

But it did not sound as if anything would be left to her choosing, not while they were in Kent ruled over by the lady of Rosings Park in any case. Charlotte would have to wait until her husband inherited Longbourn. Once she returned to her childhood village, and was mistress of her own home, her life would no longer belong to the dragon down the lane. She thought longingly of such a day when she would be truly the mistress of a house.

"I have a letter here from my cousin," her husband said, interrupting her thoughts.

"Mr Bennet has written to you?"

"No. 'Tis my cousin Elizabeth who writes to request a visit to Kent. Of course, I will want Lady Catherine's guidance on hosting a guest so soon after our marriage. It is done, is it not, my dear? I wish I had seen to my correspondence before we were summoned to Rosings today. I should have liked to secure her opinion."

"Elizabeth wrote to you?" Charlotte asked, her confusion increasing.

"Well, no. That would be rather improper, would it not? No, my dear, she wrote to you to request a visit. I have been reviewing the letter. It seems there is some trouble at home, something about her mother—but no matter."

The indignity! Not only reading another of her letters without permission, but now acting upon its contents without consulting her. How was Charlotte to form a response? Of course, she did not want Elizabeth to visit them in Kent!

"I believe it was our intention to keep visitors at bay for some time, was it not?" she asked cautiously.

She had lately persuaded him to that opinion, stating that it was only right during the first bloom of marriage for a modicum of privacy, though the truth ran much deeper. Charlotte was certainly not eager for any of her family or friends to see what had become of her life. The shame surrounding her powerlessness was all too consuming. She had no desire for anyone to see her sunk so low, particularly when she had thought it such a triumph to have secured a husband at seven-and-twenty.

"You are correct, Wife. But I do think it would bode well for Miss Elizabeth to visit Kent. She could learn something from Lady Catherine should her ladyship condescend to honour us with an invitation during Miss Elizabeth's visit. Our Sunday invitations have come with some consistency since your arrival in the county. And if I may be so bold, I could provide much-needed influence to my young cousin."

Charlotte cringed. It was more likely he was interested in proving to her friend that she had made a great error in refusing his offer of marriage. How wrong he was. The visit would only solidify her confidence in her refusal.

Before leaving Hertfordshire, Charlotte had relentlessly begged Elizabeth to visit Kent at her earliest convenience, but that was before. Since her marriage, it had become clear this was not to her advantage, and she had called off any effort to secure her visit—or anyone's for that matter.

Her marriage was still young—not yet two months—but she had seen enough to foreshadow the many years of surrender and compliance required to keep the peace. And Elizabeth would never understand her choices.

"I am eager to hear what her ladyship advises regarding your cousin's visit," she finally muttered.

She had no more to say, so she rose and nodded to her husband, who had already begun to open another letter—likely another addressed to her. He had taken to not only dictating her replies to her own family and friends but had also been intercepting her post and only reading aloud to her the parts he deemed necessary. But knowing Elizabeth's correspondence was included made her stomach churn with bitterness and embarrassment.

It should be Elizabeth in this home, not she. By refusing Mr Collins's offer of marriage, Elizabeth had secured a vulnerable future for her mother and sisters. Charlotte would never shirk duty of that kind. Marrying Mr Collins had been an easy choice for her dutiful nature. And his position as

Hunsford parson was completely respectable—and even more so his future as master of Longbourn. To marry a landed gentleman—indeed, to marry at all!—was more than she had ever anticipated for herself, and so she had taken the chance with very little consideration. Death and marriage were the only sure methods for the gentry to secure a stable future. And for Charlotte, it was only to be obtained through marriage.

While she regretted losing her dear friend's esteem when she initially accepted Mr Collins, her current state of mind was that of anger, not regret. If Elizabeth had not been so self-interested, so painfully self-centred, as to refuse an offer of marriage that would have secured a certain future for her family, Charlotte would not now be living with this loathsome man. The isolation and submission which would often subdue her spirits were instead creating a raging ferocity.

Her visit is entirely unwelcome. She was too ashamed for Elizabeth to arrive and see how right her own refusal had been. *Selfish girl!*

If long discussions about the number of chimneys at Rosings Park had been her wont in life, she would have withstood it. Alas, the long list of things she was required to give up for the sake of her marriage had only compounded as the weeks went on: her dignity, her pride, and her patience, to name a few.

CHAPTER 1

E lizabeth Bennet was free. Finally, now that she had arrived in Kent, she might enjoy some time with her dearest friend, Charlotte, and some peace and quiet —away from her mother. She was filled with anticipation for the visit and took joy in unpacking her things about her room.

Hunsford Parsonage—Charlotte's new home since her marriage to Mr Collins—was a well-appointed, lovely cottage. As Elizabeth might have expected, the best aspect of the house was the view of the neighbouring grand estate, Rosings Park. Though she had only just arrived in Kent that day, Elizabeth had already been required to hide a multitude of smiles, as her cousin produced detailed stories, histories, and financial figures for all aspects of Rosings and his revered patroness, Lady Catherine de Bourgh.

Elizabeth was given a quaint guest room at the end of the corridor. Light filtered in through a generous window highlighting a comfortable window seat fitted with embroidered pillows and a soft throw. A simple quilt covered the bed, and an overly stuffed chair sat by the hearth. It was truly inviting. The room wanted only for spring to arrive more quickly so that fresh flowers could be placed on the escritoire that sat near the window. That slight, feminine piece of furniture stood in readiness for hours of attention, for it was already equipped with fresh paper and ink.

The view out of the window offered her a glimpse of the gardens that had figured heavily in Charlotte's recent letters. Looking at them made Elizabeth frown somewhat; in truth, Charlotte's letters—the few she had received—had been the messages of a stranger, detailing household matters and gardening plans rather than the confidences one would expect of an intimate acquaintance.

She had been unsure what to expect when she arrived but was relieved to see Charlotte in good spirits, if a bit subdued. Perhaps it was merely the conduct of a wife which had altered her. Elizabeth admitted to herself that the gardens seemed quite well organised. She could see the gentle paths through the rows of soil that would soon welcome vegetables, shrubs, and flowers. She hoped she would still be in Hunsford when the first bounty was brought into the house.

Charlotte's maid was assisting Elizabeth with her toilette when she heard a quiet knock on the door. She sighed with happiness when it was Charlotte who entered. It was their first moment of true privacy since her arrival.

"Hayes, you may go. I shall ring for you when I am ready to prepare for bed."

"Oh Charlotte!" Elizabeth exclaimed after the maid closed the door. "This is a lovely home. How well situated you are."

Charlotte smiled and sat next to Elizabeth on the bed.

"Our home is comfortable, and I am satisfied with my life here, though I have dearly missed you and news from home."

"I missed you as well—most fervently. I was so lonely at home without you or Jane. She has gone to London, did I tell you? And my mother! Charlotte, you would not believe the near constant whining and moaning since Mr Bingley and his party left Netherfield Park!" She grinned widely and let out a deep breath. "I am so grateful to be here."

Charlotte smiled warmly in response and clasped her hand. The moment reminded Elizabeth of sitting up at night with her elder sister, Jane, in their shared room, and filled her with a sense of tranquillity she had rarely felt since the autumn.

Elizabeth and Charlotte shared some quiet time together, mostly discussing news from Meryton. Charlotte was eager to hear of her own family and catch up with all the goings on from the neighbourhood. For an all-too-brief time, Charlotte seemed happy; it was the old Charlotte that Elizabeth had known since she was a young girl, and the doubts which Elizabeth had carried with her to Kent began to dissipate.

After a time, Elizabeth asked a question which would prove to be the wrong one. "Charlotte, did you not bring Sarah Johnson to be your maid? I expected to see her. Is she placed elsewhere in the home?"

Charlotte's demeanour changed almost instantly, the smile fading from her face as she lowered her eyes to her lap and removed her hand from Elizabeth's grasp. She paused for a moment before she spoke, saying, "Sarah has gone back to Lucas Lodge."

"But...I thought it was all arranged. Did your mother need her after all? Or is someone in her family ill?" Elizabeth enquired further. Mrs Bennet and Lady Lucas were close. She was surprised she had not heard of Sarah's return, though she had been carefully avoiding her mother for weeks.

"No, nothing of that nature. I believe her family is all in good health." Charlotte hesitated again, then said very carefully, "I have learnt that Lady Catherine prefers to select the servants for the parsonage. Something about the relative proximity to the estate and her knowledge of the area."

"So, you sent her back? So soon?" Elizabeth asked.

Charlotte waved her hand as if to brush away the small inconvenience, followed by a tight shake of her head and a frown that made it plain she had no wish to continue speaking of Sarah. Elizabeth was not convinced it was a matter to be dismissed but decided not to press her.

"Oh!" Elizabeth exclaimed, happy to introduce a subject that would countenance no confusion. "I nearly forgot." She made her way to her trunk and pulled out a small bundle of letters tied with a lavender ribbon. "Your mother asked me to carry these to you. I believe you will find one from each member of your family. I am certain—"

Charlotte quickly reached for the letters, cutting off Elizabeth's words, "Oh, I am so very eager to hear from home and appreciate you taking the trouble to bring them to me." She looked at the letters almost hungrily, shuffling through them to see who had written, her eyes dancing with joy.

How very odd! Charlotte's delight surprised Elizabeth. Surely it could not have been many days since her last correspondence from home, yet Charlotte had grabbed the missives out of her hand in a peculiar desperation. "It was no trouble, I assure you." She gave Charlotte's shoulder a friendly squeeze.

Charlotte rose from the bed, distracted and clutching the small bundle of letters. She smiled. "I shall leave you to your book. Do not distress yourself over burning the candle too long. Lady Catherine supplied beeswax candles for your use as I explained to her that you were a great reader. As you might imagine, she wished to spare you the excessive smoke of the tallow candles. Sleep well."

Charlotte left Elizabeth's room feeling bolstered by the strength of their friendship and ties to their past. She was comforted by a familiar face and a reminder of her previous existence. She had hoped seeing Elizabeth in person would relieve some of her bitterness, and it had.

It was very agreeable to stay up late talking to her friend, and she imagined the six-week visit might not be as bothersome as she had previously assumed. It lifted her spirits to consider the visit a much-needed respite.

Even Mr Collins had been quieter that evening and performed his duties with more restraint. He allowed the ladies to dominate the conversation at the dinner table, which was exceedingly unlike him. Of course, he said much, but he was less dictatorial.

And the letters from home! Charlotte was beaming as she approached the door to her chamber. Perchance this visit would be just what she needed to be more accepting of her new life! Once her correspondence was safely tucked into the locked drawer of her dressing table, Charlotte rang for Hayes.

"Come," Charlotte responded to the knock on her door.

Hayes helped her quickly prepare for bed. Once dismissed, the maid turned to tell her, "The master asked that I remind you that today is Tuesday, ma'am."

Charlotte attempted to keep a straight face while her stomach dropped, her nascent good spirits immediately gone.

"Yes, I daresay it is. That will be all for tonight then. Thank you."

Perhaps all would *not* be well—it seemed her life would be just as it had been before Elizabeth arrived.

Elizabeth woke at sunrise, as was her habit, eager to begin exploring the park on her first morning in Kent. After a day confined to a carriage, it was invigorating to move her feet and feel the cold morning wind on her cheeks. While she needed her pelisse, Elizabeth was pleased to see signs of spring's near arrival. The ground was hard and the branches bare, but tiny hints of new growth appeared all around her.

Elizabeth remained near the parsonage. Her breath formed a continuous cloud in front of her as she stretched her legs and travelled a few paths through the woods nearby. She would have ambled longer, as there were many new paths to explore, but she was disinterested in getting lost quite so soon after her arrival.

Elizabeth pushed open the breakfast room door with energy, rosy cheeked from the recent exercise. She was famished.

It was a surprise to find her cousin and Charlotte still breaking their fast. "What a beautiful morning!" she greeted them with a fervency not mirrored by her hosts, and she found herself stopping short of the table, looking back and forth between the couple.

Charlotte did not look up from her plate as she softly greeted her guest. Mr Collins' stern countenance provided some warning to the strange tension in the air. Elizabeth gently took a seat and waited for a clue that might explain her reception.

Mr Collins broke the silence, "Cousin, as you know, I am responsible for your welfare while you are in Kent. Your father has entrusted me with your safety. Mrs Collins was unaware of your plans to take a walk this morning, as was I." His eyebrows gathered, and he shot a quick glare at Charlotte, who simply nodded and averted her eyes. He continued his speech, "I shall expect to be in full knowledge of your whereabouts while you are our guest. I daresay, that should be an easy enough task, should it not?"

Elizabeth darted her eyes to Charlotte for some guidance on how to reply and found her friend pushing food around on her plate. Charlotte's eyes were glazed over with a nothingness she had not seen there before. Aware that her natural teasing would not do this morning, Elizabeth hesitantly began, "As you wish, Mr Collins. I shall inform you or Charlotte when I plan to walk out in the future."

He looked smugly pleased with his efforts. "Thank you." He left the room with a satisfied grin and one last look to Charlotte, which Elizabeth perceived to be a warning of some sort.

Once he was gone, Charlotte invited Elizabeth to help herself to some food and join her in the back parlour when she had finished. Elizabeth ate quickly, eager to see what could be done to ease her cousin's frustration.

When Elizabeth joined her, Charlotte was already working on a basket of mending. Elizabeth offered to help and settled in beside her friend.

The first garment Elizabeth pulled out of the basket was a shirt belonging to her cousin. It was large and the seams frayed. A slight yellowing could be seen around the neck and the underarms. Elizabeth attempted not to grimace while she quickly exchanged the shirt for a pair of stockings.

Once she had begun working, she said, "Charlotte, I am sorry if I have caused any trouble for you this morning."

Charlotte kept a staid expression on her face, but said nothing, merely continuing to stitch evenly and steadily. After a few awkward moments of silence, Elizabeth tried again. "You know I love to walk in the mornings. I shall be certain to tell you or someone in the household when I plan to ramble about."

"Thank you," Charlotte said, still not raising her eyes from her work.

"As you know, I have always been allowed to walk out in the mornings when at home. Shall I leave a note each morning? Or, perhaps, I can inform your cook if you are not yet awake?"

"Either would suffice." Charlotte sighed and dropped the shirt she was mending to her lap, evidently wishing an end to the conversation. "You need not alter your personal habits on my account. I am certain I cannot keep you from your morning rambles, and I will not; but please do stop looking at me that way. All is well, Eliza."

It certainly did not seem as if all were well, but Elizabeth could sense that the conversation was quite finished.

In her eagerness to leave Longbourn, Elizabeth had given very little thought to her concerns for Charlotte. While she and Charlotte had rarely sent letters to one another in the past due to their close proximity, she had instinctively known something was remarkably altered. Even knowing this, her frustrations with her mother had outweighed her concerns.

Elizabeth was blamed for not accepting Mr Collins, and Jane had taken herself off to London to avoid her mother's disquiet over her failure to secure the affections of Mr Bingley. Elizabeth had been happy for her sister but had not fully comprehended how miserable her home would become in Jane's absence. And so, she had requested—nay, begged—Charlotte to invite her to Kent.

Elizabeth was not designed to be unhappy. Even if the air in the parsonage felt stifling with peculiar tension, and even if Charlotte was clearly not herself, Elizabeth made every effort over the next week to be an easy guest, providing stories from home and being helpful to her hosts.

She assisted Charlotte with the mending in the mornings, commented regularly on Mr Collins's garden preparations when they were at the table, but more often than not, she generally gave a wide berth to both Collinses.

It appeared they too gave each other much space. Mr Collins spent his days in his garden or monitoring those who travelled Hunsford Lane from his study, while Charlotte spent much of her time in the back parlour, which faced neither the lane nor the garden. Elizabeth surmised this was by design as there was a very fine morning room at the front of the house that went wholly unused.

Charlotte was not swayed to cheerfulness by Elizabeth's humour as she had been in the past, and as the first week of her visit wore on, Elizabeth found herself adopting a sedate attitude, attempting to emulate her sister, Jane, who was always tranquil and demure. Surely her efforts at false serenity would allow her visit to pass peaceably. Elizabeth hoped they would. Efforts to placate her mother's histrionics were often successful when she adopted the appearance of quiet submission.

The finest morning that week was the one during which Charlotte visited Rosings Park to practise on the pianoforte in the servants' wing. During those glorious hours, Elizabeth read, relaxed, and took an unreported and unsupervised turn about the garden.

Beyond that glorious morning, Elizabeth had continued her early rambles in accordance with her cousin's strictures, informing the cook, Mrs Montgomery, of her plans before she went. She enjoyed the plump and petite woman and looked forward to their friendly early morning conversations about the neighbourhood gossip and, of course, anything related to Mr Collins.

Discovering Mr Collins's love of onions was a surprise, but it did rather explain his pungent odour. Elizabeth humoured herself by composing little witticisms about the irony that a man who smelt so much like an onion should have so few layers. Like the offensive vegetable, he did seem to leave all in his purview red-eyed and weeping. Sadly, there was no one who desired her humorous observations. *Dreadful indeed to have such clever thoughts and no one to share them with!* Elizabeth thought to herself with a small smile.

The later part of the week trapped everyone indoors due to unrelenting rain. Mr Collins was particularly glum to be deprived of his daily walks to the nearby estate, and their regular invitation to dine at Rosings Park for Sunday dinner was not dispatched. It was hard to combat Elizabeth's restlessness, but she was not distraught. A change of scenery would come when the weather improved. *I suppose I shall have to wait another week to meet the grand Lady Catherine.*

CHAPTER 2

Hunsford Parsonage, Kent
March 16, 1812

My dearest Jane,

I have now been a se'nnight in Kent. I must apologise for being so long in sending news of Charlotte and our cousin, Mr Collins. The parsonage is a charming home, and Charlotte assures me she is quite comfortable here. I have seen the famed gardens and can expect to be invited to dine with Lady Catherine de Bourgh while I am here. I am all anticipation to see the great lady herself.

Pray excuse my thoughts I shall share forthwith, for I do seem to have much time to think here in Kent…I have long promised you that a certain gentleman once of Netherfield and now of London would no longer cause me worries or anxieties as they relate to you, but dearest sister, I cannot help but continue to be utterly vexed. Of course, I know you are endeavouring to banish all painful thoughts as it pertains to this particular man and his deceiving sisters (and, no doubt, a deceiving gentleman from Derbyshire as well), but I will not be silent today. I cannot believe a partnership with Miss D was instrumental in his departure. Perhaps that scheming sister of his should make more efforts to finally achieve her own matrimonial goals and thus eliminate his obligation to join the two great families?

I do wonder about Mr D's part in this business of separating such a beautiful couple. It is rather a mystery. I know you would tell me to quit my study of the situation and let your heart be—but I do lay this before their feet, whether or not you agree.

What more shall I tell you of Kent? Mr Collins does spend much time in the garden, but he is often summoned by Lady Catherine to visit the estate for various reasons. Should she bid him to bring her a silk shawl from India, I am certain he would be found aboard a great ship bound east within a fortnight, as he is ever her loyal subject.

I can say this with certainty after my first week in Hunsford—though our situation in life is not enviable nor ideal, we neither of us can accept a marriage without love, my dearest sister.

Yours affectionately,
Elizabeth

E lizabeth's second week in Kent passed much the same as the first until one afternoon when, while the ladies were having tea, Mr Collins burst into Charlotte's parlour in high dudgeon. He appeared to have run there; perspiration was beaded on his forehead, and the smell of him filled the room. He rested his hand on the mantel, bending over to catch his breath—papers crumpled in his hands, his face beet red—while the two ladies awaited some explanation for his precipitous arrival.

Once he had caught his breath, he turned on the ladies and thundered, "How have you allowed me to present this sermon to her ladyship today?"

Charlotte's mouth dropped agape for a moment before she quickly repressed any shock, but Elizabeth permitted herself the full display of her incredulity.

"My dear," Charlotte began but was quickly silenced.

"Have I not afforded you the privilege of hearing me speak? In my own parlour, I have condescended to provide you with my words, my thoughts, yet you cannot prevent me from provoking the displeasure of Lady Catherine?"

Without the ability to know her ladyship, Elizabeth had not a guess at her complaints. She knew what she herself disliked about Mr Collins' sermons—they were all arrogant and dull—but could not guess if her ladyship felt likewise.

It was a Palm Sunday sermon, was it not? Elizabeth mused. *Jesus entered Jerusalem. They waved the palm branches. What could Mr Collins possibly have altered to cause such distress? Perhaps it was his weaving the subject of female virtue into the story of Jesus's victorious entry into Jerusalem?* Elizabeth was required to cough in order to cover an obstinate snicker.

Elizabeth glanced at her friend curiously. Charlotte's eyes were lowered, and she was apologising, rather abjectly, for her error, but Mr Collins was not mollified. He scolded her like a child, and Charlotte's countenance went from an embarrassed pink to a mortified pallor while he went on about how her negligence had likely cost them her ladyship's favour. Sadly, Elizabeth watched her dear friend relent, nod, and assure her husband she would be more perceptive in the future.

Ridiculous, presumptuous man! Elizabeth fumed, wanting to defend her friend, but beginning to understand that any action she took against her cousin would no doubt also affect Charlotte. Her current practice of nodding along to her cousin's manifold long-winded speeches was keeping an escalation at bay, but it would not do. Mr Collins was a fragile creature whose ego required constant soothing, and who was nearly always on the precipice of a fit. Elizabeth's disdain of him grew daily, and the act of subduing her annoyance was beginning to grate upon her nerves.

Before Mr Collins left them, he delivered one last bit of news given with the air of someone conferring a grand consolation. "Do not fear," he said. "She has not withdrawn her invitation to dine on Sunday."

"That is very good of her," Charlotte said; but though her words were enthusiastic, her aspect was not. Elizabeth echoed some syllables of agreement though she could not imagine that any lady who inspired such terror and subjection would be a pleasure to dine with.

Elizabeth excused herself soon after her cousin and made her way down into the kitchens. Mrs Montgomery slipped her a slice of cake, and Elizabeth pulled up a stool to the table where the cook was cutting vegetables.

Mrs Montgomery reminded her of Longbourn's housekeeper, Mrs Hill. She was astute about the goings on of the home and the village, but perceptive enough to keep her thoughts to herself when Mr Collins was about.

"What is the matter with the master today?" Mrs Montgomery asked with a knowing gleam in her eye.

Elizabeth rolled her eyes and sighed. "Mrs Collins and I are unable to read minds, madam."

"Aye, miss. Mr Collins would find that unsatisfactory indeed," Mrs Montgomery responded. She lowered her voice to continue on, "I do worry about Mrs Collins. I hope she will find more friends like yourself, miss. It will be hard for her here. Most folks 'round here do not take lightly having the great lady at Rosings in their affairs."

"I cannot imagine they would."

"I heard the mistress was snubbed at the last assembly, poor thing. Her husband's duties require he call on parishioners, and he overheard details about a local quarrel while attending an ill neighbour. Took that information straight to her ladyship, he did."

Horrified, Elizabeth replied quietly, "I hope he did not create trouble for the family?"

"Aye, miss, he did. It were a squabble over a flooded field of apple trees. He caused a great deal of trouble by getting Lady Catherine involved. Would have been best to let them that was affected sort it out amongst themselves."

"But what can be done? I should speak to Charlotte. I cannot leave her here with no friends to attend her...maybe I shall encourage her to do some shopping with me, in hopes we might meet the villagers. Or we could make calls to her neighbours? I could help encourage a new friendship along. If they could meet her, they would know her acquaintance to be valuable! She is far more trustworthy than her husband."

Mrs Montgomery smiled and nodded her approval to such a scheme, but her eyes betrayed her doubt. Elizabeth was not certain it would help, but she did not like the idea of leaving Kent without knowing her friend enjoyed an alliance of some sort.

Mr Collins delivered a predictably dull sermon on Sunday morning. Elizabeth spent most of the service trying to study Lady Catherine without overtly staring—all while appearing attentive to the droning on of her cousin from the pulpit.

Charlotte visited Elizabeth's room while she was dressing for dinner and immediately complimented her gown. Elizabeth knew the simple muslin would be nothing to what Lady Catherine was used to seeing her visitors wear, but it was the finest she had brought—indeed, among the finest she owned.

Charlotte smoothed imaginary wrinkles in Elizabeth's skirts, appearing to be assembling her courage to say something.

"Thank you, Charlotte. I am eager to meet her ladyship," Elizabeth said, wanting to bolster her friend with a welcoming response.

"As you should be, Elizabeth. It is undeniably a great honour for you to meet Lady Catherine. Did you know she is the daughter of the late Earl of Matlock? The sister of the present earl, of course."

"Indeed?"

"Lady Catherine moves in the highest circles of society and thus has exceedingly elevated standards of etiquette, as you can imagine. I want to be sure you are aware of the expectation that you be punctual in your preparations to depart and also..." Here Charlotte paused, and Elizabeth watched her expectantly.

With a weak smile, Charlotte said, "I am sure your

natural wit and vivacity will be...will be tempered in her ladyship's presence? Her ladyship bestowed upon my husband the living at Hunsford, and we want to be sure you have only your best qualities on display. As our guest and a member of our family, your actions reflect on our character as well."

Elizabeth gaped at her friend—a playful retort was at the ready, but she hesitated. Charlotte appeared quite serious. In fact, she looked pleased to have finished her speech in such a concise manner. Elizabeth closed her mouth and simply nodded, never breaking eye contact. To have responded in contrition was unimaginable.

For not the first time, she wondered what had become of the friend she once knew.

At first glance, Rosings Park was just as Elizabeth expected—ostentatious and gilded, from the floors covered in exceptionally fine carpets to the painted, ornate ceilings. The opulent furnishings included elaborate mouldings, luxurious wall hangings, and furniture in velvet and silk, announcing that the house's rank, privilege, and wealth was valued over any indication of comfort. This place was an estate but could not be called a home. Liveried footmen attended the walls and doorways, and not one dared to raise their eyes to the visitors.

Lady Catherine de Bourgh was much like her house. She was a tall, large woman with strongly marked features. The lady was covered in lace—much like Elizabeth would imagine her mother would attire herself, could she afford it. She was not an appeasing woman—whatever she said was spoken in so authoritative a tone as marked her self-importance. It could be no surprise that this woman was one of Mr Darcy's relations.

Lady Catherine's daughter, Miss Anne de Bourgh, had a demeanour in opposition to her mother's. She was a tiny, frail lady—possibly in her late twenties. There was a quiet astuteness Elizabeth observed in her, though it was smothered by the many layers of shawls laid across her shoulders. With no wish to embarrass her friend, or to provoke her cousin, Elizabeth said as little as possible, and quietly observed the room. Miss de Bourgh was closely attended by her quiet but dutiful companion, an older woman called Mrs Jenkinson.

Lady Catherine had no scruple in questioning Elizabeth thoroughly about various aspects of her family and her upbringing; though none of it met with her ladyship's approval. The rest of the group said very little. Mr Collins was—for once—quiet, allowing Lady Catherine to hold court and entertain herself with Elizabeth's discomfort. Miss de Bourgh only nodded, and Charlotte appeared attentive but numb to the entire experience. The only people seeming to enjoy themselves appeared to be her cousin and the great lady herself.

At length, Charlotte was prevailed upon to exhibit. While Charlotte played the pianoforte, Elizabeth was finally free to let her mind wander, revisiting her friend's earlier admonitions about tempering her customary vivacity. She could not like that Charlotte had spoken to her so, but within the great parlour of Rosings, one could see the reverence—and yes, call it fear—that had inspired Charlotte to address her. She was so lost in her thoughts that she failed to hear Lady Catherine's address.

"Cousin!" Mr Collins scolded. "Her ladyship has just asked you a question!"

"Pardon me, Lady Catherine, I was distracted by the lovely performance."

Lady Catherine pursed her lips and nodded, "I always tell Mrs Collins that she must be dedicated to her practising. There are few people in England, I suppose, who have more true enjoyment of music than myself or a better natural taste. If I had ever learnt, I should have been a great proficient. I do believe Mrs Collins has improved since arriving in Kent."

"Yes, my lady," Elizabeth responded.

Lady Catherine looked appeased by her submissive words and attitude. "I was just telling Mr Collins to expect my two nephews to arrive this week for their annual visit. They are my late sister's son, Mr Darcy of Pemberley in Derbyshire, and the Earl of Matlock's son, Colonel Fitzwilliam."

Elizabeth stifled a gasp behind her teacup. *Mr Darcy! Here?* She ought to have done better to remain at Longbourn. Charlotte was an anxious and disinterested host, Mr Collins and his patroness appeared to be equally intolerable...and now she would suffer the company of Mr Darcy too? Likely not, Elizabeth decided. After all, Mr Darcy was no great friend of hers. She imagined he would keep to Rosings and pay no mind to the little group across the lane.

Was Miss Anne de Bourgh to be the primary beneficiary of his visit? Mr Wickham had mentioned that Mr Darcy and Miss de Bourgh were rumoured to be betrothed.

She glanced over to where Miss de Bourgh sat, her companion fussing over her shawl. Lady Catherine's daughter was as wan and disinterested as she had been all night with no evident excitement over the mention of Mr Darcy.

The evening was rather a disappointment overall. But later, after Elizabeth had prepared for bed, she began penning a letter to her father and found reason to be thankful that the evening had provided some interesting musings she could share with him. He had told her to write, though a response was unlikely.

She giggled in the candlelight as she described Lady Catherine's idea of entertainment and fell asleep later imagining her father's puckered lips and twitching eyebrows as he read her descriptions of Rosings Park. Her favourite part of the letter was the part about Miss Anne de Bourgh seeming bored by the notion of her visiting cousins, *'Perhaps she is as loath to see Mr Darcy as I am,'* she wrote. She did not finish the letter, assuming there would be many more reflections to add when the lady's nephews arrived.

CHAPTER 3

The arrival of Lady Catherine's nephews was known immediately to those at the parsonage. Mr Collins had spent the morning in great anticipation, watching the lane diligently for any unknown carriages bearing exalted personages. It appeared a trial for Charlotte to keep Mr Collins away from Rosings Park on the day of their arrival; however, on the following morning, he hastened to great house to pay his deepest respects.

To the great surprise of all, when Mr Collins returned home, Lady Catherine's nephews accompanied him. Charlotte had witnessed them crossing the road and immediately rushed to Elizabeth to tell her what an honour it was, adding, "I thank you, Eliza, for this piece of civility. Mr Darcy would never have come so soon to wait upon me. The gentleman's interest in you was clear in Hertfordshire. Undoubtedly, he will be no less captivated here in Kent."

Elizabeth had not a moment to respond or renounce all

rights to the compliment before three gentlemen—Mr Collins, Mr Darcy, and a man introduced as Colonel Fitzwilliam—entered Charlotte's parlour.

Elizabeth regarded Colonel Fitzwilliam with interest. He was charming and pleasant, bringing an ease to the small space they all shared. He was not nearly as handsome as his cousin, but his features warmed as he exhibited his effortless, friendly demeanour.

"Here I thought we would be bound only to sit and wait upon my aunt's visitors and tour her estate. I find myself much relieved to make new acquaintances during our visit to Kent," the colonel said with ease. "Is your acquaintance with my cousin a long one, Mrs Collins?"

"No, sir," Charlotte replied with perfect gentility. "We were introduced in Hertfordshire, where I hailed from before my recent marriage."

Elizabeth added, "We met Mr Darcy last autumn, while he visited his friend, Mr Bingley, who leased an estate near to my father's." She turned to Mr Darcy and said, "My sister has been in London these last three months. Have you never happened to see her there?"

Her question had two motives. She was eager to see if her sister had crossed paths with Mr Bingley. And further, she was eager to see if Mr Darcy was willing to acknowledge that theirs was more than a passing acquaintance.

But Mr Darcy said nothing; it was Colonel Fitzwilliam who replied, "Is that so? I doubt Darcy has seen your sister in London, Miss Bennet, for I have spent the last three months complete attempting to compel my cousin to join in some society with nary a success."

Mr Darcy looked on the conversation with an expression of surprise and discomfiture. *Could he not enjoy a little teasing?*

"My cousin is correct. I have not had the pleasure of

seeing your sister in London," Mr Darcy finally replied.

"I had it from Jane in my last letter that she called upon Mrs Hurst and Miss Bingley," she added. "Perhaps you have word from your friend?"

Mr Darcy murmured he had not.

"As I was telling you before, my cousin has been something of a recluse this winter," Colonel Fitzwilliam said, tossing a grin at Mr Darcy. "I was shocked enough when he summoned me to his study to inform me we would make our annual pilgrimage to Kent. It was only with two days' notice that he deigned to tell me when we would depart."

A sound emerged from Mr Darcy that could only be described as a groan. Elizabeth thought it boded well for Mr Darcy to have such a cousin. Even a man of his standing would need someone in his life who added some levity.

Their discussion was interrupted by the arrival of the tea cart. "Eliza, will you pour?" Charlotte asked, and while surprised, Elizabeth did as asked.

Three lumps of sugar for Mr Collins and a splash of milk for Charlotte. She remembered how Mr Darcy preferred his tea as well; though he seemed surprised when she delivered a cup into his hands exactly as he favoured it before asking the colonel how he should like his tea.

Mr Darcy showed no more signs of liveliness than he had in Hertfordshire, sitting quiet and still with scarcely a sign of life to him. He had hardly uttered a word, though perhaps that was because her cousin had begun to speak too much to allow for others to contribute. He did, however, stare, his gaze jerking away when he caught her attending it.

She considered Charlotte's words, inferring the attention she received from Mr Darcy implied interest. Elizabeth knew this man thought her far below his notice. His intent gazes were most likely designed to find fault, if indeed they had any purpose at all. Almost certainly, they were a mere absence of thought.

But why had he come at all? It truly was an honour for the gentlemen to call so quickly upon their arrival. Perhaps it was merely a courtesy because of their recent acquaintance in Hertfordshire. Once they completed this visit, it was improbable she would see the gentlemen anywhere but church. It was unfortunate, too, because Elizabeth especially enjoyed the colonel.

Darcy stood at the appropriate hour to depart the parsonage, thankful their visit was completed. He enjoyed seeing Miss Elizabeth once again, but her presence always mystified him. Each time he saw her, he felt his confidence in her unsuitability for him waver.

She was so different from other ladies of his acquaintance. The ladies of the *ton*—deemed well-born and gently-bred—seemed lacking in the face of Miss Elizabeth Bennet's unique charm. Her fine eyes were expressive, her air honest and generous...and her intellect—well, she consistently outshone all others in cleverness.

He knew he had a dreadful habit of watching her intently. Even when she was arguing a point against him, he was bewitched. Her arch kindness made it impossible for him to be offended by her.

Darcy always knew how he was meant to behave. Governesses, tutors, and professors had ingrained in him what a gentleman should say to certain persons and in particular situations. He had long been schooled in how to maintain control; but this woman confounded him, and he reacted likewise—mute and muddled.

Matchmaking mothers across the country spent years putting forward their daughters and introducing their many accomplishments in the hopes he would at last show one of the ladies preference. He had been guarding such notice assiduously for many years now, knowing that the wrong attention at the wrong time might lead to the unintended engagement of his honour. To no degree did he plan to allow himself to be forcibly attached to some excessively flattering and otherwise vapid woman, and if such an abundance of caution led to the general opinion that he was haughty and too reticent, then so be it.

But then came her. And now—in her presence—he had to remind himself not to stare! Not to watch her every move and observe her every facial expression! After all these years of carefully constructed reserve, numerous parties where he avoided eye contact, and balls spent dodging dance partners, he had been finally, in essence, trapped—even if it was unintended by the lady. He had been entrapped by his own fascination.

How frustrating to be so infatuated with each arch of her eyebrow and every quirk of her lips! The ladies of his sphere were typically demure and docile, but not Elizabeth. She was the embodiment of life—giving and joyful and vibrant. Even her hair did not appear to behave. Her wild, chocolate curls—auburn when the sun hit them, to be exact—were always pushing out of the confines of her hairpins to reveal rebellious locks with no intention of being forced into submission. What he would not give to touch one of those blessed coils...

So lost in his thoughts was he that it took nearly the entire visit to notice Miss Elizabeth appeared more reserved than usual. He thought, perhaps, she was nervous to be in his presence again. He ought to be careful not to raise any expectations. Charmed as he was, he still could not offer for her. She was not for him.

Thankfully, Fitzwilliam was good enough to accompany him that morning. His cousin had nearly spit out his tea when Darcy suggested they accompany Mr Collins home to greet the ladies of his household. Darcy knew he could not condescend to visit the overly flattering Mr Collins on his own. He was already tongued-tied enough in Miss Elizabeth's presence. That parson and his insistent rambling only rendered communication more difficult. How was a man to respond to his fawning and deference?

Once they were safely beyond the parsonage gardens, Fitzwilliam clapped Darcy on the shoulder. "Dare I ask why we made this call? Surely it could not have been for your friendship with Collins. That man is infuriating. Always bowing and grinning and droning on."

He theatrically shook his shoulders as if to shake off the experience. His broad smile widened to show he was quite amused.

Darcy frowned. Had his design been so obvious? "It was the correct thing to do. I made the acquaintance of Mr and Mrs Collins, as well as Miss Bennet, while I was in Hertfordshire with Bingley and thought to honour that connexion."

Fitzwilliam gave him a sceptical glance. "Was that the only reason?"

"You would rather be spending time with our aunt and cousin?"

Fitzwilliam put his hands up in defence of the statement. "I can admit the ladies present were entirely welcoming and kind, but that man! I cannot offer a guess as to whose company I prefer between Lady Catherine and Mr Collins!"

"I know." Darcy smiled. "'Tis a poor choice, to be sure."

"I do believe that man smelled of onions!"

Darcy suppressed a chuckle.

"How long must we stay in Kent? I cannot imagine finding consistent excuses to miss Sunday services." Fitzwilliam grinned. "And certainly, Lady Catherine will not stand for it more than once or twice."

"My plans are not fixed."

"By all means, please *fix* our plans to suit yourself. I do not require any particular consideration or notice," Fitzwilliam teased.

"Is she not aunt to us both?" Darcy asked. "We both have some duty to perform here."

"Yes, but I am more willing to shirk that duty than you are." Laughing, Fitzwilliam said, "Pray allow me to defer all decisions to you, Cousin. I am at your leisure. Until I am not, that is. I could be called back to Spain on a moment's notice."

Darcy rolled his eyes. Fitzwilliam did enjoy reminding him rather frequently of his impressive war history. To Darcy, the idea of Fitzwilliam off fighting in Spain brought him sadness, though his cousin's time spent with him while off-duty was a comfort. He had ever been more a brother than a cousin.

Darcy's fondest memories of boyhood all included his cousin—climbing trees, getting into mischief, and even being punished side by side. Without him, he would have been very much alone. With Fitzwilliam, he was not 'Master of Pemberley' or 'Potential Suitor'—he was just himself.

For several days following Mr Darcy and his cousin's arrival in Kent, Elizabeth and Charlotte were limited to indoor pursuits due to a succession of rain. They were days that wore long, particularly for Elizabeth who was increasingly discomfited by her hosts.

As she sat with Charlotte one grey afternoon, Elizabeth read an unengaging page of her book five times before she set it down and let her mind wander to the inhabitants of the great house across the lane. She still could not account for Mr Darcy having called at the parsonage on Tuesday. It argued against every belief of him, that he should condescend to recognise the Collinses in such a way. And then to sit so silently! He was, as ever, impossible to comprehend.

Her mind full of such musings, she spoke to her friend as she would have back in Hertfordshire. "Which gown shall I wear to church for Easter, Charlotte? I am aware of Lady Catherine's strong opinions, and I hope to endure her condescension with the finest my trunk may offer," Elizabeth said theatrically, raising an eyebrow and grinning at her friend. "Though, of course, the distinction of rank must and shall be preserved."

Immediately, Elizabeth noted the narrowing of Charlotte's brows while she kept her eyes on her mending. Sadly, it was another tease gone terribly wrong. *Charlotte truly has lost her ability to laugh in Hunsford.*

"I care not what you wear to Easter-day services, Eliza. You must know that I do not extend friendships based on one's similarities to a fashion plate, nor would Lady Catherine. She is all that is honourable," Charlotte replied, keeping her attention on the needle and thread. "And should we be invited to dine at Rosings, I am certain that what you wear will have no impact on the pleasantness of our visit. Are you dressing for one of her nephews? I should warn you to temper your expectations and be on your guard, for the sake of the gentlemen, of course. As you say, the distinction of rank shall be preserved. You are a guest in our home and family to my husband. I should think you would take our position in this community more seriously. Perhaps you could show a bit more gratitude for your great fortune."

Elizabeth barely refrained from sighing and rolling her eyes. Though Charlotte's speeches were becoming tiresome, in truth, they were more concerning than vexatious. Charlotte sounded as though she was mimicking her husband's thoughts and words, too afraid to voice any opinions of her own.

Elizabeth watched intently as Charlotte kept a steady rhythm with her needle and thread—in and out and in and out. She was a shell of her old friend—keeping up appearances and watching her tongue, day in and day out. Marriage had significantly altered Charlotte, and Elizabeth did not think it was for the better. She wished Charlotte would speak to her of it.

Lost in thought as she was, she nearly leapt out of her skin when Mr Collins came rushing into the parlour shaking a single piece of paper in his hand. Rage emanated from him. As shocking as it was humorous, Elizabeth could not smile when it appeared he would ring a peal over her.

"Cousin! What can you possibly have to say about these abusive lies outlined in this communication?" He placed his bulky person directly in front of her, and she sat further back in her chair. His fierce brandishing of the page meant he nearly struck her with it. "I shall not abide a sharp-tongued serpent in my home!"

Elizabeth looked to Charlotte for some assistance but found no help therein. Charlotte had gone still and pale, wild desperation in her eyes, and appeared unwilling to meet her gaze. Elizabeth turned back to Mr Collins. She raised her chin to look him in the eye. "I am not certain what you speak of, sir."

He shoved the piece of paper at her, and Elizabeth took it, glancing down to see her own handwriting—with horror, she recognised it was the letter she had been penning to her father. She gasped. "Mr Collins, this is my letter! How have you come to be in possession of my personal correspondence?"

"You are in my home, and as such, your possessions must be within my purview," he proclaimed. "How dare you utter such loathsome and contemptuous words about a woman so vastly superior to you! Lies, all of them! The Bible tells us that the Lord detests lying lips, Cousin Elizabeth—what can you have to say to that?"

"You had no right to enter my bedchamber and look at my letter," she replied.

His face red with rage, Mr Collins continued speaking as if he had not heard her. "I should have known after your undutiful actions at Longbourn that you would require much instruction. I am thankful your father sent you here to me, for I can lead you to true repentance. Naturally, should Lady Catherine extend an invitation, you shall not be allowed to dine at Rosings on the morrow. I shall not allow it. If you show some notable remorse, you may, at a later time, be welcome in the presence of those of such high standing. At this time, I find that possibility unlikely. One must earn the privilege of an audience with their betters."

Mr Collins ripped the letter from her hand, tore it, and tossed it into the nearby flames burning in the hearth.

"Mr Collins!" Elizabeth exclaimed, astonished by his audacity. But there was nothing for it; the flames consumed her words eagerly. No matter; it was nothing that could not be rewritten or told at a later time. It was, rather, his behaviour that surprised her most. "You are behaving in a very shocking way, sir. To enter the bedchamber of a young

lady in your care is improper, much less to remove possessions therein and burn them!"

At this, Charlotte at last rose and entered the argument.
She approached her husband carefully, laying a hand on his
arm, "My dear Mr Collins, I am sure you did not enter Elizabeth's chamber. Perhaps you found her letter in my parlour
or the breakfast room, sir?"

Mr Collins appeared to consider this. Elizabeth could
sense he was vacillating between being insulted by his wife's
suggestion and relief that she had provided him another
path. "Ah, yes—I am sure my dear wife is correct. Please,
Cousin, do be more considerate."

"I did not leave it in the parlour," Elizabeth asserted
softly. She may have stumbled into Bedlam, but it did not
follow that she would permit the inmates to have their way
with her. "It was in my bedchamber."

"Elizabeth, my dear, I am sure in your distraction your
missive was left in a public room," Charlotte insisted.

No matter how Charlotte's defence of Mr Collins vexed
Elizabeth, it did seem to mollify him. When again he spoke,
he used his customary pompous gravity, looking down his
nose at her. "I shall take my responsibilities as your superior
and elder with the greatest solemnity. I expect better
decorum from you in the future—beginning now. We shall
spend more time in deep religious studies each night, and
from this day, you are restricted to the parsonage."

"You cannot—"

"Yes, I can," he interrupted. "And I shall. I cannot neglect
the opportunity to set you on the right path, madam, no
matter how dearly you might like to continue in your wild,
animal ways."

At Elizabeth's gasp, he added, "You may maintain only
your morning exercise as a time of reflection—in order to

recount and consider the scripture discussed in the evenings."

With that, he left them, quitting the room with an air of satisfaction and sanctimony.

Elizabeth was frozen in place, perfectly still, her mind wild with anger and mortification. For several moments she stood in silence with Charlotte; when she glanced at her friend, Charlotte could not meet her eye.

At length, Elizabeth made her way to the door, intending to go to her chamber, but before she exited, she turned over her shoulder to say quietly, "Charlotte?" When she had her friend's attention, she continued. "The letter I was penning for my father was in my room. But I daresay you already knew that."

Elizabeth's pace had quickened to almost a run by the time she reached the stairs, though she took care that the Collinses should not hear her fleeing them. After reaching her chamber, she poured some water from the ewer and splashed it on her face, her breath coming fast and her heart racing.

Elizabeth sat at the writing desk, finding the pen and ink well just as she left it. She had not blatantly insulted Lady Catherine in her letter, but it was not flattering either. Her father had always been her outlet for witty repartee. During her lonely first weeks in Kent, her quips collected for his reading pleasure had brought her some levity. It did not signify; her thoughts and impressions were her own, and her cousin had no influence, no matter what he believed.

Elizabeth lifted the lid of the delicate desktop to find letters from her father and Jane, which she had carried from home, and moved them to a pocket in the lining of her trunk. She would have to be more cautious about what she left out in the open.

Surely Mr Collins did not think he could keep her at Hunsford like some prisoner? She would not remain if she were to be treated like a naughty schoolgirl, rather than an esteemed guest. She came as a favour to Charlotte—to demonstrate her support of her marriage—not so that Mr Collins could correct her 'wild' behaviour. She did not doubt that her letters to her family could be closely examined, no matter how she protested against it.

Thoughts of Charlotte made her stop and swallow hard. Charlotte had lied, blatantly. Why? To subdue him? To appease him? What had happened in this house to so alter her friend? Every instinct within her urged Elizabeth to find her cousin and object to his strictures, but loyalty to her friend tugged against it.

Just then, the maid entered her room. Surprised, Hayes quickly curtseyed and apologised, "Pardon me for the intrusion, Miss Bennet. I was unaware you were here. I was returning a few of your gowns to your wardrobe." She moved to put the garments away and enquired if Elizabeth needed anything.

"Please ask Mrs Montgomery to send a tray up to me this evening. I shall not be dining with the family," Elizabeth said with a sigh. At least she would not have to pretend courtesy through a long meal.

Moving over to the bed to rest a while, she considered that the maid's entrance had not been preceded by a knock. She knew enough about Lucas Lodge to know Sarah would never have dared perform her duties in that manner. Perhaps the great Lady Catherine appointed the servants at the parsonage for reasons more than simply preference?

The thought infuriated her, but it was less unsettling to imagine a stealthy, conniving maid than a dreadfully repulsive cousin.

CHAPTER 4

Elizabeth was not herself upon waking. The sun would rise soon, but her heart and body were weary. If the state of her bedclothes were any indication, she had not slept soundly. Charlotte's support of her husband had broken something within Elizabeth—she who had always assumed her inclination to understand people was so keen. Yet, keen it was not.

She found herself re-examining memories in her mind, looking for evidence that she had long been wrong about her friendship with Charlotte. But it was to no avail. She could find no proof. In all her memories she found a steadfast friend—fortification for dull parties and a confidante for her heart's inner workings. Theirs had always been a friendship reliant on honesty.

Elizabeth readied herself for her walk without calling for Hayes. She preferred to pull on a plain walking dress that she could fasten herself and secure a simple braid which could be easily pinned on her own. She was certain the entire world would see the havoc of her mind when they viewed the state of her tired eyes. She splashed water on her face but found no support there.

While the sun was only beginning to rise, and most of the household remained abed, Elizabeth still took care to open her door most quietly and tiptoe down the corridor. She had no energy for forced conversation.

Mrs Montgomery was lighting the fires when Elizabeth arrived in the kitchens. "Good morning, miss. Shall I find you something to take on your morning walk?"

"No, thank you," Elizabeth replied. "I do not require sustenance quite yet. I shall breakfast with the family when I return. I shall not be long."

"I'd be right pleased if you took one of those apple tarts, miss." She pointed to a small basket with an assortment of sweet provisions. "Or I could wrap up some of those pickled apples the master enjoys?" She wiggled her eyebrows at Elizabeth who pinched her face in response.

"Thank you, no."

Elizabeth wondered if she should ask her about helping to get a letter out to her father but thought better of it. It would not do to have the household talking about a disagreement between herself and her cousin. She also had a care for the woman's position in the house, which could be impacted should she bow to Elizabeth's request and be caught assisting her.

Elizabeth reached for the servants' door and stopped short when she heard, "Eliza."

She whipped her face around to find Charlotte looking nearly as dreadful as she felt. Her red eyes and the dark circles underneath them gave her to think her friend had also not slept.

Elizabeth dropped to a polite curtsey. "Good morning," was all she was willing to utter.

"Would you mind joining me in my parlour for a moment?"

Elizabeth nodded, and Charlotte led the way in a stealthy manner that suggested she too did not want to stir her husband's interest. They both settled in their customary chairs, and Elizabeth waited in silence for Charlotte to begin a conversation. She was not eager to hear excuses, but still would not snub her friend.

"I want to begin by apologising for the uproar that took place yesterday," Charlotte said while fidgeting with her dress. "As I am sure you have already surmised, I thought it best to resolve the conflict more quickly rather than waste breath determining fault."

"I see," Elizabeth responded.

"You should understand that my husband takes his duties rather seriously. And, as a visitor in our home, he considers himself your protector. As such, his authority is final. Understanding this, you should have no trouble here."

"Should I not?"

"I find peace in the *calm*," Charlotte responded with some emphasis and looked her in the eye for the first time. "Should you write your letters quickly and put them directly into my care, there should be no further conflict."

"Could you not *talk* to your husband?"

Charlotte visibly cringed. "I shall be living with Mr Collins long after you have returned to Hertfordshire, Eliza."

"Perhaps you could simply request he lift the restrictions he threatened yesterday?"

Charlotte held her gaze but slowly shook her head.

Can she not even say it? It struck Elizabeth that Charlotte would make no effort towards reconciliation. Or perhaps she considered *this* reconciliation. If so, that was a sad thought. Her silence said much.

Elizabeth aimed to offer an olive branch of sorts. "I shall endeavour to keep my correspondence private, and I thank you for your offer to carry my letters. I want peace for you too, Charlotte. I sincerely do. Is there anything I may offer for your comfort? Perhaps you should like to speak a little more. You could tell me about your marriage."

"No, thank you." Charlotte stood to exit the room.

Elizabeth rose from her chair and quickly asked if her friend would like to walk about the gardens with her that morning, but she replied only, "I am sure Mr Collins cannot spare me," and exited the room.

Darcy prepared for Easter services with extra attention. He was light in his step and cheery in his mood. He was certain his valet was perplexed by his behaviour, but considering that only caused him to smile more. He shocked even himself, tipping his hat at parishioners as he approached the church.

Fitzwilliam's interest in his visit to the parsonage had made him realise the need for greater circumspection. His cousin was too interested and too intelligent to miss any signs of admiration on Darcy's part. Thus, he had denied himself the pleasure of another call, grimly enduring the limited society of Lady Catherine and Anne.

But not today. Today he would see her. After taking his seat in the family pew, he tried to appear nonchalant as his gaze roved the sanctuary in search of Miss Elizabeth. Fitzwilliam gave him a curious glance, and he shrugged his shoulders in response. *Confound it. Why must Fitzwilliam always be so aware of my every move? He should save his powers of observation for his time in the army.*

He found her seated by Mrs Collins in the pew towards the front where the parson's wife would customarily sit. He wished he had been there when she entered, for now, in a humble, bent-head posture, he saw little more than her bonnet and a simple green gown that suited her small frame well. He felt great pleasure just merely being in her presence. *If I cannot have her, I can at least enjoy watching her while I am here.*

Mrs Collins said something to her, and as she responded to her friend, Darcy was gifted with the full view of her beautiful face. A very short observation, however, showed him that once again she did not appear to be her typical, vivacious self that morning. Her fine eyes looked dull, and their expression could only be described as despairing. There was a meekness to her that he could not like. Even the shape of her mouth as she responded to Mrs Collins felt unfamiliar and subdued.

Throughout the absurd speech the parson called a sermon, Darcy considered what he might say to her. He would dearly like to cheer her.

Following the service, Darcy moved his long legs quickly out towards the churchyard, hoping to find a moment to speak to her. He knew with certainty there would be no opportunity for conversation during Easter dinner under the watchful eye of his overbearing aunt.

He was required to pause a moment and to nod his thanks to the bumbling vicar. "Yes, happy Easter," he responded with a distinct lack of enthusiasm to the man's effusive well wishes. His greedy eyes had landed on Elizabeth in the churchyard and did not desire to leave their mark.

Once released by Mr Collins, it was the work of a moment to arrive by her side. "I am certain this sunny day finds you well," he said, and could not fail to detect surprise in her sorrowful gaze. Their eyes met, and he could not help but wonder why she was at a loss for words.

"Good morning, Mr Darcy."

"I imagine weather like this might be ideal for a great walker such as yourself. Have you enjoyed meandering through the park, Miss Bennet?"

"I have, sir, but only a little."

Her reticence discouraged him, but he proceeded determinedly, "You should visit the paths that border Rosings to the south, just outside the formal gardens. I think you would find them to your liking."

"Thank you for the recommendation, sir," she said. His words were not encouraging her as he hoped, so he flashed her a full smile and was surprised to see her dark eyes widen, a question in her expression.

"Good day, Miss Bennet."

"G-Good day, Mr Darcy."

Spending a long evening with Mr Collins brought Darcy no joy, but the promise of Miss Elizabeth's company was a superb consolation. He knew his movements were scrutinised at Rosings and was forced to linger in his rooms for above half an hour so as to not seem too eager to join the family in the drawing room.

If it were not for his aunt's constant interference and oversight, he should like to take the stairs two at a time to await her arrival. Keeping himself under regulation was to his benefit and hopefully hers as well.

Once he joined the family, he placed himself directly in front of his aunt. She considered his conversation her due, so he complied—but only for the reprieve that was shortly to be delivered.

When the butler entered to announce their guests, Darcy schooled his expression and stood as uniformly as possible— but it was no use—his eyes searched hungrily for her presence.

"Mr and Mrs Collins, my lady," the butler announced. The man and his wife bowed and curtseyed and performed all appropriate civilities.

"I should not have to remind you about the importance of being punctual, Mr Collins," Lady Catherine called out to them from across the room. She then immediately turned to speak to Fitzwilliam, dismissing their entrance entirely.

Darcy thought perhaps it was Miss Elizabeth who had delayed their arrival, for she had not yet entered the room. Had they left her behind? Was she unwell? She had seemed rather subdued in her posture and conversation that morning. Was anyone to fetch a doctor? Had the apothecary been called?

"Of course, my lady," the parson responded to his aunt, while he stumbled to a seat near Lady Catherine. "My deepest apologies for our tardiness. As you have mentioned before, punctuality is a sign of good breeding." The man looked positively pleased with himself for the response.

Darcy turned to the window to roll his eyes. Good breeding! That was a joke. Half the *ton* considered a late arrival the height of fashion, and only the most grasping arrived early.

The butler re-entered the room, and Darcy spun around to take in Miss Elizabeth's entrance. But instead, the staid retainer requested Darcy attend an express rider who had just arrived.

Darcy nodded to his family and their guests before following him out of the room.

"I shall have my share of your news, Darcy. Do not be long in relieving our anxieties regarding the contents of the express," Lady Catherine bellowed across the large room.

"Of course," Darcy responded with nary a glance at the woman.

Once the correspondence was in hand, he was relieved to see that it was not his sister, Georgiana, who required his immediate attention but news of a fire in the stables at his estate, Pemberley. He paced the front hall, taking in the details of the notice. As expected, his loyal and experienced servants had made exemplary decisions in his absence. Their quick actions had saved not only the lives of the stable boys within, but also his horses. Work had already begun to rebuild.

Darcy was relieved but knew a timely response was required. He called the attention of the butler, who was quick to lift his eyes for instructions. "Please see that the rider is provided a meal and rest before he returns north. If this note is any indication, he has ridden hard and fast for two days."

The butler nodded in reply. "Also, I require use of her ladyship's study so that I may pen a response. You may notify my aunt that our family is in good health."

By the time the note had been written, sealed, and sent back to the rider, Darcy had little time to prepare for the onslaught of questions when he returned to the drawing room. Once the details of the correspondence had been shared, the entire party stood to dine.

The meal held little pleasure for Darcy who spent most of his time wondering why Miss Elizabeth had not come. He hesitated to ask in front of his aunt; his only consolation being that if she were extremely ill, he thought her friend, Mrs Collins, would have stayed back to attend her.

Even if Miss Elizabeth was only slightly ill, it did seem in rather poor form to not mention her absence. Perhaps he missed their explanation while he attended the express?

Mrs Collins appeared as she ever did in Hertfordshire—capable of rational and shrewd conversation. Nothing of the sort could be said of her husband who crowed his own accomplishments rather loudly—if you could call them such. Celebrating the manner in which he had reprimanded one of his servants sung of a rather foolish master. Seeking his aunt's approbation for his choice words, even more absurd. A self-satisfied gleam in the man's eye set the hairs on Darcy's skin on their ends. To his satisfaction, Fitzwilliam was examining the man closely as well.

"...I told him, I did, that only one man would be master of my domain," Mr Collins proclaimed. "And I shall not dictate the rest of our exchange while in the presence of ladies."

Darcy could not be happy with the turn of conversation. It was in poor form, and the man was altogether too pleased with himself.

"Perhaps Mrs Collins will play for us this evening? I have not yet had the pleasure," Fitzwilliam said, turning to his subject. Darcy was thankful for his cousin's intervention.

"I shall second that request, Cousin," Darcy joined in and sent a small smile to Mrs Collins. She blushed at the attention and thanked the gentlemen for their kind request.

Of course, as they were only on the second remove, it would still be some time before they would have the pleasure of music to drown out the need for conversation. A long night it would certainly be.

CHAPTER 5

Elizabeth rose early the next morning to exercise her feet and her mind with a walk through the park. The day held the promise of early blooms and sunshine. She was delighted to forgo her pelisse for her cheery yellow spencer and nearly skipped down the lane to attend to her favourite byways; her morning walks were, apparently, the only outings she would be allowed for many weeks to come. She decided to put aside her hurt and anger —to ignore her humiliating banishment from Rosings—for a beautiful morning such as this.

Before she committed to taking the path she was most accustomed to, she remembered Mr Darcy's suggestion and turned in the other direction. She made her way towards a trail through the woods bordering the formal and ornate gardens of Rosings Park to the south.

After walking some miles, she found a sturdy log to sit on in order to enjoy the biscuits stashed away in her pocket at the behest of Mrs Montgomery. The cool morning air had chilled her cheeks but had also rejuvenated her spirit. Feeling clear-minded and energised once again, she prepared to return to the parsonage, the house which had become her temporary prison.

Elizabeth had not gone far when she was surprised to see someone approaching. The gentleman rider sat tall on a magnificent black beast with a fine beaver hat fixed smartly atop his head. Though she cared little for horses, she could see he had a fine seat. She enjoyed the view of his person at a distance and was rather disappointed to see it was, sadly, only Mr Darcy. She felt all the perverseness of the mischance that should bring him to the same path she walked. To prevent their ever meeting on this path again, she considered informing him that she planned to walk it daily, for surely that would discourage him, though she did not speak a word of it. A desire to converse with someone—anyone—beyond the Collinses stunted her impertinent speech.

He pulled his horse up beside her on the path and dismounted in one swift move, tipping his hat and bowing to her as his only greeting. "You mean to frighten me, Mr Darcy," she teased. "But I will not be alarmed."

"You could not honestly believe me to entertain any design of alarming you, Miss Elizabeth. I have had the plea-sure of your acquaintance long enough to know that you find great enjoyment in occasionally professing opinions which in fact are not your own," he said, looking pleased with his response.

She was surprised to receive the second smile in only two days from the typically staid man—remarkable! His expres-sion was so friendly, she could not help but smile at his rebuke, and he appeared satisfied.

"Where do you go on this fine morning?" he asked.

"I have been walking for some time and must return to the parsonage."

He nodded. "May I accompany you?"

While she knew it must only be a sacrifice to general politeness that urged him to offer, she was, nevertheless, easily persuaded.

"You may," she responded and took his offered arm. He made a clicking noise in his cheek and immediately his horse began following their sedate pace. Of course, only Mr Darcy could compel such a grand creature into submission.

He did not say a great deal as they set off, merely responding to her avowed love of solitary rambles with a remark upon the excellent weather. She could find nothing wanting in his conversation, even if she would have preferred his more gregarious cousin, Colonel Fitzwilliam, as a walking partner. She could admit Mr Darcy possessed a calming presence about him in this scenery, observing the flowers and sharing about the variety of local species as well as an abbreviated history of Kent. His reflections and knowledge of the area were significantly more interesting than the trivial stories Mr Collins had provided upon her arrival, and she found herself less irritated by his unexpected presence on the path and more attentive than she would have previously imagined.

The subsequent morning found Mr Darcy joining her ramble again, although for what reason she was uncertain. Exercise helped to clear the cobwebs from her mind, and she had much to contemplate with all the odd happenings in the parsonage, that she did not pay the vagaries of Mr Darcy much mind. At least the gentleman did not interfere with her need for contemplation. His company seemed much elevated after the sanctimonious dialogues she was forced to attend from her cousin.

His long legs allowed him to keep up with the brisk speed she was accustomed to and also desired. Silence was often their companion, but she found the stillness welcome. She was learning Mr Darcy preferred the quiet, and when he did speak, it seemed the consequence of obligation rather than preference.

When Mr Darcy met her once again the next morning, he suggested they take a new route. She followed, always enthusiastic for outdoor exploration and ever curious to learn more about the county.

Winding through thicker brush, Mr Darcy was remarkably kind to move nettles and branches out of her way.

"Perhaps you might tell me where you are taking me?" she quipped.

He did not turn around to face her. He held back a branch and indicated she should proceed ahead before answering, "Colonel Fitzwilliam and I took this same path many times as children. There was a hidden glade where we would retreat during our visits. I have lately wondered at its location."

She was eager to help him find it once again. "And I have lately yearned for some adventure. Lead on, good sir."

After some time, the dense trees opened up to reveal a clearing filled completely with wildflowers—a carpet of bright colours stood before her. Stepping into the glade, she was overwhelmed by the mass of bluebells and primrose covering the ground and the rough, natural edges of the space, outlined by vines that climbed the surrounding trees. The glade overwhelmed all her senses—smelling the floral blooms of early spring, viewing the vivid colours, and feeling the warmth of the sunshine that the break in the trees allowed to pour in.

She knew all the flowers and trees growing in the vicinity of Longbourn, but some of these blooms were foreign to her.

"Mr Darcy," she breathed, turning in a full circle to take in the beauty of her surroundings. "This is a piece of heaven!"

He smiled, "I knew you were fond of nature. I thought you might enjoy this, but I was not sure if we would find it. These paths were more attended to when I was a child. My late uncle, Sir Lewis de Bourgh, enjoyed these woods and saw the paths were kept clear. He was a spirited and active man. He regularly took us on morning walks when we were children.

"After he died, Colonel Fitzwilliam and I would often retreat to this spot during our visits. We enjoyed many imaginary adventures here—pirates on the rough seas, military men fighting fearsome battles. They are fond memories. Unfortunately, Lady Catherine prefers the structured and manicured gardens of Rosings Park, which you have no doubt visited. The wilds of nature cannot be controlled by her, and thus, she allows them to exist beyond her bordered parklands but does not put forth any effort into maintaining them."

"Sir, I believe that may be the longest speech I have ever been honoured to receive from you," she said with a smile.

"Yes, perhaps."

She wanted him to remain as he was, so she smiled and arched her eyebrow to tease him plainly, "I suppose it would surprise you to know I can be reserved at times."

"I could be convinced. One does not converse much when they spend long hours reading," he said slowly.

"Ah yes, accomplished women do improve their minds by extensive reading." She remembered their conversation at Netherfield Park and Caroline Bingley's comprehensive list of what was required to be an accomplished lady. She smiled playfully. "Perhaps Miss Bingley has taken your advice and visits Hatchards with more frequency. Though, it is unlikely she would employ her time emulating my preferred activities. I doubt she considers my example exemplary."

He contemplated this and responded, "Perhaps not. I cannot admit to being an expert on the thoughts of Miss Bingley. Yet, I would argue that no one honoured with the pleasure of knowing you should find anything wanting at all." He looked at her with complete seriousness, and she believed he meant it.

To be praised by Mr Darcy was a surprise after their many contentious interactions the previous autumn. She imagined he did not offer compliments often, so it softened her to him. But it also reminded her of the shortcomings Charlotte had been frequently impressing upon her during her stay. Perhaps she was truly lacking.

"Of course, they may, sir," she said, now distracted by her own frustrations. "In fact, I fear I have been told very recently that my behaviour wants for more refinement." She sighed. "It is hard to disappoint those you love," she said solemnly. She meant it as a witty rejoinder, but she knew it came out more seriously than intended—though, equally, she was serious.

She knew she was disappointing Charlotte, but she was becoming miserable in the fragile harmony they continued to mend together each time Mr Collins erupted into another embarrassing outburst. Were it not for her concern, she would have already returned home; but she could not, not until she knew if there was anything she could do for her friend.

He considered her and nodded. "I can certainly understand a concern for disappointing those you love. I have spent the five years since my excellent father died trying to care for those under my protection—to live up to his expectations. I have many responsibilities—to my family, to my tenants, to the communities that Pemberley supports, to the Darcy legacy. Each decision I make has the potential for significant impact..." He trailed off. They had ceased walking, and he kicked the dirt with his highly polished boot. She knew there was more, but she did not want to pry.

She held his gaze in silence, allowing the quiet to be enough. She did not want to disrupt the mood or say the wrong thing. Her heart was stirred on his behalf.

Elizabeth had known of his deceased parents and that he was a guardian to a younger sister but had not yet considered the great number of lives he was responsible for. That considerable task would be challenging for anyone. Her frustration with Charlotte and Mr Collins certainly paled in comparison to the weight of all who were under his care.

They returned quietly, side by side, and she was surprised to feel a moment of regret when he turned down the lane towards Rosings.

The next morning, Elizabeth was unsurprised to once again find Mr Darcy along her now favoured path. *How easy and completely different he seems from the man I met at Netherfield Park!* He immediately offered his arm, which she accepted quite happily.

Elizabeth was finding these mornings a respite from the parsonage, even with Mr Darcy as a companion. He was quiet and thoughtful and asked very little of her. She knew there were people she respected who enjoyed his company. Was this the version of the man they were accustomed to? If the good-natured Mr Bingley would seek a friendship with Mr Darcy, how could he not have redeeming features?

They sauntered in companionable silence for some time before Mr Darcy asked after Mr and Mrs Collins.

"They are both well, thank you."

"Do they never walk out with you in the morning?" he asked lightly.

"Mrs Collins has never preferred being out of doors. If they have already broken their fast this morning, then it would follow that Mr Collins is likely monitoring the hedge near the lane or tending to his garden. Such that he is out in front of the home, it is equally probable that Mrs Collins is in her back parlour, enjoying a wholly different scene from the nearest window."

His lip slightly lifted, as if he were tempted to smile or laugh, but he quickly adjusted his features. "It appears Mrs Collins has married well," he said hesitantly, as if to offer it as a question.

She considered that for a moment. Had Charlotte married well? Perhaps Mr Darcy would consider this a well-suited match per Charlotte's station in life. Had not Charlotte inferred she married for comfort? Was this the comfort she once desired? She answered, "On her wedding day, she was prepared to be perfectly happy."

"And how do you consider her now?" he asked.

It was a heavy question whose answer was laden with Elizabeth's deep regrets for her friend. Charlotte seemed now to be everything *but* happy, but that was a bit more information than propriety would allow she answer to him. "Now? Now I would consider her...comfortable."

In his silence, he offered her the space she needed to think. Teasing and provoking being her general nature, she was not often pressed to consider such serious subjects. Her father often challenged her mind over histories or philoso-phy, but it was much easier than sorting out this business of one's dearest friend being seemingly lost to her.

"I believe Charlotte is happy to have the safety and secu-rity of marriage. That was her reason for accepting him— though it would not be mine."

Mr Darcy looked at Elizabeth with concern. Uncomfort-able being solemn too long, Elizabeth smiled and said, "Or, perhaps, she simply desired a man as verbose as her own father. Though at the risk of being ungenerous, I must own, I would much rather listen to Sir William Lucas speak about St. James's than hear Mr Collins rehearsing his sermons."

He released a soft chuckle and flashed her a wide smile. Had she less vanity, she would have felt nothing at the reac-tion her comment induced. His happy expression reached his eyes, and she enjoyed a first sight of his dimples. His hand-someness almost surprised her. Almost...for it was surely not the first time she had seen it, only the first time she had seen it without her general distaste for him obscuring it. Encour-aged, she forged on, "Or, conceivably, she was lacking proper guidance and desired an attentive lady of the peerage to shower her with advice?"

His response was a laugh so deep and sincere it nearly occasioned her to gasp. She joined his laughter, leaning a bit more upon his arm as she did so. When she caught her breath, she apologised for her dreadful speech. "You will have to forgive me. I did not intend to be so mean-spirited. Staying with my cousin has been utterly vexing, and it felt good to laugh."

"There is nothing to forgive."

She believed him—again. In fact, she believed he was always honest to a fault. He raised his other hand and placed it on top of the hand she rested on his arm. She was not surprised by his gesture, because he was so kind to her of late—but she was not prepared for the fire of emotion surging through her. The feeling of his hand comforted her— a comfort long absent during her stay in Hunsford, and possibly longer. She was pleased he could be a retreat from this otherwise undependable part of the world.

After a time, she said, "I have lately been attempting more caution with my impertinent tongue."

"Are you sure it is impertinence, Miss Bennet? Could it not be cleverness?" he challenged with a kind expression.

She shrugged, "Indeed, Mr Darcy, you bring up a good point. I would prefer to think it the latter, though I am certain you have more to say on the subject."

"I am happy to offer some intelligence, Miss Bennet. The former implies insolence and unmannerly behaviour, while the latter implies a quick intellect. I see no malice here today, though it appears you may believe otherwise at present."

"And I dare say, you have come to your own conclusion."

"Indeed, I have, Miss Bennet." He smiled and kept walking in silence. Then, ever so quietly under his breath, he whispered, "Clever girl."

CHAPTER 6

Darcy always woke with a purpose. In the five years since his father's death, all within his realm had relied on him. His habit of rising early was now sweetened by the possibility of walking once again with Miss Elizabeth Bennet.

He only saw her in the mornings, but he found himself amused by the memories of their brief interludes throughout the rest of every day. At times, he was forced to quickly remove the smile on his face in order to not draw the attention of his aunt, which was often, because Miss Elizabeth was perpetually on his mind. Each cloud in the sky was a threat of spring rains he hoped would remain at bay so he might meet her.

On Friday morning, he hurried through his morning routine, moving with eagerness to the paths just outside the formal gardens. The gardens were covered with a mist that had settled in overnight, bending the light of the first rays of sunshine which suggested a crisp, cool morning full of promise.

Miss Elizabeth, too, offered a promise of light in his day. He approached her quietly, wanting to have a few uninterrupted moments to watch her before she perceived his arrival. With her bonnet in her hand, he was able to take in the beauty of her hair, which was damp from the morning air. A few wild curls spilled out over her shoulders, glistening in the sunlight. He could not yet see her fine eyes, as her face was tipped upwards, with eyes closed. The early morning and its quiet possibilities seemed to invigorate her as well.

"Good morning, Miss Bennet," he whispered when he came upon her.

He was greeted with a quiet, "Good morning to you, sir." She immediately took his offered arm, and they strolled slowly in their practised manner.

Just being near her was pleasurable. He was undeniably drawn to her. Darcy was uncertain whether he would ever take action upon his feelings, yet he already knew forgetting her would be impossible. He had tried to forget her before, in London, over the winter. He had lost many nights of sleep wondering what she was doing and if he would see her again. Putting her out of his mind, even then, had proved unbearable.

He began to realise it would be harder to leave her this time—after five beautiful mornings spent together, and he meant to spend more. One week was rather not enough. It was perhaps improper that they continued meeting this way, but they never planned their meetings, not in the strictest sense. These were not secret assignations—even if he admitted to himself he was seeking her out quite plainly. In fact, he was abundantly aware of the marked attention he was giving her and the implications of that.

If she were a lady of the *ton*, there would already be rumours of an impending engagement after all the time spent together, and the lady in question would most assuredly be visiting Bond Street to begin planning her wedding clothes. But not Miss Elizabeth. Warmth spread through his chest at the recollection of their past exchanges and the charming manner in which she challenged him. She was no fawning miss. She was not hanging on his every word. She defied him and rebuked him and invigorated his mind. He was always hoping to be one step ahead of her, but she repeatedly surprised him with her wit.

He was pleased that she seemed livelier on these walks than she had appeared on Easter morning, but his concern from that day was still itching at him to be sure she was well. Her sullen eyes at church, coupled with the fact that she had not come for dinner that evening, worried him. When they had been at Netherfield Park together, and in Hertfordshire in general, she had been confident and self-assured. Not so in Kent. In Kent, even in her teasing, she was quieter and more cautious, and even apologetic.

"Pray forgive the impertinence of my question, but I hope you are well?" he asked tentatively.

"I am, sir."

She seemed to take the question lightly, distracted by the trees and the birds, running her free hand across the leaves of a nearby shrub and pausing to examine its buds.

He ventured again, "You did not seem yourself at Sunday's service. When you did not attend Easter dinner at Rosings, I was concerned for your health. I hope you are quite...recovered?"

She stopped her study of the shrub and turned to looked up at him, her brow arched elegantly. "Did my cousin say I was unwell?"

"He did not. In fact, he did not mention anything about your whereabouts. Those were my own conclusions."

She looked thoughtful for a moment. "I was not able to attend."

"Might I ask why?"

Her discomfort was obvious, and he hastened to apologise. "No mind. It is none of my business, naturally." He gestured along the path, indicating she should go ahead...but she did not. She remained still and pensive, and he sensed that perhaps she wanted to tell him more. At least he hoped she did.

"You would honour me if you should choose to confide in me," he said gently.

Quietly, she said, "I was not allowed to go to Rosings because...because..."

He waited while she trailed off and then appeared to come to some resolution to finish. She turned her face from his when she finally continued, "Due to my misbehaviour."

Her words were a jolt. "What? Surely my aunt has not...has she barred you from Rosings?"

Miss Elizabeth brought her hand gently to his arm, and dimly, he thought what a mark it was of her character that in the midst of her distress she sought to reassure him.

"No, sir. It is nothing of that sort." He was hurt to hear the ambiguity in her answer. He was quickly searching for a polite response when he only wanted the truth—but she was not his to ask. If only he could demand the truth! If she was his, if she was under his protection...

She must have seen the turmoil in his expression, for she responded, "It was simply a disagreement with my cousin."

Darcy's brow wrinkled, bewildered at such a notion. He could only be more baffled when she looked away from him and said, "Nor am I permitted to partake of any further invitations."

He was not at all satisfied with her answer, his concern only increasing. She was staring down at her feet, so he could not read her facial expression. "Miss Bennet, I hope you will allow me to help if you are in any distress."

She looked up at him, her face a mixture of sadness and hope, "Thank you, sir. I shall."

She turned towards the path once again and softly pressed his arm with her hand. His anger was tempered by her gentle touch. She may not desire to share all with him, but she appeared to trust him. Her hand pressed a second time on his arm, gently urging him to move his feet, one in front of the other.

It was in her favour to move him along, because inside his mind a storm of anger was brewing. *What in the devil would occur to cause that bumbling vicar to punish his grown cousin, a guest of his wife? Nay, not only a guest but his wife's most intimate girlhood friend! I could thrash him!*

He and Fitzwilliam would call on the parsonage more often. The past two mornings after he joined her for a walk, Darcy had visited the stables for a long ride to clear his head before returning to Rosings. It was vital to find some physical exertion in order to prepare for an afternoon and evening of stale conversation with unlimited amounts of gossip and unwanted advice.

He could relinquish his morning ride this day, though, to check on the state of the parsonage. He must.

She interrupted his chaotic thoughts with a cheerful sounding tone, "I have been dealt worse punishments, Mr Darcy, I assure you. When I was much younger, my mother, in particular, was not fond of my skinned knees and ripped stockings earned from climbing trees. She has many times prohibited me from reading or walking out, and you well know these to be my most treasured pastimes. As you can see, I am out of doors now. No one has taken my walks, nor has Mr Collins limited my reading. I am no prisoner, sir."

She looked for a response, but he did not give it to her, frustration binding his tongue. She continued, her voice becoming even more light-hearted, though surely she must have felt anything but that. "And I have brought several books with me from Hertfordshire. It will take some doing, but I am sure Shakespeare may provide me as many follies and amusements as a dinner at Rosings Park."

With that, he chuckled. He liked very much the vision of a stubborn, young Miss Elizabeth climbing trees to the chagrin of her mother. Darcy envied her spirit and determined good humour. If she were content, he would try to be as well.

"The punishments of young ladies sound far preferable to that of young men. Richard and I—that is, Colonel Fitzwilliam and I—had countless times to line up for the veritable firing squad that was my father's temper. Even when we were old enough to understand what harsh punishments were possible, we still threw our energy thoughtlessly into mischief, causing all kinds of trouble, only to end up in my father's study to face his judgment. And he could be quite severe. His expectations for us were exceedingly high. Richard, as you can imagine, always the military man, would provide as much distraction to the enemy as possible in order to lessen the punishment or direct it away from me."

She smiled up at him. "He rendered a great kindness. Have you always been close friends?"

"Yes, we have. We grew up together. His family's estate, Matlock, is not far from Pemberley. Since he joined the army, he is often gone for long periods of time, but he is entirely devoted to his family. We share the guardianship of my younger sister. When his time is his own, he often spends it with us. I had not a brother, but he has been nearly that to me."

"I always wanted a brother," she said wistfully.

"I can imagine a house full of sisters was fairly different from the quiet home I was reared in. Not to mention *your* particular sisters," he said, hoping to see her smile.

She feigned offence, gasping and bringing her free hand to her chest. "You wound me, sir!"

He laughed and was relieved to see her join him. Her full, honest smile brought his senses all to attention. He was so overwhelmed with joy when she enticed him to laugh. It was a freedom he was unaccustomed to. In that moment, both of them grinning widely, he imagined pulling her by her hand deeper into the woods and kissing her soundly. His smile grew even wider, and she stared at him, as if she had never seen him thus.

Laughingly, she said, "I am particularly unlucky in meeting with a person so well able to expose the real character of the Bennet women! Not to mention being in a part of the world where I had hoped to pass myself off with some degree of credit. What will your aunt think if you describe my silly and unruly sisters? Indeed, Mr Darcy, it is ungenerous of you to mention all that you know to my disadvantage!"

"Your secret is safe with me, Miss Bennet. As always, I am at your service." He bowed deeply, almost reverently, in the same manner as Mr Collins, and found himself laughing once again as he came back up. They were caught up in the moment, both smiling and attempting to catch their breath.

"I do thank you, sir, both for your secrecy and the distraction you have provided this morning. I do dearly love to laugh, and humour is in short supply at Hunsford Parsonage," she said, somewhat breathlessly.

He could not say more, so he simply responded, "I know."

Clouds were beginning to block the sharp morning sun, threatening the possibility of rain. Both nodded in understanding of the darkening sky and began making their way back to the parsonage.

After accompanying Miss Elizabeth to the fork in the road that would take her to her cousin's home, he felt a twinge of regret to say goodbye once again. He could not bring her with him to Rosings and openly pay court to her in public, as he dearly wished—not yet. And especially not in Kent.

If he did decide to accept her attentions and choose to court her, he would want her as far away from his meddling aunt as possible. And their engagement would have to be of a short duration in order to remove her from her family promptly as well. Their impropriety and connexions to trade would make her entrance into London society even more strained.

Her family truly was a nuisance. She agreed with him on this, as was evidenced from their earlier tête-à-tête. Should he decide to marry her, the distance between Longbourn and Pemberley would appropriately burden those relationships. He froze in the middle of the lane, turning his gaze back in the direction of the parsonage. *Am I truly contemplating marriage?*

The thought shocked him, and he began walking once again in the direction of Rosings. The *ton* would assume she had entrapped him in some way. It would be necessary to be seen in London with her for a time before an engagement was announced and to introduce her to Lord and Lady Matlock, ensuring their support early on.

If Lady Matlock understood his intentions, she would take Miss Elizabeth under her wing and thrust her into society properly. Her acceptance and supervision would be key.

He thought of Miss Elizabeth's excitement and joy if he were to finally tell her that he too felt all she felt, and his pace quickened. After all her teasing and faux quarrelling these many months, he imagined she would be quite overjoyed to see her efforts had succeeded in securing him. He smiled at the thought.

Once she was his, he would ensure no one ever occasioned her to look the way she had the previous Sunday. Never again. She may truly be banned from Rosings if he made her his wife, but that alone would be an incentive to woo her. He hoped he possessed the courage to make this choice, but he was yet uncertain whether it was all worth it.

It was easy enough to convince his aunt that he and Fitzwilliam must attend to business out of doors that afternoon. His aunt was made agreeable to their scheme to venture out in the rain, as Darcy intended to inspect the eastern fields for the drainage concerns shared by her tenants.

Fitzwilliam smirked even less than anticipated when Darcy suggested they call on the parsonage before returning to Rosings.

As expected, their visit was accepted with wild enthusiasm from the vicar himself. Darcy allowed his cousin to guide the discussion and share good-humoured tales about the war on the Continent. His cousin was an experienced conversationalist and always put others at ease. Darcy, while enjoying his cousin's banter, found it hard to sit still. He crossed and uncrossed his legs. He moved over to the window to observe the rain. He sat back down and accepted tea. All the while, he watched Miss Elizabeth. And watched her cousin.

The man could not stop talking, but he seemed harmless enough. It was hard to imagine him punishing Miss Elizabeth when all Darcy observed beyond the profuse and ridiculous flattery the man uttered was the beaded sweat on his brow; the man was nearly quivering in excitement and nervousness over his esteemed guests. He did not seem to be a danger, but merely a fool.

Miss Elizabeth appeared well too. He enjoyed watching her respond to Fitzwilliam's stories—relishing the tilt of her head or the curling of an unruly lock of hair around her finger while deep in contemplation, as well as the way her eyes sparkled when she was rather amused. She was not the woman of the woods from four hours prior, but she did not seem unhappy either. She rather reminded him of her elder sister Jane—quiet, appeasing, and serene.

In all, it was a mystery, but one he was well pleased to figure out.

While attending church the following Sunday, Elizabeth found herself trying to avoid looking at Mr Darcy. How greatly one week improved the way she saw the man! One week of pleasing weather and fulfilling exercise with her friend. A friend? She was surprised by her own notion.

The man was in many ways completely infuriating—ruining lives one day and being a gentle confidant on another! She reminded herself that it was mere curiosity driving her interest in him. He was like a specimen in a rather intriguing experiment. She needed more evidence before drawing any conclusions, that was all.

Watching him enter the church with Colonel Fitzwilliam, she found it perplexing that these two men of such opposite natures were so close; however, Mr Bingley too was a man of cheery smiles as well as an open and welcoming character. How was it that these two talkative and hospitable men relied on and befriended such a serious creature? Perhaps Mr Darcy enjoyed being around more effusive individuals? He had certainly enjoyed her teasing antics that week.

After the service, Elizabeth noted Mr Darcy making his way to her. She blushed at his approach—her cheeks hot, she lowered her face in the hopes that her bonnet would guard her discomfiture. He was followed closely by Mr Collins, hastening after him to bow to his patroness's revered nephew and thanking him for his continued condescension.

Mr Darcy's entire appearance changed from that of an approaching friend to the defensive and haughty demeanour she had long been acquainted with. Her cousin asked no less than three questions before allowing a space in time for Mr Darcy to respond, to which Mr Collins received merely a nod. Not shrewd enough to see the censure in Mr Darcy's silence, her cousin continued babbling on without any encouragement.

Once Mr Collins moved on to speak to Lady Catherine, Mr Darcy's demeanour softened, and he leaned down to ask quietly, "Has the vicar lifted your restrictions on this charming Sunday, or shall we miss the opportunity to entertain you again this afternoon, Miss Bennet?"

His manner surprised her. *Is Mr Darcy flirting?* The thought enlivened her.

She mirrored his gesture, leaning towards him as if to

share a divine secret. "It is a pity I shall not be joining you this afternoon, sir, for I shall miss the diversion," she said archly. *And am I flirting with Mr Darcy?*

Composing herself and acknowledging a few onlookers, she adjusted her expression to a more neutral countenance and continued, "The weather appears to promise another afternoon of rain, Mr Darcy. I am sure a book will be all the amusement I require today."

CHAPTER 7

The day that followed was plagued by a driving rain that kept everyone inside. Mending clothes from Charlotte's charity basket and Elizabeth's embroidery were only sufficient diversion for so long. Elizabeth had also depleted her reading material and had not yet received any letters from home, nor from Jane in London. She could not imagine she was welcome to the contents of the library at Rosings. She equally could not imagine Mr Collins having any book that would interest her. She had already suffered sufficient examples of his book collection during the nightly religious lessons he required her to sit for.

Hoping to help Charlotte along in making friends in the village, Elizabeth coaxed her friend to go shopping the next day if the weather improved. Mr Collins reluctantly allowed them the time for their 'frivolous' walk to town.

After Charlotte assisted Elizabeth in posting a letter to Jane in London, they visited the local milliner and hosier, a bookshop, and eventually stopped at a bakery for some fresh scones. The baker's wife introduced the ladies to their other customer, a Mrs Jacobson, whom Charlotte later identified as a young, wealthy widow of the area whom she had not yet had the pleasure of meeting.

Mrs Jacobson was surprisingly welcoming, though she had little of substance to say. Elizabeth was bored by the conversation but could feel Charlotte's excitement at the possibility of a friendly neighbour. The ornate and overly decorated bonnet upon the lady's head was diverting enough to pull at Elizabeth's curiosity. A lavender ribbon, matching the lining of the bonnet, was tied into an ornate bow under her chin. If the lady had ceased in her decorations there, the bonnet would have been pretty—but no. A dark blue bird perched in a nest sat atop, inquisitively staring Elizabeth in the eye. Concentration was beyond her capabilities at the sight of it.

Mrs Jacobson pulled her from her amusement to ask about each of their purchases that day and related her own. Their new acquaintance was particularly excited about some red ribbon she had purchased. Elizabeth wondered if she would consider mounting a pigeon on her next bonnet.

It was disappointing to know instinctively that her friend would not be entertained by her musings, though Charlotte did seem a little happier on their walk home. Charlotte had been informed of numerous members of the gentry in the area but had yet to meet many neighbours beyond their parishioners who frequented Sunday services. Her friend appeared genuinely delighted to have been introduced to someone new, and for that, Elizabeth would be grateful, no matter what she thought of the lady's bonnet.

A windy morning was the setting for Elizabeth's next walk with Mr Darcy. She had been forced to wear her pelisse and warmer gloves and to tie the ribbons of her bonnet tightly under her chin. Even with the wind howling, Elizabeth could not be kept from her own moment of solitude every day— even if her walks could no longer be called solitary. She still found this part of her day to be a safe haven from the anxious air of the parsonage. Elizabeth continued to wonder what possessed Mr Darcy to deviate so greatly from one version of himself to the next—from this amiable man to the reserved gentleman he had given her to expect at Netherfield.

Searching for answers to her mind's unresolved questions, Elizabeth asked Mr Darcy to tell her more about his life. He spoke extensively about his many houses and tenants and projects. She had not imagined there were more properties than the house in town and the renowned Pemberley. His responsibilities were great, and she felt guilty for ever imagining he had any improper pride.

He also spoke expressively about his sister, Georgiana, and her preferences. It was, indeed, a joy to hear him speak so lovingly about her. He was detailed in his description— she was tremendously timid but came to life when playing the pianoforte. Though she lacked confidence in most of the traditional feminine endeavours, she was truly passionate about music, and it showed.

While Elizabeth was aware Mr Darcy was not verbose, it was surprising to hear him speak openly about his own reserved nature. "Like my sister, I too am ill qualified to recommend myself to strangers," he told her. "I certainly have not the talent which some people possess of conversing easily with those I have never seen before."

This information gave Elizabeth further understanding of him. When they first met, he had been surrounded by unfamiliar society. She had immediately judged him, assuming him only haughty and prideful. *He did insult me the first time we met—but he was also being compelled by a much more sociable friend to dance in a room full of strangers.* Never had she considered an imposing man such as he, with so much experience in the world, would be uncomfortable in society!

She had formerly speculated it was his station, far above all others in Meryton, that kept him reticent; when, it appeared, it was likely his private nature. She was slowly learning he was prideful, but not to a fault. There were further layers to his personality, and his pride was not unjustified. There was a great deal to be proud of, and his self-importance may have been more a mask than arrogance.

His deep affection for his sister was evident, and allowed Elizabeth to see a softer side of him. She kept quiet when he told her about a disappointing event that occurred the previous summer. He spoke of leaving his sister in the charge of an untrustworthy companion who put her in harm's way. His withdrawn expression revealed he was even now very affected by this, still burdened by what had occurred.

How well did she understand this! She too was learning what it meant to put trust in another person who later turned out to be unworthy of it. While she would not press him for further details of what had happened to his sister, Elizabeth could sense his wretchedness. The impenetrable Mr Darcy had been shaken by whatever had occurred, and she rather enjoyed seeing this exceptionally unguarded side of him. He cared for his family deeply and detested those who would bring them harm. She wanted to return the comfort he provided during their last walk together, so she moved closer, leaning on his arm and giving it a little squeeze. She hoped if the gesture alarmed him that he would consider the chilly gusts of wind a motive.

Darcy was elated when Miss Elizabeth held his arm more tightly and pressed herself against him. While her bonnet now blocked his view of her expressions, he was delighted to feel her warmth. His body reacted immediately to her closeness. He gently covered her hand with his but had to make a concerted effort to concentrate on the conversation.

When they entered the glade he had shown her once before, she pulled away from him, closing her eyes and tipping her face heavenward. In that moment, he thought her the loveliest creature he had ever beheld.

He was surprised by how comfortable he felt sharing details of his life with her. There were many gentlemen of his long acquaintance who knew much less about him. Watching her just then, he considered how dearly he would like to introduce her to Georgiana. Miss Elizabeth's spirit could bolster Georgiana, and a friendship would undoubtedly provide his sister some needed confidence.

Back at the parsonage, Elizabeth and Charlotte settled into their routine of sewing in the parlour after breakfast. The hour was early for callers, so when Hayes entered to announce visitors, they were surprised. Elizabeth could not see the cards that had been handed to Mrs Collins, but she immediately straightened and smoothed her skirt, assuming it would again be Mr Darcy and the colonel. To her surprise, however, it was Mrs Jacobson bringing two friends to call on Charlotte.

Mrs Summers and Mrs Oliver were both on a smaller scale than Mrs Jacobson, and not just in the sense of height. Both were smartly dressed for morning calls, but neither of the ladies could claim the same creative and exaggerated style that Mrs Jacobson was clearly known for. Atop her head sat a crimson velvet bonnet with large black feathers jutting from just over her ear. The other ladies followed her in quietly and stood in eagerness for an introduction.

After all were introduced, Charlotte called for tea and refreshments and settled in to hear the neighbourhood gossip. Charlotte eventually manoeuvered the conversation to boast of her best attribute—her connexion to Lady Catherine. The ladies were amazed by her regular visits to the estate and invitations to dine. They fawned over her, and Charlotte was nearly glowing with pride as she described with great detail the ornate rooms and the two elaborate sets of china she had had the pleasure of observing while taking tea.

Elizabeth was mostly quiet, allowing Charlotte to form her friendships where she could, but enjoyed studying the characters of the women as they spoke. She decided these ladies must operate beyond Lady Catherine's dominion to be interested in the Collinses' intimacy with her ladyship, rather than be repulsed by it.

How odd it was to listen to Charlotte go on and on about Lady Catherine, sounding very much like her husband! But Elizabeth knew how much Charlotte would wish to be on even-footing with these wealthier women, to establish her position with them. Nevertheless, it was alarming to watch Charlotte fall in with the neighbourhood gossips, contributing titbits of her own knowledge of neighbours as she could. If Elizabeth closed her eyes, she fancied that Charlotte had become Lady Lucas. *Are we all to eventually become ladies of nervous tendencies and spiteful gossiping? Are we destined to become our mothers?*

After the callers departed, Elizabeth went upstairs to rest. She meant to settle her mind, but it was filled with concern for her friend. Was she truly to leave Charlotte in Kent with these insipid ladies and her vexing husband?

Before travelling to Kent, Elizabeth would have believed that Charlotte would run her household with little interference from Mr Collins, whom she had imagined simply pottering in his garden and speaking nonsensically from the pulpit once a week. Yet, the anxieties and unspoken air of uncertainty in the home were clearly beyond Charlotte's management. Elizabeth did not envy Charlotte having to spend her days and nights with Mr Collins.

Charlotte had paid a dear price for the privilege of having her own home, and Elizabeth shuddered to imagine how near she might have been to finding herself in her friend's position. Did Charlotte resent her for it? Surely not.

In any case, Elizabeth could not feel guilty for exercising the one power women held, which was the authority to refuse! Surely Charlotte could not hold it against her now, not when she had so vehemently opposed the match that Charlotte had calmly and thoughtfully accepted.

Granted, this was all before Hunsford—before Lady Catherine made clear her complete control over the parsonage household—and before the daily interference of Mr Collins in all of Charlotte's affairs. How could her friend not be miserable?

A knock below stairs brought Elizabeth from her thoughts. Shortly after, the maid came to tell her there were more callers downstairs. This time, it was the callers she had first anticipated.

Their visit was all that was to be expected: the colonel was jovial and entertaining, while Mr Darcy was all that was civil and polite.

There was no sense in Mr Darcy feigning indifference, as Elizabeth had long been aware of his frequent looks. She was even becoming more accustomed to his unending stares. No longer considering them brooding or disdainful, she was a bit discomfited by the notion that they may, in fact, be rather the opposite. She blushed just thinking of it.

During an especially dull conversation about the accumulation of spring rain, Elizabeth brazenly decided to stare back. She wondered if he would break the gaze first. She stared rather plainly at him with a tranquil expression that she had been recently assuming while in Kent. When he did not look away, she smiled a bit to see if she could effect a change in him. She witnessed his jaw clench and a straightening of his back, but he would not avoid her gaze. His observation merely became more intent.

Since tormenting Mr Darcy was the only enjoyment to be had on that dreary afternoon, she arched her eyebrow in a quizzical manner in an attempt to unsettle him. She watched his lips begin to turn upward; he tried to repress the movement, but it appeared to make it even more inevitable.

Suddenly, he stood and moved to the window rather quickly. Following him with her gaze, she observed in the reflection of the panes of glass that his lips did turn up into a full smile once his back was to the room. She likewise grinned at the sight of his dimples. She felt quite satisfied with herself and considered the game won.

Allowing her attention to appear engaged in the conversation once again, her mind began to wander. She must

consider Mr Darcy's marked kindnesses and the implications. She could not conceive why she had challenged him in
that way—was she becoming like her youngest sisters, Lydia
and Kitty, with their unrestrained and heedless flirting?
What did she want from Mr Darcy? Surely, she understood
the consequences of provoking the man in such a manner!

She was certain he understood it was merely a study of
his character, or rather a game intended to push him to a
point whereby he might show himself more openly. But, no.
It was not only that. She was beginning to comprehend there
was something drawing her to him, and that he, against
every expectation, appeared to be just as interested in teasing
and flirting with her.

Elizabeth was forced to contain her amusement in this
conclusion. It was nonsensical to say the least. Mr Collins
and Mr Wickham had both informed her in Hertfordshire
that Mr Darcy was promised to Miss de Bourgh. If marriage
was not a consideration, she ought to protect herself from
these attentions. Mr Darcy was a wealthy man who was likely
doing nothing more than seeking to relieve his boredom
during a visit to his aunt. He would be forgiven such an
indiscretion as the natural tendency of a man, but in her
case, there could be rumours, and her reputation could be
ruined—or worse, she might begin to care for him and be
hurt.

After the gentlemen departed, Charlotte made her way to the
kitchen to confer with the cook. A soup of potatoes and
onion, a roasted chicken, and a simple apple tart would
round up the evening meal quite charmingly. Charlotte felt it
was in her favour to prepare a lovely table while Elizabeth

was visiting, for surely news would travel back home. She would not be pleased if her hosting abilities were mocked back in Hertfordshire. At least her husband's interference with the menu had lessened in the last month as she began to better understand his particular preferences.

Charlotte went back to her parlour to ensure all was in readiness for the evening scripture, and checked with the footman for the location of her husband. She was relieved to hear he was still out of the house. Naturally, she did not wish illness upon her neighbours, but when her husband was called to attend to families during their last hours, she enjoyed a short-lived respite.

After seeing all was in order, she retired to her room to dress for dinner. She felt a little lighter after the busy day. It was not often the parsonage received callers, and two parties was, indeed, unique. The eventful day rather lifted her spirits.

She sat at her dressing table to attend to her toilette, pleased with herself as she recollected her day. The visit from Mrs Jacobson, Mrs Summers, and Mrs Oliver had been a first and had been sorely needed. She could hardly contain her excitement to have neighbours call on her. It was all she could do to pour the tea and try to follow the many twists and turns the conversation took. And to think! She was even able to offer evidence about why the Price boy had not shown up for work at the Oliver house. Her husband's long-winded speeches about all the goings on in the village might be of some use after all.

She hoped that even though her husband was generally disliked by most of the villagers, it was conceivable her connexions to information and Lady Catherine would assist her in making a few friends—and she deeply longed for local acquaintances. Even with Elizabeth under her roof, she had felt alone. Her marriage had severely altered their long, valuable friendship and left a distressing emptiness in her heart.

The second party of visitors was equally astounding. Lady Catherine's nephews were unusually kind to visit once again. She was especially happy for her husband's absence so she could enjoy the colonel's good humour more fully. Although, it was hard to focus on his tales when she was often distracted by the looks passing between Elizabeth and Mr Darcy.

Charlotte frowned at the recollection of that. How had Elizabeth managed to gain the attentions of a man like Mr Darcy? A wealthy man of the highest social circles— following her around with his eyes like a puppy! But she knew the truth of the matter. She smiled, albeit guiltily, considering that Elizabeth would have her just deserts soon when Mr Darcy wed Miss de Bourgh. It would surely reward her previous selfishness towards Mr Collins. Elizabeth should have considered more carefully what she was capable of attaining and what she most certainly was not.

CHAPTER 8

Elizabeth woke the next morning long before the sun was completely risen, but could already see that it would be a beautiful spring day. And spring it truly was, for she noticed the trees leafing and the flowers' early buds from her window.

Nothing could lessen her temperament on a morning such as this! Even Mrs Montgomery was particularly lively that morning—flitting about, talking of all the new vegetables rising from the earth in the kitchen gardens. Elizabeth thanked her for the rolls and biscuits already wrapped for her morning walk.

This may have been the first morning Elizabeth truly hoped Mr Darcy would accompany her. While she had enjoyed a few solitary walks since his arrival, she admitted to herself that she preferred when he joined her.

Her feet carried her energetically to a path where she might be easily discovered. When she spied him approaching, she could see the look of mischief and humour on his face and laughed outright at his childlike manner. "Might I enquire as to the source of your amusement, sir?"

"I was recalling a particular expression I saw on your own face yesterday. I think, perhaps, you meant to vex me, but I will have you know that you certainly did not." He was then attempting a stern face, but she could see his eyes smiling at her.

"Vex you?" She laughed heartily. "Of course not. I would never, Mr Darcy."

"I shall have you know I too can play at your game. Perhaps I shall punish you by asking Mr Collins to recite a favourite sermon the next time I come to call. We shall see if you can remain as perfectly composed as I was able to."

"You would not!" she said, feigning offence and laughing. "I am certain I shall manoeuvre this to my own amusement, sir! When you come requesting a sermon, I might tell my dear cousin of your preference for Fordyce's sermons on the virtues of young ladies."

"Clever girl," he said most seriously, but with a great admiration that made Elizabeth's heart pound and her breath come short. Fortunately, he offered his arm just then, and she took it quickly.

He was watching her, and she could feel it, sense it. She could hear his breath coming fast just over her shoulder, perhaps waiting for her to look up at him, but she could not. A fierce blush rushed hot over her face, but she was not about to give him the satisfaction of flustering her.

His hand came up to cover hers and set off a response unlike any she had experienced before. She tried to imagine other sensations that could be compared to the feelings such an action caused; but it was entirely foreign to her. His presence provoked an upheaval of emotions and sensations—the comfort of home, the excitement of a new book, and a slight sinking feeling in her stomach, like when you have been caught doing something you should not.

Once reaching the glade, they separated while appreciating the beauty around them. Elizabeth spoke, saying, "Mr Darcy, I was given to believe at Netherfield that your preferred morning exercise was riding. Are there not satisfactory horses at Rosings?"

"I do favour riding." And that was all. He was not going to fall for that playful trap after all. She was a bit disappointed, but he continued, "Do you ride, Miss Bennet?"

"Not if I can help it."

"I wondered as much," he said. "You have the right disposition for it. I would imagine you a great rider one day."

"Perhaps."

"My cousin Anne also prefers to keep her feet firmly on the ground," he said with a smile upon his handsome face. "However, I did encourage her to purchase a phaeton so she may take drives. It arrived just yesterday."

"I would very much like to see that! I know not if I would feel safe on such a thing, with a perch so high off the ground!"

"I can assure you it is quite safe."

"It sounds delightful. I imagine learning to drive it will take some time."

"Fitzwilliam and I plan to take Anne out and instruct her in the afternoons." He smiled as he offered, "I could teach you as well."

"I do not imagine that being necessary. I can assure you, my father will never buy a phaeton. He would deem a vehicle assembled for the purpose of providing pleasure and gaining attention to be far too impractical."

"Do you not agree that pleasure and practicality can both

be achieved?" He looked deep into her eyes, and she wondered if they were still speaking of phaetons and ponies.

"I am sure they can be, sir," she responded in an unfamiliar, husky voice—quickly clearing her throat.

His eyes darkened as he stared at her, "I would by no means suspend any pleasure of yours, Miss Bennet." The look caused a shiver throughout her entire body, and she instinctively averted her eyes.

Suddenly, his hand was on her cheek, tucking a stray, unruly curl back up under her bonnet. Elizabeth felt a delightful lurch in her chest as she looked up at him. The simple touch alerted all her senses in a way she had never felt before—his breath, she could hear; his smell of sandalwood and soap, she breathed in deeply; the warmth of his fingers, the darkening of his eyes. Of all these, she was simultaneously aware.

The space between them grew narrower, and she was unsure whether it had been she or he who closed the gap. His fingers lingered on her cheek and moved slowly down her neck. Her own breath was now coming rapidly, as if to match the pace of his. She tilted her face upwards, instinctively, looking into his eyes for an answer to a question she was unsure of, when suddenly he dropped his hand.

"We should, perhaps, return," he murmured.

"Of course." Left out of breath and still rather shaken by the emotions whirring through her mind, she stumbled in her first few steps back towards the path.

What a maddening man! First the proud, quiet man in Hertfordshire, and now...? This gentle, witty man? It was a shocking transformation from the Mr Darcy she first knew. She was aware that her attachment to him was growing—likely much against her better interests. But, how could she have feelings for a man she still distrusted? Which was the real Mr Darcy?

As they wound their way back towards the parsonage, Elizabeth asked him how he spent his days at Rosings.

"As you suggested earlier, I do often ride. In addition to my own pleasures, my aunt requires a great deal of my time. I have reviewed her ledgers and attended to estate business, much to the chagrin of her steward, I am sure."

Elizabeth smiled at this image. "I imagine Lady Catherine's steward is very capable."

"Aye, he is. He has cared for the estate since I was a child. He does not require my oversight, whether or not my aunt desires it."

"And do you not entertain callers every day?" she asked pertly.

"The ladies of the house do—and often Colonel Fitzwilliam as well. I am not typically at my leisure to join them in the drawing room until just before dinner—and of course, after. Occasionally, Mrs Jenkinson plays the pianoforte in the evenings, but more often than not, the ladies retire early."

Elizabeth remembered playing for Mr Darcy in Hertfordshire. At the time, she had unwittingly thought his intense observation was a desire to examine her inaccurate performance. She had imagined him congratulating himself with each missed key. How her motivations had altered! Today she sought out the self-same scrutiny—but she knew better of it. His attentiveness had not changed, but her interpretation of his fixation had been utterly transformed.

Mr Darcy brought her back to the present, asking, "And how do you spend your days while here in Kent?"

"Mrs Collins and I are often together throughout the day. In the evenings, Mr Collins is on a quest to save my soul, sir. I, his only pupil, sit for a lengthy lesson each evening."

He thought her merely teasing at first, but she assured him that the lessons were a requirement of her stay. That he was appalled by her forced schooling confirmed her own affronted feelings.

"The religious studies are an effort on my cousin's part to exact repentance for the misdeed I mentioned before."

She could tell he wanted to know more, but she was not sure how to tell him without insulting his aunt. If she had written enthusiastically about the number of chimneys and windows at Rosings in her letter to her father, she would not be in this position.

"Your cousin's behaviour is a disgraceful presumption! Have you written to your father to tell him of this treatment? I cannot think he should suffer it."

After a moment of pained hesitation, she confessed, "Mr Collins came across a letter I was writing to my father containing a subject of which he did not approve. This was my misdeed, and if the truth must be known, I cannot deny that I wrote that which offended him. How he came to be in possession of my private correspondence, I know not—not through any honourable means, of that I am sure. Nevertheless, his wrong does not make my error right, and I shall not attempt to write to my father again."

When Elizabeth looked at her companion, she was amazed and a bit fearful of the thunderous hues which had arisen on his brow. "Miss Bennet, that is frankly an unpardonable presumption on the part of Mr Collins. He had no business seeing your private correspondence." He stopped and paced a bit, obviously irritated by the new intelligence from the parsonage. "I could send your letter to your father. No one would question any letter I asked to be posted."

"That is very generous, but I believe unnecessary. Charlotte has made an offer to help should I desire to write home. Just last week, we were discreet, and I was able to send a letter to Jane in London. Besides, I shall be leaving Kent in just over a fortnight. I am certain if I sent a letter to my father now, I should be home before he brought himself to respond. I am sure I can tolerate Mr Collins and his strictures for that long."

Mr Darcy did not like this reply. She found herself rather flattered by his clenched fists and stony glare. But he eventually replied with a nod and offered his arm to continue walking.

They meandered in silence for some time before Mr Darcy finally said, "I know you are not within my care; however, I hope you will oblige me by telling me, at any time, if you are in need of my assistance."

She blushed at the thought. "Thank you. I promise I shall."

Darcy was yet unsure of his intentions towards Miss Elizabeth, but he was persuaded he would protect her as a friend, particularly against the likes of Collins.

Instead of visiting the stables for a lengthy, exertive ride, he turned his steps to the house. Upon entering, the butler took his hat and gloves, and he walked into the smaller dining room to break his fast. Food had already been laid out, even though he was doubtful he would find anyone else in the house had yet arisen.

After filling a plate and accepting the offer of coffee and a newspaper, he sat down to eat. Unfortunately, his anger had taken root, and he found the food could not tempt him. Even the newspaper failed to hold his attention. The coffee, he owned, was welcome, for he always enjoyed a hot beverage in the morning. Beyond that, there was little to satisfy his frustration.

Hearing the click of the door opening, he turned, surprised to see Anne enter. Anne was all that was meek and good. She was a reliable friend, but a fragile person. She could offer listening ears and a weak smile, but little else. She was a welcome distraction on this particular morning, for she offered no offence, no advice, and no conversation.

Darcy considered the long-standing demand from his aunt to marry Anne. Her wishes were never going to come to fruition, even if she would not cease telling others of their inevitability. His aunt's interference was abhorrent, but Darcy worried about how it affected Anne. They had decided between themselves not to wed many years before, yet he felt guilty for letting her continue in this state of waiting due to his reluctance to inform her mother of such.

Until he married or explicitly rejected his cousin, she would be kept at Rosings. How he wished he might take her away and introduce her to more society! She deserved more than this small, suffocating life. She could have had a Season in town and been introduced to many eligible suitors. No doubt her entrance into society would have been welcome, for she possessed a kind soul and enjoyed a sizable fortune, to say nothing of her property.

His mind wandered to Miss Elizabeth. What would Anne think of that choice? While he had spent many months questioning whether she was worthy of his attention, he could not help now wondering whether he was worthy of *her*—her resilience, her wit—so clever and full of life. Even with her poor connexions and lack of fortune, she was the only woman he had ever pictured as Mrs Darcy.

Anne interrupted his thoughts with a quiet enquiry, "Cousin, I am impatient to drive my phaeton. Shall we take a drive today? I am eager for time out of doors. The weather has been quite comfortable this last week."

"Fitzwilliam has examined the phaeton. He took it on a drive yesterday, so I do not believe we should delay."

"I have always envied the ladies in London who drive. Mother says I should have been a celebrated horsewoman had I ever learnt to ride," she said quietly, with a slight hint of humour in her voice.

"No doubt she did," he said with a low, quiet chuckle. Speaking carefully, he added, "I believe Miss Bennet enjoys outdoor pursuits as well. Should we invite her to join us for a lesson?"

"Miss Bennet would be a lovely addition to our party. Shall I send her a note?"

"Pray, do."

Charlotte Collins sat quietly, watching her husband pace about her bedchamber. First to the bed and then to the chair, then to the window and back to the bed again. He was incapable of sitting still, the source of his dismay being the fact that he had missed their many visitors the day prior.

Despite her husband's obvious frenzy, Charlotte remained calm, offering practical answers in sedate accents.

"First, my dear, we were visited by a Mrs Jacobson, whom I became acquainted with during our recent shopping excursion. She is a gentlewoman of some means and brought with her two friends to call on us, a Mrs Summers and a Mrs Oliver."

"And has Lady Catherine heard of these ladies?"

"I am certain that Lady Catherine is familiar with all the gentry in the area. Besides the ladies, her nephews were our other morning callers. The visit, I am convinced, would not have transpired had not her ladyship sanctioned it herself. I am sure you are honoured by their condescension, my dear."

Charlotte, motivated by peace and a sense of control (even if a false sense of it), attempted to steer her husband's mood in a more positive direction. Even the wide berth she gave him every day would not protect her from his interference if their servants were making reports to him of her activities while he was away.

Her husband was motivated not by peace, but by approval. While he nodded along with her counsel, his uncertainty prevailed. "Lady Catherine, in all her splendour and generosity, has made it clear to me that it is my responsibility to ensure you are properly trained to host guests. She has concerns about your father's fortune being acquired in trade, and of course, she is always correct and so thoughtful to offer her help."

"My father was knighted. I am sure Lady Catherine cannot find him or his manners offensive." Charlotte bit her tongue, knowing to say more would be unwise. Unable to help herself, she added, "I can also assure you, my dear, that I am perfectly capable of managing this home and hosting guests."

"Perfectly capable? How am I to know that or reassure her ladyship if I have had so few opportunities to observe you?"

Observe me? "My mother has counselled me in the ways of the gently-bred, and I am sure you do not intend to insult her teachings."

Her husband drew up, attempting to mollify, even as he debased her further. "Lady Catherine believes you may one day be a capable hostess, but nowise does she think you ready now for guests beyond those from Rosings Park. Your excellent mother notwithstanding, the society of Meryton could hardly have prepared you for nobler visitors."

And now I need permission to meet friends? Charlotte's skin fairly prickled with rage. She was a woman of seven-and-twenty and had been capable of entertaining callers for above a decade now. If anyone needed lessons in hospitality, it was her husband who she had found reading a letter from Jane addressed to Elizabeth a week prior!

"If you have no faith in my capabilities as a wife, pray tell me why you asked me for my hand in marriage." Charlotte heard the peevishness in her own tone.

"I could not return to her ladyship without an impending marriage! I went to Hertfordshire because she decreed I should visit and bring back a wife. After my humiliation was delivered by my wicked cousin, there were a mere five days at my disposal before my scheduled return to Kent."

He took her hand, "I thank God you were in such desperate need of a husband, for I had no other ready choices in the county."

Charlotte stood agape. She had always known her husband made a hasty decision when he proposed marriage, but she had unreasonably hoped it was performed with good intention. She had never expected love, but respect, even a little admiration, might have been nice. But no. It was merely her *availability* that drew him. Her availability to suit the whims of his patroness, it appeared.

There was nothing more to say. She simply nodded and averted her eyes.

"We shall turn away callers unless I am home to supervise you, my dear," he said while patting her hand and smiling at her in a belittling manner. She imagined herself a pitiable creature.

The following morning found Elizabeth trapped in the parlour with Charlotte for many more hours than she found pleasant. A dense fog had laid itself across the area, stifling her ability to walk out and, it appeared, also settling a gloom about the home. Charlotte had a vacant look in her eyes and her movements were slow.

Elizabeth held up the small infant's gown she had been sewing in triumph. It was not her best work, but she was proud to add it to the pile of completed items. "Charlotte, I think we need a break. Let us take a short walk. I shall not drag you far in this weather. Perhaps a turn about the garden? Please say yes."

Elizabeth looked at her expectantly and found her friend staring off into the distance, her needle suspended in the air as if frozen in time. "Charlotte?" she asked a bit louder.

Charlotte shook off her distraction and responded, "Pardon?"

"I wondered if you might take the air with me for a time?"

"Oh," she looked around the room before responding in dull tones, "I do not know. I shall ask Mr Collins."

"Pray, do not, Charlotte. It was merely a suggestion. Perhaps another day," Elizabeth offered quickly and followed with a warm smile for her friend. She would rather commence sewing another item than to request her cousin's permission.

Charlotte nodded her approval and began her sewing once again.

A loud commotion brought them both to their feet as Mr Collins sprang into the parlour, barely catching his breath. Elizabeth steeled herself for another possible confrontation but was relieved to see a glow of elation on his face.

"My dear Mrs Collins, come see! A note has arrived by footman from Rosings. I wonder at its contents!" His eagerness surpassed even the notion of opening the missive, so excited was he.

He tore open the note and skimmed the words within, his enthusiasm fading into a surprised grunt. "Cousin Elizabeth has been invited by Miss de Bourgh to ride in her new phaeton on Saturday morning at ten o'clock. She will be accompanied by one of her cousins."

"How have you managed this, Eliza?" Charlotte asked coldly, but quickly adjusted to a false smile. "I had no notion that you and Miss de Bourgh had taken an interest in one another."

Elizabeth looked back and forth between the two of them, unsure how to respond, as she too was surprised by the invitation. A note from Miss de Bourgh? It was shocking. Theirs was a passing acquaintance, nothing more.

Mr Collins hurried to offer his opinion. "I am certain Miss Elizabeth has met Miss de Bourgh on a number of occasions —dining at Rosings and at the Sunday services." He was frantically nodding as if to convince himself of the possibility. "You will not be insensible to the honour, I am sure. Lady Catherine herself must have sanctioned this outing. How fortunate you are!"

Though her cousin's words were eager, his tone and narrowed eyes held suspicion. Clearly he considered these ill-gotten gains. Elizabeth was unsure how to answer him. A look to her friend did not help; Charlotte's false smile made her feel ill. "Yes, well, this is a surprise. I am pleased and quite honoured by the gesture."

"Please do mind your manners and remember your place," Mr Collins scolded. "This condescension is quite extraordinary."

He asked Charlotte to pen a quick response in the affirmative to send with the waiting footman. Taking the note with him out of the parlour, she heard him repeat, "Extraordinary."

Extraordinary, indeed! Elizabeth was excited for the planned activity and knew which cousin would undoubtedly be accompanying Miss de Bourgh.

CHAPTER 9

When Saturday arrived, even the overcast morning did not diminish Elizabeth's excitement. When the sunshine came out and rendered the sky cloudless, she began to anticipate Mr Darcy's imminent arrival, and Miss de Bourgh's, of course.

Mr Collins called Elizabeth into his small study to remind her to behave and to outline the diverse and countless glowing qualities of the grand Miss Anne de Bourgh. She found herself unable to make eye contact with him, and during his long-winded speech, decided to occupy her mind with a thorough evaluation of the room.

The room was as poorly kept as Mr Collins himself. Dusty old tomes lined the walls, evidently untouched by the current resident. Ink spills on the top of his desk illustrated either a compulsion towards clumsiness when writing his sermons or an inattentive maid.

"...and you must not forget the superiority of her blood line..."

She continued to nod and smile, keeping her mouth shut, all while feigning interest in her cousin's speech about the heiress of Rosings Park.

While wandering about the room, her eyes were drawn to familiar handwriting in an open letter that sat upon his desk. Her father had written to Mr Collins? Elizabeth tried to appear attentive to her cousin's rambling harangue while clandestinely examining the letter to see if it were truly from her father, who was a self-proclaimed negligent correspondent. She could only imagine what devious bits of humour lay within—and what a long letter it appeared to be! Leaning a bit farther, without directing attention to herself, she observed with some surprise that the salutation was 'My dearest Lizzy'.

She was so surprised by the appearance of her own name that she confirmed it not once but many times, even going so far as to blatantly bend over his desk and eventually to hold it up to him and interrupt his speech.

"Perhaps, sir, instead of speaking to me about virtuous behaviour, you might explain how a letter written by my father and addressed to me is in your possession." She spoke evenly despite the angry flush that heated her cheeks. "Nay, not simply in your possession, but unsealed and lying open on your desk, and therefore, presumably *read*."

Mr Collins flushed as well, but far from chastened, he went on the attack. "Give me that!" He grabbed the letter out of her hands. "I shall decide what reading is appropriate in my home."

"A letter from my father is hardly to be compared to deciding whether the nature of a book is appropriate. You must give that to me!"

"Must I?" His voice got louder, and he rose to his full height to loom over Elizabeth. "I am master of this house, and master of *you* while you reside here. You have not shown yourself to be of good judgment and upright character—"

"I beg your pardon!"

"Lady Catherine herself was informed of your behaving in a manner that was not ladylike and advised me to correct it while you reside under my roof. She insisted that it was my duty to nudge back that which was going awry."

"Informed of unladylike behaviour! By whom? I may be under your roof, but you have no authority over me." Elizabeth's thoughts immediately turned to Mr Darcy. He would come and remove her—she was sure of it. If only he were here now!

Right then Charlotte opened the door. She exchanged a glance with her husband and then looked self-righteously at Elizabeth before saying, "Whatever have you done now, Eliza?"

"What have *I* done?" Elizabeth asked, incredulously. "I found a letter addressed to me from my father on your husband's desk—*opened*! Your husband is reading my personal correspondence."

And Charlotte, incredibly, replied quietly, "It is his house, Elizabeth, and anything that enters into it is within his purview."

She sounded as if she spoke by rote, repeating the words that no doubt she had heard often. Elizabeth could scarcely form a thought through the astonishment which beset her.

"That is not true. My own father has not examined—"

"Your father has allowed you too much liberty," Charlotte replied sharply. From the corner of her eye, Elizabeth saw Mr Collins nod approvingly.

"I beg your pardon!"

"You always were a selfish creature, Elizabeth. Why you could not simply visit your dear cousin and enjoy our hospitality with a semblance of gratitude and maturity, I shall never know."

Elizabeth was astonished by the aloof, cold response from her once-dear friend. Mr Collins appeared distinctly satisfied with his wife and repeated smugly, "My wife is correct. Cousin, you must learn gratitude and humility and forget these wild ways your father has allowed you."

Wild ways? Since when is reading a letter wild? The thrum of her temper surged along with her rapid heartbeat until she was nearly out of breath. She had stayed in Kent for Charlotte, wanting to know what was happening in her home and wishing to see what she could do to help her; but it was clear that Charlotte had chosen her path.

It took all the patience and poise within her to accept this. In a remarkably steady voice, enunciating each word, she said, "Do not ever call me 'cousin' again. You are no longer my family. I shall no longer recognise you. You need not be in my presence another minute." She said these things to Mr Collins but took the time to give Charlotte one last meaningful, pleading look—which went unanswered. "Please give my excuses to Miss de Bourgh."

Elizabeth grabbed only her bonnet before tearing out of the house. She was always agile and quick on her feet, but in her desperation to move as far away from the Hunsford parsonage as possible, she had quite lost her bearings. She stopped after some time to put her hands on her knees and draw in a deep cleansing breath, willing her racing pulse to slow, and wishing the heat on her face would be cooled.

She moved to lean against a large, old oak tree, employing the shade of the branches to catch her breath and take in her surroundings. Once she oriented herself, her feet moved her forward before her mind caught up, taking her at breakneck speed down the familiar path.

Darcy was all anticipation as he drove the phaeton towards the parsonage. Anne, in turn, appeared to be struggling against laughter. His intentions, his eagerness, must be so obvious, but he found himself uncaring. According to Fitzwilliam, she had been an apt pupil all week, and she likely thought this scheduled morning of instruction an amusing ruse. Nonetheless, he was thankful that she had invited Miss Elizabeth.

"I fear you have gone distracted, Darcy. Perhaps you should have let me drive."

"I was under the impression this outing was to be a learning experience for the ladies?"

"As you wish," she replied, "But I shall remind you that I went out on my own just yesterday. While you were busy inspecting the empty tenant dwellings these last two days, Fitzwilliam has been instructing me. He thought I was ready."

"You know your mother's opinions regarding the necessity of diligent practice to attain proficiency at any skill," Darcy replied drily.

Anne murmured an inaudible response towards the passing scenery.

Darcy drew the phaeton up in front of the parsonage and hopped down, handing the reins to Anne and tipping his hat to Mrs Collins as she rushed out to meet them. The lady was twisting her hands in front of her and greeted them with a trembling voice and shaky curtsey, unable to meet their eyes. "It appears that Eliza has gone off on one of her rambles and must have lost track of time. I did remind her of her engagement this morning. I am sure she will be saddened to learn she missed you."

Mr Collins had arrived during his wife's speech and added eagerly, "As I am sure you agree, I shall tell my cousin that it would be best if she kept to herself here at the parsonage for the remainder of her visit. She is unused to and quite unsuited for your noble attentions. She is wholly unaccustomed to the elevated society we enjoy here in Kent. I shall be sure to remind her about the consequences of offending you both."

Her husband's speech seemed to embolden Charlotte, who became more certain of herself. "Please allow me once again to apologise, on behalf of myself and my dearest husband. It will not happen again. She will not be given the opportunity."

Darcy was confused by their abruptness and before he could respond, the couple was already returning into their home.

Darcy watched them go, his eyes narrowed. Disappointment coursed through him but more than that—anger. Had they lied outright? Where was Elizabeth? Could she be in some danger? He would not have believed it possible, but in light of what Elizabeth told him before of Mr Collins's behaviour, perhaps it was.

"What are you thinking, Darcy?" Anne called from her perch.

"Am I so obvious?"

Anne replied to that with a mischievous grin, then asked, "You are concerned for Miss Bennet?"

Darcy, disconcerted by Anne's directness, said, "It is unlike her to be late or to forget an engagement."

"Perhaps you should look for her and be sure she is not

injured somewhere." Anne recalled herself then and said, "Of course, that would be the responsibility of Mr Collins, would it not?"

Darcy shot her a droll glance. "Neither Mr Collins nor his wife seemed to think anything amiss. But for me..." He looked off towards the forest.

"Go and seek her," Anne said. "I shall return to the house." At his look, she added, "You said yourself I was quite the apt pupil. It is a short distance, and I shall do perfectly well, I am sure."

Darcy nodded, and then watched as she set off, driving very well indeed. He then secured his hat, took note of his surroundings, and began stalking towards the nearby wood. At the very least, he knew he needed to find Miss Elizabeth and discover what kept her from their outing. No matter what the Collinses believed, he did not think it was by choice that she had missed their excursion.

He tried to recall what he last said to her. *Perhaps she did not want to join us after all? No. She was quite clear in her interest.* His feet kept moving, one boot in front of the other—to her. His pace quickened as his agitation grew.

His thoughts were a tangle of emotions—all revolving around her. He had long realised he was drawn to her— happier with her—even with her teasing nature that often discomposed him, but now the depth of his devotion, coupled with the extent of his concern for her, made his wishes perfectly clear to him. *My duty, my family, my sister—I have always done what was right and what was expected, but I cannot deny Elizabeth anything. I want her to have all that I have to give— all my worldly treasures—for my family to be her family, my sister to be her sister, my children to be her children.*

The revelation nearly stopped his forward movement. *I love her.* He loved Elizabeth Bennet of Longbourn in Hertfordshire, and he wanted to marry her, to be with her, to care for her always. No one else would ever take the place as mistress of Pemberley with the same wisdom and grace. No—Elizabeth was clearly the partner he longed for, the equal he had not thought possible. When had he begun to think of her as merely *Elizabeth?*

He had an abrupt notion of where to find her—*she must be in our glade.*

To be betrayed by a friend was surely one of life's greatest pains. The tumult of her mind coupled with the agitation of her spirits meant that Elizabeth arrived at her destination faster than she had anticipated. She must have been running —and she surely looked wild! Her heart felt like it was breaking. *How could I be so wrong about a dear friend?* She had known Mr Collins was an imbecile long before her visit and had deduced from her correspondence that Charlotte was altered, but she never imagined such a breach of loyalty and friendship.

Her friendship was a thing of the past, and Elizabeth steeled herself to find strength for the rest of the wretched visit, for she knew well enough she would not be packing up her things and abandoning Kent early. How would she explain her sudden departure and abrupt appearance in London to her family? Would Mr Collins even permit her to arrange travel?

Elizabeth had known grief before. She had mourned the death of a beloved grandmother and cried alongside Long-bourn's tenants during hardships. But not this—this felt so different. None of her previous experiences compared to this turmoil—this pointed and personal betrayal.

Was this keen meanness years in the making? Or had it been the whim of a moment? Had her entire friendship with Charlotte been a ruse?

Elizabeth considered what she knew. Mr Collins was a controlling, overbearing man who clearly grasped at any shred of authority he could. He held terribly little power in the world, even less with Lady Catherine at the helm of his church, his words, and the running of his home. She could imagine two explanations equally likely for his behaviour— either he deplored his loss of control in all aspects of his life and thus ruled with an iron fist over the women under his power; or he was simply cruel. Perhaps it was a little of both.

It was a juxtaposition of two extraordinarily different men —the Mr Collins who had visited Longbourn and Mr Collins of Kent. One was a babbling, self-serving idiot, but the other was completely punishing. How her father would laugh at her if she wrote a letter explaining the Collinses' current behaviour! He would consider it the greatest of comedy and thank her for the fine joke—and, in all likelihood, ask if the basis of the characters outlined were drawn upon from sheer boredom or madness. She could hear him now, telling her to take up novel-writing to relieve her wild imagination!

But how had Mr Collins exacted such a swift and complete control over Charlotte? Was it merely his words or were there actions as well? While she would not wish his cruelty on anyone, she resolved that her friend was reacting to his viciousness. It appeared Charlotte, once her most reasonable and sensible friend, had been reduced to a bitter woman full of spite.

While considering Charlotte's deceit, Elizabeth was distressed to admit to her growing knowledge of the strong appearance of duplicity in the natures of all people. Even Mr Darcy had recently shown her such an honest and kind nature—a fine, handsome figure who was attentive, gentle, and caring. But she also knew another Mr Darcy—one who was arrogant and proud; one who most certainly reduced his childhood friend, Mr Wickham, to near poverty and—she was fairly sure—one who had pushed Mr Bingley away from Jane. He could be insufferable as easily as he could be kind, it seemed. How was she to trust anyone?

She paced back and forth, her discomposure growing with each step. She had long considered herself a student of character yet Charlotte, known to her since birth, had become a stranger to her in the space of a few months. Her cousin, stupid as he was, was capable of being two wholly different persons in one setting versus another. If she could not even understand those two, how could she even hope to understand a man like Mr Darcy? To reconcile all this behaviour that was perfectly contrary to her previous understanding of him?

And, why has this become about Mr Darcy? She wondered. *I am upset about Charlotte—why does this man persist in invading my thoughts?* She pulled her bonnet off and pointed her face to the sun. She hoped the rays would calm her and provide her strength. As it had always done, nature began to soothe her.

After some time, Elizabeth heard movement in the brush and turned to look, to see what it might be. Taking in the tall, striking form of Mr Darcy, she coloured and felt her ire begin to flood through her entire being. Why did he have to appear here now? He looked so handsome and greeted her with gentle concern.

"You cannot know how relieved I am to see you are not injured. I was very alarmed when the Collinses told me you could not go driving with us. I am afraid I feared the worst."

His kindliness so hard on the heels of her confusion made

her tremble. Bravely, she said, "It is none of your concern, Mr Darcy."

He strode directly to her, standing closer than was strictly appropriate. "I would be happy to make it my concern." His eyes searched her face, and she responded by averting hers.

His imposing stance—so close and protective—nearly broke her. She pressed her lips together tightly to ward off tears and turned her head to hide her face.

His defensive stance softened, and he lowered his voice to speak more softly, leaning into her. "Whatever has happened, please allow me to help."

She knew in that moment she could reach for him, and he would reach back. She was sure he would calm her—but could she trust him? His changeable nature might be just as ruinous as Charlotte's! Could she depend upon anyone in this world? Elizabeth might find it entertaining to be contrary in order to amuse her company, but in matters of the heart, she required constancy.

"I have long believed myself discerning and have valued my ability to read others' characters, particularly those I have known my entire life. In my vanity, I believed I was worthy of true friendship. It is a bitter thing to find yourself surrounded by people of such duplicitous manners. I wish I had never travelled to Kent. There is not one person here I can trust."

"Not one?" He looked hurt and stepped closer, "I hope you know you may trust me."

"How can I? No, you sir have confused me most of all."

"Have I?" He reached out to touch her arm, and she withdrew. He retreated just as quickly. "What reason have you to distrust me? If I have provoked you in some way—if, if I have alarmed you..."

Her anger, her distress on this morning were not founded

upon Mr Darcy's actions or character, yet he was here and he was asking her questions. When else might she have the opportunity to understand him? He had, at the ball at Netherfield, refused her the chance to sketch his character. Perhaps he would answer for it now.

She straightened to her full height, raising her chin to look him in the eye, and steeled herself for a denial. "Mr Darcy, here, in Kent, you have been all kindness to me, all concern for my well-being and my equanimity. A true friend, I might say. However, please tell me how I may trust the man who ruined, perhaps forever, the happiness of a most beloved sister?"

His astonishment was clear, and he coloured in response —a flash of his true emotions. She saw him replace the concern with an immediate defensiveness, and so she continued, "What motive can you have to be a party to that breach? Even if you were not the primary instigator, I am certain you did not act in her defence."

Still astonished, he hesitated. "Yes." Clearing his throat, he continued, "I will not deny my part. Bingley may have *believed* himself in love, but that distinction is rather unremarkable. The material reason I endorsed his departure was that your sister appeared unattached. I watched them most particularly and did not perceive in her a deep regard for my friend."

He took a step back, and hesitantly resumed his speech, "I was aware that Bingley's attention to your sister had given rise to a general expectation of their marriage. I did not want to see him made a fool. For him to marry her without shared affection—"

"You thought her indifferent?" she interrupted.

"Yes. I did not wish for a marriage of unequal affection for my friend."

She was not satisfied, but she understood. He was wrong, but if he had been right, she could agree that she would not wish for an unequal love for her sister either. He was not the first to point out Jane's appearance of indifference. Her sister's serene manners and reserved nature did not often permit others to perceive her thoughts or feelings.

Even with Mr Darcy's participation, Mr Bingley did, in fact, make his own decisions. If what she was learning was true, it was Mr Bingley's indecisive nature and uncertainty that truly separated the two. At least in Mr Darcy's decision-making, he was confident. His truth might be painful, but he did not put on airs to simply ease her comfort.

This still did not explain his general disdain for the people of Meryton or his officious treatment of the good-natured and charming Mr Wickham. He left the man nearly impoverished and forced to join the militia when a respectable living had been entrusted to him by Mr Darcy's own father.

"You are good to your friends and do not hesitate to involve yourself in their concerns." Elizabeth bit her lip a moment before adding, "I suppose I might be more alarmed by how you treat those who are not your friends."

"Who do you see that I have mistreated? What do you accuse me of?"

"Did I not have a very plain view of your disdain for strangers at our first meeting when you refused to dance with me and insulted my appearance?"

His eyes were wild, searching for the truth. She felt a sort of pity that he was having trouble recalling what she was referring to.

"You heard me at the assembly?" he finally asked.

She nodded, and he was shocked into silence, eyes wide and mouth hanging open. "And what of Mr Wickham?"

"Wickham?" he repeated, clearly abhorring to hear even the name. He took a step backwards.

"How am I to reconcile the man you are here in Hunsford with the man I long decided to dislike? Your character was revealed to me by Mr Wickham many months ago. Yes, I would say you are very good to your friends but woe to the man that you have decided is no longer worthy of your consideration!"

"You take an eager interest in that gentleman's concerns," Mr Darcy retorted. "It should not surprise me—many young ladies have been taken in by his charm."

"His charm!" She huffed. "It is not his charm that made me feel pity for him! You have reduced him to his current state of poverty, yet you feel no concern for his misfortunes!"

"His misfortunes!" he spat. "His misfortunes have been earned by his actions! George Wickham was a favourite of my father. Our fathers greatly respected one another—his being the steward at Pemberley. George was my father's godson, and we were raised like brothers."

He began pacing while he told a long, detailed story of a childhood friend turned spiteful rival. It was the most Elizabeth had ever heard him speak, and she knew instantly that not everyone was afforded this vulnerable, effusive version of Mr Darcy. She felt the honour of receiving his confidences in parallel to her great dismay at learning of Mr Wickham's numerous misdeeds.

She was appalled to learn that Mr Wickham resigned all claim to the living promised by Mr Darcy's father in favour of three thousand pounds. To think he persuaded all of Meryton to think Mr Darcy a monster! He elaborated, sharing a long list of scandalous inclinations seeming to bring him pain to simply utter—debts, cruelty, dishonour.

Mr Darcy was brief on the subjects that should not be

heard by young ladies, but she could not misunderstand his meaning—Mr Wickham's history included seducing vulnerable ladies. She was aware of this type of behaviour but would hardly expect it from someone she had admired.

She was struck by the realisation that Mr Darcy retained the support and friendship of many honourable people, while Mr Wickham had only his amiability and lovely words to recommend him. That she had put more trust in Mr Wickham's capriciousness than the obvious superiority of Mr Darcy, including weeks of gentle kindness directed at her, was alarming!

How could she have been livid at the deceit and duality of those around her when she herself spat her disapprobation of Mr Darcy to anyone who would listen in Hertfordshire and then sought his kind attentions once in Kent! This final thought depleted her of all control.

She cried outright, "I could not have been more blind! My prejudice. My ignorance. Until this moment, I never knew myself. How vain I must be to fall for his slick charms and decide, without proof, that he was a victim in the worst sense. Forgive me, though little I deserve it—I was a willing contributor in his plan to slander you across Hertfordshire." She covered her face with her hands, feeling the great shame of it all.

Mr Darcy was directly in front of her in an instant. He put his hands on her shoulders, earnestly offering, "Do not blame yourself for believing him."

It was devastating to realise how unreliable her own discernment was. She had been blind to Mr Wickham's behaviour and gave credence to his every word. Indeed, she especially enjoyed criticising Mr Darcy with him and furthering his complaints to any willing listener in Hertfordshire. Her behaviour had been disgraceful. She believed

Wickham because he gave her attention and satisfied her vanity. Mr Darcy, who met her with honesty and disinterest, she deemed untrustworthy. She withheld her respect because he wounded her pride. How could she ever trust *herself* again?

Sobs choked her, disorienting her thoughts and words, and robbing her of her breath. "You have no idea what I have done, what I have said...I thought...my dearest friend would aptly agree...could not understand...duplicity...conceited and selfish." Elizabeth was shocked to feel his fingers squeeze gently on her shoulders, pulling her closer.

Her sobs were also combined with the shocking reaction her body was having to his close contact. She was unused to being touched by a man. She should not be allowing such liberties, but Elizabeth was so desperate for comfort after weeks of being cautious, even secluded. And although she had not been willing to admit it to herself, his presence had become a safe haven for her. Her sobs and uneven breathing continued as he pulled her head to rest on his shoulder. Her hands came down from her face into tight fists against his chest.

When her breathing once again slowed, he stepped back just enough to tip her chin up and ask if she was well. She nodded.

There was a quiet, unspoken understanding as they stared into each other's eyes. While her crying ceased, her heart was beating fast and her breath coming quickly, in anticipation of what, she was not certain, but she was comforted by the fact that he seemed equally affected. And without warning, his arms wrapped around her back, and his lips were on hers.

He kissed her gently at first, tempting her slowly, teaching her how to move against his mouth. She was at once tentative and eager. The distance between them felt too great. Her fists resting against his chest relaxed and made their way up to his neck, effectively removing what little space remained between them. Warm hands stroked her back and brought comfort.

His fingers slowly made their way to twist through the curls that had escaped their pins at the nape of her neck—a thumb trailed a blaze of heat from her hairline down her neck and across her collar. She instinctively gasped and threw her head back as his mouth moved to follow the same trail and settled into soft kisses on her shoulder.

Her eyes flew open, taking in the sight of him in this state of abandon—this vulnerability she had never seen in him— this leap from his generally controlled manner to this distinctly passionate man. When he brought his mouth back to her, she surprised even herself by opening hers for exploration, and what followed ignited her even more. How was it possible to feel so much and then continue to build upon what you thought was the limit?

A wave of heat moved through her body, bringing confidence in her movements. His lips were so soft and his kiss so completely overwhelming. Removing one hand from the back of his neck, she traced his chin, the line of his jaw, his neck. She could feel his pulse beating as quickly as her own. A muffled sound escaped his mouth and drove her to stop her attentions.

He moved to bestow a long kiss upon her forehead and whispered against her skin, "Forgive me, Elizabeth. I should not have—"

She twisted her fingers in his hair and looked him deep in his eyes—she was not sorry, and she was not afraid of what had just occurred. She was only disappointed the moment had passed, so she allowed their broken connexion to transpire slowly, continuing to caress the back of his neck, then his shoulder, and down to his chest as she slowly backed away—never breaking eye contact. "Please do not apologise, sir."

"Fitzwilliam," he said hoarsely.

She gasped. "The colonel?" She quickly looked over her shoulder for his cousin. When she did not see him, she turned back to Mr Darcy. "Where?"

After a moment of silence, Mr Darcy broke into hearty laughter and she, rendered giddy by the release of all the contrariety of emotion she had experienced in the last half an hour, joined him.

"My name," he said, somewhere in the midst of it all. "My name is Fitzwilliam."

"I see," she said, suddenly aware of their precarious position. If his dishevelled appearance was any indication of her own, she would do better to return to the parsonage promptly. "That is...well, I am glad to know your cousin is not lurking about then. But...I should perhaps leave you now."

"Leave me? But..." He paused and then admitted, "Yes, it might be for the best."

With that, Elizabeth made her way down the lane, turning back only once to see him watching her silently. She kept her face neutral until she turned back towards the path, only then allowing a glowing smile to overtake her.

CHAPTER 10

Elizabeth entered the parsonage quietly and went straight to her bedchamber. How she longed to escape! The sweet little guest chamber had become more like a gaol to her, though she felt it was impossible to leave.

For a brief, mad moment, she thought about setting off walking. If she was any judge, it could not be much more than ten miles to Bromley—could it? But even as she considered it, she knew she was not in earnest. She was stuck there.

While she must remain, it did not follow that she must spend time with Mr or Mrs Collins. She would follow their guidelines and give them space. So resolved, Elizabeth curled up in the chair by the hearth in her chamber. She was quite capable of remaining composed and polite—and at a distance. Perhaps she would remain in her room all week. She did not delight in being in their company any time soon and could not guess at their reception after her earlier outburst.

She felt reckless and unsettled and humiliated. Even if Mr Collins was in the wrong, she had reacted to his behaviour abominably. Renouncing their familial attachment? And she thought herself the rational one!

She felt foolish, but her mind was under too much duress to contrive a sounder plan than one of avoidance. And she was not even certain she would leave if she could—not with Mr Darcy so near. The shock of the morning was still coursing through her—the anger, the mortification...and the kiss. Oh, that kiss.

She still could not credit that she had been kissed by Mr Darcy—and moreover, she was surprised that she had been a willing recipient. How easily had her desire overcome her restraint! She had always believed herself made of sterner stuff.

But what did it all mean? That moment when she had believed his cousin approached, she was first struck by fear—fear that they would be forced to marry! But hard on the heels of that came acceptance. Did it mean she secretly wanted to marry Mr Darcy? Was she falling in love with him?

She shook her head to clear it of such confusing thoughts.

"Mrs Collins!" Charlotte could hear her husband's heavy step the moment he crossed their threshold. She followed his progress as he stamped towards her parlour, still shouting, "Mrs Collins! Mrs Collins!" Did he expect her to shout back?

He was heaving and panting when he entered the parlour, and Charlotte thought she ought to encourage him to exercise more often. Surely it could not be good that a man as young as he was could be overcome by running the short distance from his garden to her parlour.

"Mr Darcy and Colonel Fitzwilliam, the nephews of our beloved patroness are come...the colonel, you will recall, is son to the Earl of—"

"Mr Collins, they have been here some time now, of course I know who they are." Charlotte forced herself to smile, to take the sting from her words. "My dear."

For a moment, he looked like he wanted to scold her but stopped himself, no doubt recalling the two esteemed gentlemen would be there shortly.

"Shall I call Eliza, do you think? She has returned and has been in her room for some time now."

Charlotte was not certain how Elizabeth might feel or how she would answer any questions about her whereabouts that morning. *What if she tells them of my husband's behaviour?*

Thinking better of it, Charlotte continued, "I think she ought to remain where she is. She was in quite a state this morning." But her efforts only sent things sideways.

"I think not," he replied abruptly. Charlotte believed it was likely that he only wished to oppose her, but it did not signify. "I shall not allow my cousin to embarrass us further today. She has already snubbed Miss de Bourgh. I shall not allow her to now insult the benevolence of her ladyship's nephews. If she wishes to remain under my roof, she will come and greet our guests."

Mr Collins rushed out to request that Hayes retrieve Elizabeth.

When the two gentlemen entered, Mr Collins was quick to speak, giving a lengthy monologue about Lady Catherine's reputed character, esteemed recommendations, and her advice about the keeping of poultry (though not one of them believed she had ever been in contact with the birds until they rested under sauce on her plate). Charlotte, ever the polite hostess, waited for her husband to take a breath before inviting the gentlemen to be seated.

Just as the gentlemen were choosing their seats, Mr Collins received a note from Lady Catherine summoning him to Rosings Park. He set off in a fluster, dismayed to abandon the illustrious gentlemen, yet not daring to displease his patroness by being anything less than alacritous. Charlotte watched a strangled greeting between Elizabeth and her husband as she entered the room and he bustled out of the parlour. She turned her attention to the tea cart to prevent her own clumsy welcome.

Mr Collins's exit allowed Charlotte to breathe a bit easier. *Perhaps his departure will subdue Eliza.*

Charlotte considered the distraction of preparing the tea a blessing. The colonel's good humour also deflected any apparent awkwardness while she delivered steaming cups to everyone's hands. When finally taking her seat, she noticed a strange occurrence in progress. Elizabeth had glanced at Mr Darcy, catching his gaze upon her. Then she smiled, and Charlotte watched her cheeks redden.

The gentlemen enquired of the ladies' health and exchanged pleasantries about the weather. Colonel Fitzwilliam talked energetically about a particular news item from the morning papers. Charlotte could only listen with half an ear, paying greater notice to the furtive glances and little smiles exchanged between Elizabeth and Mr Darcy. It was fortunate the colonel was the garrulous sort; Charlotte was too interested in Mr Darcy's and Elizabeth's behaviour to do much speaking herself.

Something was going on, and it must end. No good would come of it—especially for her husband and herself. Anne de Bourgh would *not* be thrown over for the likes of

Eliza Bennet. To selfishly abandon her family's needs for her own gain, only to be rewarded with an honourable, rich, and handsome husband? Oh no, she would not succeed—not if Charlotte had anything to say about it. Had this been Eliza's design all along? Was this why she had been so insistent on coming to Kent? Vexation grew as Charlotte imagined herself an unwitting pawn in Elizabeth's schemes with Mr Darcy.

"Elizabeth," she began with false brightness, "I shall be sorry to see you return home in a se'nnight, though I am certain you will be eager to ascertain the well-being of your family and renew your local friendships."

Elizabeth looked as if she had been caught with her hand in the jam jar. "Um, yes, of course."

"I am sure you are especially missing your friends in the militia, particularly your favourite," she said with a knowing nod and false grin.

Elizabeth's face dimmed a bit. "I am sure I do not know who you mean."

Charlotte clearly saw the look of warning on Elizabeth's face, but had no intention of being subdued. She turned to Mr Darcy. "Mr Darcy, am I correct that you have a past acquaintance with Mr Wickham?"

"I do." He replied tersely, his eyebrows furrowing.

"Mr George Wickham?" Colonel Fitzwilliam was nearly on the edge of his chair, looking at both ladies. "Do you know him?"

Mr Darcy said, "Wickham has joined the militia currently stationed in Hertfordshire, not far from Miss Bennet's home. Both of the ladies are acquainted with him."

"The militia? It seems they will have anyone these days." Colonel Fitzwilliam looked offended. Turning to the ladies, the colonel said, "I implore you to keep your distance from that man. He is no gentleman and is not to be trusted."

Elizabeth's colour was high, and her eyes shot angry darts in Charlotte's direction; but to the colonel she was serene. "Yes, we are acquainted, and I believe acquainted is a far friendlier term than he deserves. Never fear, Colonel Fitzwilliam. I admit to believing him to be a gentleman for a time, but I shall not be taken in by a scoundrel. I do, however, worry for his betrothed, Miss King."

She looked to Charlotte, one brow raised. "Mrs Collins, I am sure you remember that Mr Wickham is newly engaged to Miss Mary King."

"Of course." Charlotte nodded. Her attempts at distraction had not gone as well as planned, but they had certainly discomfited both Elizabeth and Mr Darcy and had brought their exchanges to a halt.

The gentlemen rose to take their leave soon after, and Elizabeth ventured to the lesser used morning room. In accordance with the typical behaviours of the parsonage, Elizabeth knew it would be best to rely on physical distance from the other residents to keep the peace. This space also allowed her mind to wander to all the hard places her equanimity required.

Elizabeth's feelings for Mr Darcy continued to be a bit of a tumult. She had learned enough in the past few weeks to understand that most of her early perceptions of him were inaccurate. His austere manner could be explained by a shyness she had not comprehended early on. He was a private man; what seemed like arrogance could be explained by the manifold responsibilities laid at his feet due to the nature of his wealth and holdings.

Mr Bingley, she was coming to realise, was a fickle man

easily led by the whims of his friends and family. And while Mr Darcy owned his part in separating Jane from Mr Bingley, she was unconcerned by his reasons; the protection of his friend was admirable. She would have done the same for Jane. Yes, the full accountability lay with Mr Bingley.

And Mr Wickham—oh, that enlightenment stung the most. Pretty words and compliments had entirely clouded her discernment on that front. His conniving nature concealed his true person. While she was astonished to learn he was dishonourable, it was her own perceptions and decision-making that hurt the most. To be so deceived! To be so ignorant!

And if all this were true, then her deep connexion and friendship built in Kent was also the truth—this was the real Mr Darcy.

Sifting through this knowledge, she felt finally free to allow herself to recognise her true feelings for Mr Darcy. This confident, intelligent gentleman had taken hold of her heart in a way she had never expected to experience. She felt drawn to his steadiness and comfort. Of all which he was responsible, she dreamed she too could be under his complete protection.

Elizabeth rarely considered marriage, for she dreamed only of marrying for love. She was intelligent enough to recognise protection in itself was valuable as well. Her decision to refuse the marriage proposal from Mr Collins was truly selfish. She could have put an end to her mother's fear of being 'tossed into the hedgerows' months ago.

Mr Collins's proposal and her subsequent refusal recalled her deepest fear and that of her mother. One day, her family would be removed from their home, and without a married sister to take them all in, they would be subject to the worst type of depravity the world offered poor gentlewomen—

poverty and a displacement from their current social status in the world, conceivably one of them may even be forced to enter into service, as a governess or paid companion. It was a bleak notion.

The type of security Mr Darcy offered was not only the protection of her family but of her heart. Since Elizabeth had long imagined herself a spinster, this introduced a new sort of trepidation and joy.

Her parents were not an encouraging example of marriage. While her respect for her father was great, he was of the neglectful sort—devoting his time to sarcasm and solitude as if they were his dearest friends. She enjoyed the attention he gave her, since she lacked such attention from her mother. They exchanged witticisms and both valued intelligence—but in comparing her parents' marriage with that of the marriage she was now hoping for, she could only see Mr Darcy as the ideal.

What would Mr Darcy think of her after she had attacked his character so fully? Did he understand her warm glances during their morning call? Could he perceive her greatly altered feelings?

Mr Collins interrupted her thoughts by entering the morning room to look out of the window to the path running in front of the parsonage. "Did you see her, Cousin?"

"Pardon me, Mr Collins. I was wool-gathering. Of whom are we speaking?" Elizabeth requested calmly.

"Only Miss Anne de Bourgh! Did you not see? She condescended to drive by in her little phaeton and ponies. If only I had been outside to greet her."

Elizabeth never responded, so he continued, "I am curious why Mr Darcy was not attending her. I am sure Lady Catherine would prefer her betrothed was by her side for her protection, would she not?"

Betrothed. The word shook her to her core. Mr Collins had insinuated their betrothal many months before, but this time the word stung. Was Mr Darcy in fact to marry his cousin? How had she forgotten to ask?

"I cannot speak to Lady Catherine's preferences, Mr Collins," Elizabeth answered weakly and immediately quitted the room.

Once in the relative privacy of the empty corridor, Elizabeth leaned against the wall and closed her eyes. If only her breathing would regulate itself. She knew better than to rely on Mr Collins for news, but it was undeniable that hearing of Mr Darcy being betrothed to another did affect her. Fallacy or truth, the mere thought of it stole her breath.

Delusion strongly influenced her cousin's turn of mind, so she willed the heels of her feet to stop bouncing and her fists to release their hold on her skirt. Taking a deep breath, she quickly took herself up the stairs.

Once settled on the end of her bed, she found that the privacy of her chamber only allowed her mind to assume the worst. For if her cousin was not the fool, then she most certainly was.

The next morning, Mr Collins entered Charlotte's bedchamber unannounced while her maid was helping her dress for church. His eyes darted about the room, and he wiped his hands on his breeches. Charlotte sent her maid away immediately.

Once alone, her husband began, "I have been up all night with worry. I am concerned we have not yet been issued an invitation to dine at Rosings today. You know as well as I do that her ladyship intended it, for she mentioned it last week."

"Perhaps she will extend the invitation in person this morning. She has been known to do so."

"I do not think so," he said, seeming agitated. "And I know what must have happened."

"I do not believe anything happened, sir, other than Lady Catherine neglected to send a note."

This was met with a withering look. Evidently, Lady Catherine was beyond commonplace things such as forgetfulness.

"No, I know you will agree with me, for I favour myself wise to the behaviours of young females, when I say that I believe my cousin has been poisoning her ladyship against us! That can be the only explanation for this rejection. I believe she used her charms to influence Colonel Fitzwilliam and Mr Darcy when they came to call yesterday—my cousin may have spoken against us to the gentlemen, and thus, they took false and defamatory information to her ladyship. To think that I may have been able to prevent her doing so should I not have been called to Rosings myself!"

Mr Collins began to pace the room, his stride causing his belly to bob up and down. She could feel they were teetering on the precipice of peace—a place she had become all too familiar with. Her immediate agreement and support would strengthen the chance of his calming down. "I think you must be right," she said. "How clever you are to observe it."

"I have noticed a particular interest between my cousin and Lady Catherine's nephews. She wants to seduce one of them, to be sure. Mark my words, Lady Catherine would be none too pleased if one of her nephews became entangled with Miss Elizabeth. Particularly, if my cousin would attempt to ensnare Mr Darcy and succeeded, it would damage forever the holy matrimony that Lady Catherine has endorsed for her daughter and her nephew!"

Charlotte simply nodded and responded, "Yes, dear."

"I am certain it is within your power to ensure that the sanctified union of Miss de Bourgh and Mr Darcy occurs as Lady Catherine has ordained. You must control Miss Elizabeth. I expect this of you. I shall not tolerate any less than the full support of Lady Catherine and her magnanimous daughter."

"Yes, dear," she repeated.

"As Miss Elizabeth's male relation, I have authority over her behaviour and must protect her virtue as well. I expect you to do everything in your power to keep her away from those gentlemen. I hold you responsible."

"Yes, dear."

After her husband's departure, Charlotte called Hayes back to complete her preparations for the day. "Has Miss Bennet gone for one of her walks?"

"No, ma'am," Hayes answered. "Owing to the weather, I am sure. She is still abed."

Before Charlotte excused her, she ordered Hayes to tell Mrs Montgomery not to send Elizabeth a tray. She would be expected to break her fast in the dining room.

Once Elizabeth joined her, Charlotte watched her most carefully. Her friend was deep in thought, smiling to herself as she ate—chewing for long periods and occasionally blushing.

Elizabeth's mind appeared to wander, her eyes glowing with repressed feelings. Watching her, Charlotte's resentment grew.

Elizabeth and Mr Darcy's demeanours had undergone a significant change with each interaction she observed, and she wondered if they might be meeting in secret, likely during Eliza's many prolonged rambles through the wood. Their shared glances spoke of something much deeper than their limited conversations after Sunday services and a few fleeting morning calls. How could she imagine herself reaching so high above her own station in life? And Mr Darcy —what was he thinking, entertaining these possibilities when he was promised to his cousin? Poor Miss de Bourgh! Must Elizabeth's selfishness influence yet another innocent young lady's future?

A union between Elizabeth and Mr Darcy would be harmful to Charlotte. If Mr Darcy became aware of Elizabeth's treatment at the parsonage, they could lose the necessary support of their patroness. Even if her ladyship were unable to remove the living, she could easily make them miserable. It was in Charlotte's best interest that Elizabeth's attempts to ensnare Mr Darcy be stopped.

Additionally, Charlotte knew Mr Collins would hold her responsible should Mr Darcy not fulfil his duty by Miss de Bourgh. He would think she had misguided her friend or failed to check her behaviour, and she would suffer accordingly for the error. She would not stand for Elizabeth's continued interference in her life.

During the church service, Charlotte continued her observation. Her friend may think she was concealing her interest in Mr Darcy, but to the keen observer, it was clear enough that there were unspoken words being exchanged in their glances.

Mr Collins had whispered his concerns in her ear during the walk to the church, still alarmed by the lack of an invitation to dine with Lady Catherine. Charlotte did not particularly enjoy dining at Rosings, but her equanimity was disturbed by her rattled husband. In her short marriage, regular invitations to dine at Rosings on Sundays had arrived nearly each week when the weather was fine for walking. That morning, the sun was shining, and the temperature was comfortable; there was no apparent reason that the invitation should not have been proffered, save for one. Her ladyship was displeased with their houseguest. In this, her husband appeared correct.

In order to thwart anything more than coy gazes and fluttering eyelashes, Charlotte necessarily affixed herself to Elizabeth following the service, preventing any conversation between her and Mr Darcy. The Rosings party did offer civilities to her and Elizabeth, but no more. She could sense a desire for a tête-à-tête by the way in which Elizabeth attempted to manoeuvre the conversation and distract Charlotte, but she was resolute in making private conversation impossible for them.

To the delight of her husband, a note was later that day dispatched to the Hunsford party with an invitation to dine three days hence, with the explicit instruction that her ladyship desired Miss Elizabeth Bennet be in attendance. *Interference indeed.*

Her husband beckoned her to his study shortly after the arrival of the invitation. Mr Collins was so distraught by the possibility of Elizabeth behaving badly while at Rosings that it nearly robbed him of the joy the invitation should have imparted.

"I need not remind you," he began, "of the promise you have made me to ensure Miss Elizabeth is kept away from the visiting gentlemen on Wednesday. Her ladyship is providing every courtesy to our guest, and we shall not thank her with a scandal."

Charlotte's ire paralleled her husband's on this occasion. Let Elizabeth attempt to raise herself in society by other means. Charlotte would not contradict her husband's position, nor would she neglect to obey his request.

"I shall have a talk with Eliza before Wednesday. You may trust in my shared conviction, my dear."

"Please see that you do," he responded, then flicked his hand to dismiss her.

Charlotte's thoughts wavered greatly between affection for the past and bitterness for the present, but ultimately she concluded that if Elizabeth was capable of making selfish decisions, then so may she.

CHAPTER 11

Elizabeth stared out at the steady rain on Monday morning and felt deep regret that it was to be yet another day she was kept inside—away from Mr Darcy. Her sadness felt like a crippling exhaustion. Hoping to prevent Mrs Collins from ordering her down for breakfast, she asked Hayes to carry a message to her mistress about a headache that kept her abed.

Hayes did later come to inform her when Mr Darcy and his cousin called that morning, but she was too fatigued to perform false contentment—even if only for a quarter hour. She had no desire to see him in company. She longed to see him, but avoiding the Collinses was key to her composure. *Only five days until I am in London.*

She did wonder at the excuse Charlotte might have offered the gentlemen but felt Mr Darcy would assuredly interpret any deception. Though surprised by her accusations in the glade, she thought him perceptive and certainly not disbelieving. Did he worry for her when she was not present for their call? Had whatever reassurance Charlotte provided been persuasive?

Lying in her bed that night, she imagined him riding to the parsonage by moonlight and climbing the trellis outside her window to take her away. She practised her shocked expression when he climbed through her window and quickly smothered her unruly laugher in her pillow at the girlish fantasy.

Charlotte woke much earlier on Tuesday morning than was her wont. She had not slept well, and the weight of her anxiety sat heavily in her chest. More than once in the night she had found herself short of breath, anticipating the confrontation she would instigate with Elizabeth. Each time she practised her forthcoming conversation, she saw the possibility of being outwitted. Her friend's cleverness must be taken into consideration.

It was another dreary, rainy morning, which kept Elizabeth from walking out once again. Charlotte immediately attended Mrs Montgomery and Hayes, explaining that a tray should not be sent to Elizabeth's room that morning. She must break her fast with the family. Charlotte could delay the conversation no longer.

Elizabeth appeared weary when she arrived at the table. She spent more time moving food around on her plate than eating. When Mr Collins finished his second plate of food, he stood and nodded to his wife, expecting her to follow his instructions. Leaving the two ladies alone, he was summoning her to do his bidding—now.

It took some five minutes for Charlotte to muster the

strength to begin a conversation. She had rehearsed it in the night, but in the face of Elizabeth at her table, her confidence wavered. She took a deep, fortifying breath and let it out slowly. "I am sorry you have been kept indoors once again. Perhaps the rain will abate for our visit to Rosings tomorrow."

"Yes; I do hope the rain will subside soon."

"My husband tells me it shall be a grand celebration. I wonder if her ladyship will serve four or five courses?" Charlotte said lightly, making every attempt to avoid eye contact.

"A celebration?" Elizabeth looked a little lighter at the thought. "How lovely! It will be delightful to leave the house. What occasion shall we be celebrating?"

"Miss de Bourgh's engagement."

Elizabeth stiffened, her mouth falling agape for a moment with no less horror than Charlotte had expected. Charlotte looked down, not wishing her smirk to be seen.

"Miss-Miss de Bourgh's engagement? I was not aware that she—"

They both turned to the sound of the door closing, cutting off Elizabeth's words. Hayes had entered the room and stood to the side of the buffet, eyes wide with visible interest in their conversation. Charlotte shook her head at the maid to dismiss her and turned back to Elizabeth, only to see her eyes cast down at the table, her spirit visibly deflated. Charlotte had to shake off the momentary distraction in order to continue the conversation.

"I may go to Rosings today to practise a new song on the pianoforte," Charlotte resumed. "I am sure her ladyship will want some entertainment after dinner."

"Yes, quite right." Though Elizabeth made every attempt to appear calm, she was breathing more quickly, and Charlotte could hear her foot tapping furiously under the table.

Charlotte wanted to be certain there was no confusion. Being explicit was the only way to ensure the correct response. She could not look at her as she said it, but say it she did, "Yes, it will be a festive evening. The joining of two grand estates like Rosings and Pemberley must be thrilling to anticipate. I daresay Mr Darcy will be one of the wealthiest men in England. I wonder if they will create an earldom for him?"

Elizabeth rose promptly, unable to look at her friend. "Perhaps. You will have to excuse me, I appear to have a headache again. I did not sleep well last night."

"You do look a trifle pale," Charlotte said with false concern. "I shall have Mrs Montgomery send up a posset."

Elizabeth murmured something unintelligible as she took her leave, and Charlotte congratulated herself for successfully achieving the task assigned to her. Mr Collins need not know the method she had employed.

The result of the conversation would certainly erect an obstacle between the two young lovers. Elizabeth would keep to herself while at Rosings. Even in the absence of a true celebration at the dinner, Elizabeth would never be so improper as to ask about the engagement, nor would she be eager to wish the couple joy. Charlotte hoped it would reduce the likelihood of her approaching Mr Darcy during their visit. She also considered that Elizabeth may feign a headache to leave the dinner early. *Better yet!*

Elizabeth was not eager to remain at the table with Charlotte, but neither was she eager to be alone in her chamber once again. To think she had escaped to Kent for some peace and quiet!

Just as she was about to gain the staircase, she turned and moved her feet towards the kitchens instead. She could apply to Mrs Montgomery for something to settle her aching head and also remain out of the way of her maddening hosts. Unfortunately, she found only the maid. Hayes curtseyed and asked if Elizabeth needed anything.

"Thank you, no. I was looking for Mrs Montgomery."

"Sorry, miss. She is off to the village, something 'bout the butcher, I believe."

Elizabeth nodded and began to leave.

"The butcher can't be bothered over the needs of the parsonage when Rosings Park is preparing a menu for a wedding, I s'pose."

Something in Hayes' smile rang of satisfaction, and Elizabeth's stomach dropped to her feet. She could not flee fast enough.

The act of crawling into her bed and pulling the quilt over her head made Elizabeth ache for Jane. How dearly she wished she was curled up next to her sister, trading secrets rather than hiding from her own foolishness. If she closed her eyes tightly enough, she could gain her composure once again, could she not?

But it was a misleading notion. Nothing in Kent would calm her now.

Charlotte took a deep breath of satisfaction knowing all had resolved as she desired, and looked forward to the quiet day ahead. Hands shaking, she picked up her embroidery and attempted to begin stitching once again, but it was no use. She was not created for this type of deception. A single tear fell down her cheek as she silently mourned for the past.

Yet crying only served to make her feel weak, and a heated internal battle began. She hated feeling weak—it supported her husband's claims that she was unworthy and incapable. Carving out her own future, that is what she was doing. Her decision had been sound, and she was decided not to allow even the anxious voices in her own head to change her mind.

Even in her eagerness to quiet the concerns whirling in her mind, Charlotte was unable to feel confident that the conversation with Elizabeth would provide the results she and her husband desired. They needed her mute and subdued, but Charlotte was worried she had only fuelled an ember of frustration that could be coaxed into a flame, destroying them all. What if Elizabeth wished them joy at the dinner? What if she asked Mr Darcy about his betrothal directly?

Charlotte climbed the stairs with renewed conviction and knocked on Elizabeth's door. When she was acknowledged, she entered, finding a rather sad version of her formerly high spirited friend sitting up in the bed. Her hair was wild, her eyes swollen, and the bedclothes pulled up to her chin.

A wave of sympathy coursed through Charlotte. Eliza was melancholic, and it was her doing. She nearly turned around to abandon her task but forced herself forward. She imagined her husband's satisfaction when he discovered her usefulness, and the thought of his approval bolstered her courage. "Elizabeth, I fear there is more bothering you than a headache. Shall I have Mr Collins call an apothecary?" Charlotte sat on the edge of the bed and tried to seem at ease.

"No, no." Elizabeth said, appearing quite defeated. "I never should have come here."

Charlotte began to rub Elizabeth's arm and whispered, "I am sorry you feel that way. Though you may be right, I do not see how we can return to the past to change our decisions."

Elizabeth grunted in response and turned away from Charlotte.

"I do wonder if any of your hurt has to do with Mr Darcy? I have noticed you seem rather more...friendly...than I remember from last autumn. I hope his attentions have not been untoward?"

"Pardon?"

"Soon after I arrived in Kent, I began receiving reports from locals that Mr Darcy has a penchant for giving young ladies in the area special attention. In fact, I was concerned to bring you here based on what I had learned. These rich young men do tend to act in accordance with their own pleasures."

Very faintly Elizabeth replied, "My uncle has always said the wealthy tend to be whimsical in their civilities."

"Apparently, Lady Catherine turns a blind eye to his behaviour, and has even been known to pay off those affected by his dalliances. It is all, you know, to ensure he does his duty by Miss de Bourgh. So, I want to be sure he has not injured you."

Elizabeth's response was enough to confirm some truth to her speculations. Her breath was coming in and out quickly, and her eyes were wide with agitation.

"Elizabeth?"

Elizabeth dropped her head into her hands, and although Charlotte could not hear, she imagined she must weep. She laid a hand on her friend's arm. "Oh, my dear."

"I have nothing to reproach him for," Elizabeth said, her tone muffled by her hands. "You need not be alarmed on that account."

"But there was an attempt?"

"Of course not!" Elizabeth raised her face. "He is simply my friend...or so I thought. He would occasionally walk with me in the mornings when our paths would cross."

Charlotte began to rub her back. "Was that all? Just walking?"

Elizabeth looked away from her. "I feel such a fool."

"Had you begun to care for him? Perhaps as...more than a friend?"

At length she admitted, "A little. To have the attentions of such a man as Mr Darcy...to imagine him under my power? Yes, I suppose it may have gone to my head."

Even with her previous suspicions, it was a surprise to Charlotte to hear her friend admit to having feelings for any man. But to set her cap at Mr Darcy! It was shocking, indeed. To think she would aim so high! Eliza had certainly set herself up for disappointment.

Charlotte focused on the movement of her hand, rubbing back and forth. "Does Mr Darcy know of your...interest?"

Elizabeth shrugged, not looking in Charlotte's direction.

"I may be a married woman, but as you know, my marriage was decided upon with little thought for romance. I know not about such things, but perhaps you simply got carried away...I could never look at your father again if I knew I had failed to keep you—"

"It was only a kiss, Charlotte."

A kiss! Charlotte remained calm and answered only with a pat on her friend's back. "I see."

"I cannot be at Rosings to celebrate his betrothal to Miss de Bourgh—I simply cannot! It is in every way impossible to imagine."

"I am very sorry you feel so. Should you like to go home?"

Elizabeth looked at her then, hopefulness piercing the

despair in her gaze. "I would hate for you and Mr Collins to think me ungrateful for your hospitality...but, yes, I think I would like to return home."

Charlotte knew Mr Collins would be infuriated to receive Lady Catherine's ire when it was made known that Elizabeth had fled Kent early, but the idea of having control of her home once again won over. She would have to think of a creative way to convince him that assisting Elizabeth on her journey was in Miss de Bourgh's favour, and their favour too, if Elizabeth had been successful in her efforts to charm Mr Darcy. "I shall speak to Mr Collins and have Hayes prepare your trunk. All shall be arranged."

Elizabeth woke early the next morning after little sleep. Her eyes were heavy and swollen from crying, and she felt changed from the woman who arrived in Kent a short five weeks prior.

She took her leave of Mrs Montgomery early and privately. The two embraced and wished each other well. Hayes had ensured all her things were packed and brought downstairs before Mr and Mrs Collins awoke.

Mr Collins was as he ever was—spouting platitudes in a limitless manner with nary a listener about. Charlotte was cold to her throughout the morning meal, the warmth of their conversation the previous day long forgotten, it seemed. Elizabeth was disappointed to see it; she had dared to imagine that her friend, the Charlotte of old, had returned.

The goodbyes were devoid of emotion and hardly polite. Elizabeth was relieved that Mr Collins had elicited the aid of one of his parishioners to drive her to meet the post coach.

"Lady Catherine has been all condescension to you," Mr

Collins said. Being that it seemed he might launch into yet another of his harangues about her ladyship's beneficence, Elizabeth quickly interrupted him.

"Thank you, Mr and Mrs Collins, for your hospitality. Please also convey my thanks to Lady Catherine for her kindness and welcome to Kent."

"Cousin, I am certain this visit has been good for you. When you injured your family by way of refusing me at Longbourn these many months ago, it was God himself who told me, he said, 'Collins, you must arrange for your cousin's salvation'. And, I am pleased to have made some progress in the improvement of your character during this visit."

And so, with a nod from Mrs Collins, Elizabeth took her place in the gig and waved goodbye to Kent.

CHAPTER 12

An overwhelming feeling of loneliness overtook Elizabeth on the ride to catch the post coach. She was ashamed of her behaviour over the last months and what it had wrought.

Was Mr Darcy merely a rake as Charlotte had implied? He had not behaved thus in Hertfordshire, but perhaps, as Charlotte said, he only acted so when he had an aunt behind him to cover up his indiscretions. But considering what he had implied about Mr Wickham's behaviour and what she had come to understand of Mr Darcy's own nature, it remained hard to imagine he would take advantage of young ladies.

No, she was certain they were unfounded rumours. They had to be.

It took many hours, but sometime in the middle of the night Elizabeth had reconciled herself to understanding that while his behaviour had been inappropriate, it did not change the fact that she had become attached to him—foolishly so.

Even as Charlotte had comforted her, she had a strong feeling that it was he—not Charlotte—who could be trusted; however, on some level, Charlotte was right. He had kissed her knowing he was promised to another.

Even if he shared her affection at one time, how could he continue to feel the same once he had time to consider all she had said in the glade—how she had so vehemently defended Mr Wickham and denounced his character? How could she have been so naïve as to imagine the man would align himself with her? If possible, the misunderstandings only strengthened her resolution that Mr Darcy was the truest person she knew—but how could he know her current sentiments now? How could he discern them on the strength of a few pointed glances and half-hidden smiles? And what did it signify? He would never be hers.

But perhaps none of this had anything to do with her, with what she had or had not done. This allegiance was long-standing. She never had proof of its authenticity, but she also never enquired. She could forgive Mr Darcy this, as she understood the betrothal had been arranged in their youth. She could even be satisfied knowing his heart might truly lie elsewhere—with her—and, perhaps, that possibility would be enough to sustain her.

Darcy rode his horse hard that morning, frustrated that he had been unable to locate Elizabeth on any nearby paths. Would a little mud keep her from rambling about? He thought not. Her apparent desertion left his mind reeling.

He had not had a chance to speak privately to her since their shared kiss. Mrs Collins had determinedly steered Elizabeth around by the elbow after church on Sunday—speaking to all in the congregation but him. It had been plain she had no intention of letting Elizabeth converse with him.

The damnable rain had also deterred their morning strolls, and morning calls had only been possible twice due to the amount of business his aunt asked him to look into. There seemed to be a confederacy about him, all designed to keep him from her.

Fitzwilliam's expression revealed he perceived Darcy's irritability, but fortunately he did not know the source of it—for if he did, the teasing would be unending. Brooding, he had learned, was an expected mannerism of his, so no one took great notice when he exhibited it.

Perhaps he should not have encouraged his aunt to cease inviting the Collinses to dine on Sundays. Even if Mr Collins required Elizabeth to stay back at the parsonage, she may have enjoyed the peace and quiet. His cousin Anne, though, seemed intent on securing a friendship with Miss Bennet, and so an invitation had been dispatched to the party to dine that night. *Only six more hours,* he thought to himself. Even if he could not hold a private conversation with her at Rosings, he would fondly relish being in her presence.

At length, a footman entered the morning room to provide a note to Lady Catherine. Darcy quelled his vexation, knowing the vicar would undeniably follow that note forthwith. Surprisingly, it appeared, though, to *not* be one of the numerous notes exchanged between the parson and his aunt throughout the day.

"The nerve of that insolent girl!" Lady Catherine was immediately agitated by the contents written, scowling, with high colour appearing on her cheeks. "Miss Elizabeth Bennet has taken her leave of me in a note! After all I have done for her!" This prompted a tirade from her on the deplorable manners of the younger generation, during which Lady

Catherine laid the piece of paper on the table next to her chair. It would be, Darcy hoped, forgotten; and soon enough it was, her ladyship sweeping from the room to consult her housekeeper.

Darcy moved to grab the note before a footman could collect it.

Hunsford Parsonage, Kent
April 15, 1812

My Lady,

I wish to thank you for your hospitality these five weeks in Kent. I travel today to be with my family and send my apologies for not being able to properly take my leave of yourself and Miss de Bourgh.

Respectfully,
Elizabeth Bennet

Darcy dropped the note. She was gone. When? Why?

More answers were required than were to be had in the very short missive. Darcy exited the room with haste and found the footman who had delivered it.

"You there! I believe you brought the message from the parsonage?" Darcy enquired.

The young man—Darcy believed he was called James—immediately snapped to attention. "Yes, sir. Mrs Jonas sends me various times of the day to collect any letters from the parsonage."

"And the guest at the parsonage? She was there? Or already gone?"

"Miss Bennet was being handed into a gig when I arrived —to catch the post, I daresay."

Darcy nodded and waved the man away. A million plans and schemes tumbled about in his mind. He wished to go to her immediately but could not just turn up at Longbourn uninvited. No, he would have to travel to London to speak to Bingley right away about opening up Netherfield Park. It may take a fortnight, but he resolved it should sort itself out quickly.

A note was dispatched to her uncle Gardiner when Elizabeth's coach reached the Bell in Bromley to change horses. She was relieved to have an excuse to stretch her legs. She hoped the note would arrive before her, and perhaps, her uncle might be waiting to take her to their home when she arrived in the city. She was three days earlier than planned, so she included a message that all was well. She had no interest in worrying her favourite relations.

The road to London carried families of all stations, and the stops along the way offered Elizabeth the opportunity to observe their accents, dress, and demeanours.

One lady attired in a particularly fine lavender silk gown caught her eye. Her dark black curls were pinned up in a singularly fashionable manner, and she had an air about her that spoke of great wealth. Elizabeth imagined her the daughter of an uncommonly grand gentleman, returning to town from their vast estate by the sea.

Elizabeth felt rather enchanted by her beauty until she saw the woman react unkindly to a footman. The young lady first looked around to see whether she was being watched before giving him a set down that shocked even Elizabeth. Though she could not hear all of what was said, Elizabeth deduced that he had retrieved the wrong trunk from atop their carriage. The lady's pale skin turned an unattractive shade of purple as she pointed to the correct trunk to be lowered. The poor man nearly toppled down attempting to retrieve it for her. Setting it on the dirt, he was dismissed with a flick of her hand just as an older woman, presumably her companion, arrived to console her.

Elizabeth sighed. At least the young lady retained enough dignity to hide her immaturity when she believed she was being observed—that was more than Elizabeth could often expect of her youngest sister Lydia, who would traipse about Meryton shouting a 'hallo' to any handsome young man in a uniform who looked her way. The elegant young traveller's mistreatment of those in her service was another reminder to Elizabeth of how utterly wrong first impressions may be.

Perhaps the young lady's behaviour was common for some families. Elizabeth had witnessed Miss Bingley's dismissive approach towards those in service at Netherfield, but then again, she had also once dined at the home of an earl who went to university with her father and had seen how kind and gracious those elevated personages had treated their household.

Behaviours and nuance fascinated her, and she continued her observations outside the busy inn until, at last, it was time to again board the carriage for the last stretch of her journey. She was thankful to have been provided a seat inside the coach for the long trip. The older woman seated beside her had an odd manner and spoke endlessly about her cat. She informed Elizabeth that he was a dignified little feline, named for the Prince Regent, and she longed for his company. She endeavoured to assure Elizabeth he was not some plump, spoiled animal. He was an agile thing who worked for his supper and was prone to keeping the mice from her kitchen. Elizabeth listened with kindness and appreciated the diversion.

Elizabeth imagined old Mrs Fitzgerald sitting on an over-stuffed, excessively frilled settee with a thin tabby cat moving about her person and purring his great achievements. Why could people not be as easy to understand as animals?

Her companion fell asleep just as they entered bustling London. Mrs Fitzgerald's lace cap fell slightly over her face, and as Elizabeth observed a slight smile on her slumbering face, she suspected the lady dreamt of home.

If only Elizabeth could find sleep so peaceful. The last night had been dreadful. She woke three times to find her bedclothes disrupted, a reflection of her perpetual, menacing dreams. Unfortunately, reality was nearly as dreadful.

Her future was unclear, and while it had been for as long as she lived, a foreign hope had taken root nonetheless—hope for something more, or rather *someone* more. To lose that future before she had a chance to embrace even her own feelings was devastating. And removing Mr Darcy from her mind was nearly impossible. During that dreadful stay, he had been her sanctuary. If only she had realised it sooner.

A sense of relief shuddered through Elizabeth as she spotted her uncle waiting for her upon the coach's arrival in London. His smile was a breath of fresh air among the dirty, foggy streets of the city. She was welcomed into a warm and familial embrace—finally. For the first time in days, she felt secure.

"How is it that I find myself retrieving my niece from a coaching inn today? I thought you were to stay in Kent for six weeks complete?"

"Can a lady not miss her family?" She smiled mischievously to cover her consternation in his perspicacity.

"Yes, of course, my dear, and I am glad to hear of it. You are most welcome! Your aunt will be delighted to see you."

Elizabeth was nearly as excited to see her aunt Gardiner as she was to see her sister, Jane. Her entrance into their town home on Gracechurch Street was met with a roar of laughter and questions, as well as warm embraces—none so tight as the one shared with her dearest sister. With young cousins bustling around her, grabbing at her skirts and exclaiming in joy to see her, Elizabeth was quite out of breath with delight to be in the bosom of her family once again.

Before they could even sit down, Jane was at her side asking questions, while her aunt took the children up to the nursery. "Lizzy!" Jane cried. "How happy I am to see you! My dear uncle did not inform me that you were to arrive today. Are Mr and Mrs Collins in good health?"

"Yes, Jane. All in good health."

"I am relieved to hear it. We were without a letter from you for nearly a month. I hope your visit was a pleasant one?"

To answer in the affirmative was not the truth, though the visit was not entirely unpleasant. No—Mr Darcy had created a fire of desire and joy within her that could be described as all that was pleasant, but the loss of him was considerably disheartening. But, where Mr and Mrs Collins were concerned, unpleasant was a keen description.

"I was fond of Kent, but I am overjoyed to be here with you." Elizabeth saw her aunt return, and added, "As well as you, Aunt."

Her aunt begged the two to sit down so she could serve tea. Then she delivered a plate of Elizabeth's favourite treats directly to her hands. "Lizzy, your uncle and I were all excitement and concern when we received your note. I hope all is well?"

"Yes, although, London is a welcome change of scene," she answered.

The three women enjoyed a merry conversation about the weather, the state of the roads, family, and news from Hertfordshire. Elizabeth was pleased to find some quiet time to rest before dinner. She lay on her bed and pulled the quilt up to her neck to savour the feel of safety and comfort. She thought she might even enjoy some sleep. Thoughts of the last time she felt at home filled her mind before she drifted off.

CHAPTER 13

"**L**izzy, I know you too well," Mrs Gardiner began. "You do not have to share all with me, but I shall listen, should you desire to confide in me."

Elizabeth had been allowed only one day of rest before the enquiries began. She had reassured Jane all was well, saying that she had simply missed her family, which was easy enough because Jane always saw the best in all people and situations. She would never doubt Elizabeth. Her aunt, however, was impossible to evade.

Mrs Gardiner was only ten years Elizabeth's senior, and her greater understanding, not to mention more genteel behaviour, made her an ideal companion and model for Elizabeth. Their mutual respect and similar dispositions allowed for an open and loving relationship to thrive between them.

"You need not be alarmed," Elizabeth told her.

"I daresay, I may be alarmed, but I shall hear it nevertheless."

Elizabeth joined her on the settee and sighed. With Jane having just left the drawing room to dress for dinner, it was as good a time as any to explain herself with relative privacy. "Kent was lovely," she said to the drawing room, not meeting her aunt's eyes.

A quick glance at her aunt's raised eyebrows told her that would not be enough. "I took long walks and enjoyed the countryside. Lady Catherine was just as expected—a woman I would imagine was quite beautiful when she was young but whose pleasures now rest chiefly in ordering about the concerns of others. Mr Collins enjoyed endorsing her every edict, and Mrs Collins—well, I venture to say that while she is comfortable in her home, I do not believe her selection in a partner was...was a good one."

Mrs Gardiner nodded and gently persuaded her for more details, "Your friend is unhappy?"

"She would never admit it, but yes, I think she is vastly unhappy. Some might call it misery hidden beneath contentment."

Elizabeth hesitated before continuing, "She has altered considerably from the sensible, reasonable friend I have always enjoyed. She wanted, above all, to be married, and though she has what she desired, it is less, I think, than she hoped. But she is resigned to her life, I suppose. It is certainly not the marriage I would choose for myself, and it has made my friend into a stranger."

"I see." Her aunt put a hand on Elizabeth's back and rubbed slowly, waiting for the truth of it. Elizabeth could sense that her aunt knew there was more to the tale.

"I found it difficult to live under their roof, with Mr Collins, especially. He felt it appropriate to oversee incoming correspondence, even mine."

Her aunt's eyebrows rose. "Surely he did not read letters addressed to you?"

"Indeed, he did," Elizabeth said, remembered indignation making her warm. "He even confronted me about the subjects of a half-written letter to my father I had left on the writing desk in my chamber!"

Her aunt looked appalled, shaking her head. "Some men do abuse their positions as head of household. I had not expected it of him, from what I have heard. I pictured him a rather silly man."

"He is silly, and foolish, and weak. And while he has learning, he has not understanding. And he compensates for these defects by being quite strict; not only with me, but with Mrs Collins as well. She did not assist me during her husband's regular outbursts, as I would have expected her to do."

"You argued with your cousin?"

"Pray do not refer to him as my cousin!" she said with the full force of her temper. Seeing her aunt's shocked expression, she continued more mildly, "I long to forget that he is connected to me."

Like a boulder set loose from its perch on a cliffside, once jostled, Mr Collins would roll through the parsonage and flatten everything in his sight. So much effort was necessary to keep his fragile pride intact and steady so that others in his midst might find some little harmony. Elizabeth had no desire to expand on her experiences in Kent—to create undue concern over events that were no longer within her control to resolve, nor her aunt's. Her aunt would only worry needlessly. It was rather shocking, indeed, that Mr Collins had banished her from Rosings and forced her to tend to her spiritual education. A fleeting wish to tell all was quickly dismissed by her desire to simply enjoy the peace and comforts of her family. She was tired of being angry and cautious and alone.

"I would not have you worry. I enjoyed a variety of walks, both in the woods and in the beautifully manicured gardens at Rosings Park. We also had regular morning callers. Lady Catherine's nephews, Mr Darcy and a Colonel Fitzwilliam, were also visiting Kent."

"The same Mr Darcy who visited Hertfordshire last autumn?"

"Yes. One and the same."

"And what of Mrs Collins?" Mrs Gardiner asked. "Did you not enjoy her company, even if she was much changed?"

"I wish I could say I had. It will be hard to forget her actions and words. She was quite clear that she felt I was demanding something very unreasonable with my expectations of privacy. But I have given it much thought, and I believe the bitterness and anger I oftentimes found directed towards myself were in truth a response to her husband. She extended much effort to ensure his equanimity was not disturbed. I believe my visit only rendered her life harder, reminding her of what she had lost and forcing her to mediate between her husband and me."

At the questioning look on aunt's face, she added, "I hope my departure brings her some relief."

Her aunt looked less than appeased, but it comforted Elizabeth that she allowed that to be the end of their conversation. She patted Elizabeth's hand and rose to dress for dinner.

After their meal, Elizabeth and Jane were surprised by her uncle's suggestion that the ladies remain in London for some time. "We had long planned a tour of pleasure this summer, perhaps to the Lakes, but my business will confine me to the city for some time, and I know your presence will cheer my wife."

"I daresay," Mrs Gardiner said, looking intently at Elizabeth, "you could do with some amusement. Let us say six weeks. Will that do?"

"My dear, dear aunt," Elizabeth exclaimed, "what a delight!"

She beamed at her family. Indeed, she felt certain that by the time she returned to Hertfordshire in six weeks, she would be quite recovered.

It was not long before her days quickly filled with shopping, dinner parties, visits to parks, and pleasant conversation with her aunt and Jane. The London Season was at its height, and there were many invitations and events to consider for their amusement.

Night-time was the hardest. At night, she thought of Mr Darcy. She had confessed most of her interactions in Kent more fully to her aunt, but of Mr Darcy, she had been silent. It would not do her any favours to share her broken heart when there was no means to fix it.

Is Mr Darcy still in Kent or has he returned to London? Perhaps he travelled to Pemberley. She wondered often, and she longed to know what was passing in his mind—in what manner he thought of her, and whether, in defiance of everything, she was still dear to him. Or had she ever been?

New evening gowns were offered to both Jane and Elizabeth by their generous uncle for the opening night of a play at Covent Garden in a fortnight. Mrs Gardiner was elated to spend the day at the dressmaker's as well as perusing Mr Gardiner's warehouses for the newest fabrics, while Elizabeth was enticed by promises of book shops, which made the long days of shopping ahead more agreeable. Jane, as usual, was simply content to spend time with them both.

Due to her husband's business interests—Mr Gardiner brought exquisite and exclusive fabrics into the country—Elizabeth's aunt kept a custom with some of the most sought after dressmakers in London. Such connexions allowed the ladies to move freely and quickly as they shopped, without any thought for appointments.

Thus, they were found in one of the most fashionable shops on Bond Street, sorting through a new selection of silk gloves, by none other than Miss Caroline Bingley. Elizabeth was only alerted to her presence when she heard Jane's quiet gasp and felt her hand cover her own. Following Jane's gaze, she saw Miss Bingley had entered the shop.

While a naturally beautiful woman, Elizabeth had long thought Miss Bingley to be one of the most dull and vain creatures of her acquaintance. Not to mention her overt disdain for her brother's previous interest in Jane. Over time, Elizabeth had come to think of her as a mere puppet for the general opinions of the *ton*. There was nothing original, nothing remarkable, and certainly nothing kind about her.

Miss Bingley wore a gown of the most outrageous orange velvet and, not surprisingly, a displeased expression. "Miss Bennet, Miss Elizabeth," she said with a nod in their general direction. "You can imagine my astonishment to be walking down the street and to see you! I just had to be certain my eyes had not deceived me!"

Jane and Elizabeth curtseyed, and with far more civility, Elizabeth responded, "Miss Bingley, how lovely to see you today. I hope your family is in good health."

Miss Bingley merely nodded. "My dear friends—" She looked around a bit in awe of the shop and came closer to whisper, "as someone most particularly accustomed to life in London, I should warn you of this establishment's exclusive clientele. Even those ladies of the highest ranks must wait months for an appointment, and the cost of their creations is generally considerable."

"You are too good," Elizabeth said, hiding a smirk. "How kind of you to inform us."

"I would hate to see you disappointed. Should you desire it, I would be happy to provide the direction of a more suitable establishment for your..." Her eyes swept over Elizabeth before continuing, "...simpler tastes. Are there dressmakers in Cheapside? I would not know."

Miss Bingley's smug smile made it impossible to pity her. Elizabeth knew she ought to be tolerant but found she could not resist throwing back her own dart.

"Thank you for the advice, Miss Bingley. Have you had any success securing an appointment here?"

"Louisa was required to wait nearly a year, and I myself have been waiting upwards of six months!" Miss Bingley replied. "I am sure you know I cannot throw my connexions around in order to secure you an appointment, if that is what you seek. You understand. No, no—you see, shops such as these must show restraint and be selective about whom they allow in. They cannot simply dress just anyone!"

"No, no, of course not," Elizabeth replied.

"I was just telling my dearest friend, Miss Asher—I am certain you are not acquainted—that we shall be lucky if we have an opportunity to have one of their renowned dresses made in time for the next season!" Miss Bingley leaned over the table displaying gloves to add conspiratorially, "Though, I doubt that Miss Asher will have need for an entirely new wardrobe next Season if she continues to spend so much time with my brother. We have attended engagements

together nearly every night this week! And I ought not spec-
ulate, but should a desired, advantageous outcome come to
fruition, we shall all be well situated at her estate in Surrey
by mid-summer."

Elizabeth's head spun at the rapidity of topics Miss
Bingley spat at them. It was bad enough that the lady had
suggested Mr Bingley was attached to Mr Darcy's sister in a
letter the previous autumn. But to bring up another lady in
Jane's presence?

One quick glance at Jane revealed her sister was greatly
affected. She had averted her gaze, but a soft pink blush
coloured her cheeks, and her hands trembled at her side,
fiddling with her skirts in nervousness. Miss Bingley's insen-
sitivity and callous words were not to be borne! Elizabeth
squeezed Jane's nearest hand in staunch support.

And with that, the goddesses of humility aligned their
powers for a perfect moment of revenge. Their aunt returned
to them from the back rooms to announce, "Lizzy! I have
finished, and they are ready for your measurements. Do tell
me you have decided on a pattern and have not spent this
entire time looking over gloves!"

Elizabeth curtseyed to Caroline, "You will have to excuse
me, Miss Bingley. It appears it is time for my measurements
to be taken." She could have left it at that, but she turned
over her shoulder for one last remark, "I do hope you are
able to secure an appointment soon. My generous aunt was
gracious enough to send a note over, just this morning, to
obtain ours for today. I am sure your time will soon come. As
you have said yourself, they must be selective."

Elizabeth was soon in raptures over the plans for the soft
yellow silk she had discovered at a warehouse earlier that
day. They discussed wildflowers embroidered around the
bustline as well as trim at the hemline. She considered a

modest pattern with the dressmaker with capped sleeves that her aunt thought would be flattering for her light figure. In truth, she was having this gown crafted for Mr Darcy. When she saw the fabric, it reminded her of the sunlit morning surrounded by wildflowers where he kissed her neck and shoulder. Each choice she made that afternoon was a nod to their time spent together. It forced her to shiver, imagining the look in his eyes if he saw her in this gown.

She spent the rest of the day trying to distract herself and appear attentive to her aunt and sister. She knew she was being rather standoffish, but she could not let them in—not entirely.

Each time she considered sharing her heartbreak over the loss of Mr Darcy with Jane, Elizabeth thought better of it. To utter the words would make it real, and the finality of their time together, and the pain associated with it, would still be hers to bear alone. Keeping her recollections of him secure and private in the depth of her own mind felt the safer choice.

Jane's gentleness was also bolstered by an impenetrable optimism, even in the face of true malice, that could not lend itself to the kind of support she desired. When Elizabeth one night confided in her sister that she had come to understand Mr Wickham's true nature, her sister suggested it impossible.

"I cannot think so ill of him," Jane replied.

"I have it on good authority that he is a scoundrel of the first order!" Elizabeth cried from across the room.

Jane flinched at the thought, and Elizabeth crawled into bed next to her sister and calmly added, "Even Mr Bingley and his sister attempted to tell us that he was by no means a respectable young man."

Jane seemed thoughtful and then at once her eyes drifted

off across the room. She was lost in thought. Elizabeth should not have brought up conversations from the Netherfield ball. The last thing she wanted was to upset Jane. She was clearly not thinking of Mr Wickham any longer, so Elizabeth kissed her cheek and left her to sleep.

Of course, Jane could not believe such things of Mr Wickham, not after Elizabeth herself had been so vocal in her support of the man. She was coming to realise she had long surrounded herself with those who would stroke her vanity, but now found that sincerity was more welcome. Blowing out the candle next to the bed, Elizabeth's last thoughts before sleep were that she dearly missed the steady honesty of Mr Darcy.

The next day found Elizabeth declining a shopping trip to enjoy a book she had recently purchased. She curled up in a cosy chair in the drawing room for the entire afternoon. And that is how Mrs Gardiner and Jane found her when they returned from their excursion.

Jane came to join Elizabeth, taking the chair next to her. "Lizzy, I believe I saw Mr Darcy's carriage today."

"Mr Darcy?" Elizabeth immediately set her book on the nearby table.

"I recognised the crest, and I was sure it was him I saw inside," Jane answered.

Her aunt approached and joined in, "This may go against what you have told me of his behaviour in Hertfordshire, but I would rather like to meet the gentleman. His father was a good man. Growing up only five miles from Pemberley, we knew of the family. They were highly regarded in those parts."

Jane responded, "I have always said Mr Darcy was all that was honourable—Mr Bingley certainly thought he was."

He is the best of men. Elizabeth smiled gently at her sister, though her heart thudded painfully with just the mention of his name. "I have no doubt that you and Mr Bingley—both being so amiable—would never utter an unkind word about Mr Darcy, nor anyone." She continued softly, "I confess, I found a great improvement in his manners whenever I met him in Kent."

"Did you meet him often?" Jane asked.

"Almost every day."

The two ladies exclaimed over this, exchanging a small glance.

"I was unaware you were much in company, Lizzy."

Elizabeth, resolved not to divulge the fragility of her heart, answered carefully, "Mr Darcy and his cousin, Colonel Fitzwilliam, called on the parsonage with regular frequency during my stay."

"Was the colonel much like his cousin?" Jane asked.

Elizabeth chuckled. "In some ways, yes, and in others, no. They are both, as you would expect, well-educated and with good understanding, but Colonel Fitzwilliam is much more talkative, abundantly at ease in any place I saw him. He is a natural storyteller with good manners."

Jane said, "What of their cousin Miss de Bourgh? Is she sickly as Mr Collins suggested? Is she truly promised to Mr Darcy?"

This question nearly stole the breath from Elizabeth's lungs. *Promised to Mr Darcy.*

Elizabeth hid her shaking hands under her skirts and replied as evenly as possible, "Miss de Bourgh was in good health when I left Kent. She is a quiet woman—an unassuming lady, I should say. It appears our cousin and Mr

Wickham were correct about Mr Darcy and Miss de Bourgh. Mrs Collins told me just the day before I left Kent that their engagement was soon to be announced."

She was pleased with her response. Though her voice was unsteady, she hoped that her pretence of indifference would deter her aunt and sister from further questioning. Apparently, it had, because there were to be no additional questions on that subject. The ladies soon dispersed to dress for dinner.

On their way, Jane whispered to Elizabeth on the stairs, "Did Mr Darcy happen to mention Mr Bingley while you were in Kent, Lizzy?"

Elizabeth, who was hesitant to do anything but show the utmost kindness to her sister, replied in the negative and wrapped her arm around her as they ascended.

CHAPTER 14

Fitzwilliam Darcy was used to getting what he wanted, when he wanted it. He had spent many years avoiding the young misses who were husband hunting as well as their strong-willed mamas attempting to place their daughters within his reach. Never before had he been forced to imagine himself chasing after a lady—never before Elizabeth.

Her precipitate disappearance was confusing, and in darker moments, he feared the worst. Had she learnt to be offended by his actions? On further reflection, had she revived her initial poor opinion of him?

After her note arrived at Rosings Park, little time passed before Darcy was asking his valet to pack his bags and notifying Fitzwilliam of their imminent departure the following morning.

Sitting down to dinner that night with Mr and Mrs Collins as guests was dreadful. He made every effort to allow disdainful stares to fall on both characters throughout the evening—it was easy enough to do, as he felt ample contempt towards them. Mr Collins took no notice of his brooding, but he could sense some apprehension in Mrs Collins.

Mrs Collins had been seemingly determined to appeal to his softer side, complimenting him here and there, as if a mirror image of Miss Bingley, or perhaps she was parroting her husband's behaviour.

An empty chair sat to his left, which he assumed had been intended to hold Elizabeth. How differently the evening would have been with her by his side.

The gentlemen decided to forgo separating from the ladies after dinner in favour of a scheme to encourage their guests to depart sooner. When the rest of the drawing room's inhabitants were well distracted, Mr Darcy placed himself next to Mrs Collins and in low tones asked her, "I understand Miss Bennet left this morning?"

"Yes, sir. She longed to see her family."

"I hope they are well."

"Yes, I believe they are all in good health. They were impatient for her to return to them." Almost as an aside, the lady added quietly, "Equally, I believe she was eager to escape Kent, in order to avoid certain persons who would take advantage of her trusting and naïve nature."

Mrs Collins did not afford him a glance as she said so, nor did she sound censuring, but more provoking words she could not have uttered. Darcy felt himself flush even as he wondered at her meaning.

"What is it you are talking of?" Lady Catherine interrupted, "Let me hear what it is."

Mrs Collins rose and cast Darcy a disdainful glance as she

moved to sit nearer to his aunt. "We are speaking of music, your ladyship."

Darcy coughed and stared after her, some part of him astonished by the ease and speed with which she had lied—but equally alarmed by her suggestion. He resolved that as soon as he could, he would speak to her again, though by the end of the night, he had not been afforded the chance to do so.

The next day, they departed Kent at first light and were back in London well before the noon hour. His instinct was to follow Elizabeth directly to Hertfordshire after dropping Fitzwilliam in London, but he hesitated. His mind had been busily replaying each and every one of their meetings, and he found himself disappointed by his own conduct with her. He had allowed himself to shed all principles of propriety. Did it make her feel that he had no respect for her? Why else would she leave with no word at the first sign that the roads would allow travel? Why else would her friend have seemed censuring of him?

Reluctantly, he decided that he could not merely rush off to Hertfordshire but instead would bide his time in London and hope to return at a later date with Bingley.

Once in London, he was thrust back into the daily responsibilities expected of him. His days were dictated by a mass of correspondence waiting on his desk as well as a younger sister eager for his attention. Friends began leaving their cards and invitations arrived. All of these were accomplished with little enjoyment, yet a semblance of routine began again.

Bingley made quick time of his arrival at Darcy House, coming the very day Darcy sent his cards around. Darcy was happy to welcome his friend into his study, though uncertain of the conversation's outcome.

Rather than remaining behind his large mahogany desk, he rose to shake Bingley's hand and indicated they should sit in two comfortable chairs situated by the marble fireplace. Before he could offer refreshments, Bingley asked energetically, "When did you return to London?"

"Two days ago, now," Darcy replied.

"And your family in Kent is in good health? As well as Georgiana?"

"They are, I thank you. And your family?"

"Hurst and Louisa remain in Scarborough, while Caroline and I returned last week," Bingley replied. "She is eager, as you might imagine, for all that London can offer this Season. I believe she has left her card at every house in Mayfair in under three days' time! I am impatient for Hurst and Louisa to return in a fortnight to take her off my hands."

"I imagine she is, as you say, eager to be entertained by all the *ton* has to offer," replied Darcy evenly.

The two friends discussed upcoming events and planned to meet for lunch later in the week at their club, when Bingley providentially steered the conversation in the right direction.

"And how did you keep yourself busy in Kent?" Bingley asked.

"We had the unexpected pleasure of some acquaintances staying nearby."

With Bingley's questioning glance, Darcy continued, "You might remember that Mr Bennet's cousin is my aunt's rector? He is newly married to a young lady from Hertfordshire. Mrs Collins was formerly Miss Charlotte Lucas."

"Ah, yes!" Bingley's recognition and general joviality were immediate. "I do remember Miss Lucas. A kind woman. I had not heard about their marriage."

Darcy continued, "From what I gathered, it came about

rather suddenly after we departed the area. In any case, Miss Elizabeth Bennet was with them. We were not often in company with those residing in the parsonage, but we did spend some time together."

Propriety dictated Darcy should protect Elizabeth's reputation by keeping their time together private, though Bingley would be a logical person for Darcy to confide in, especially as he was familiar with both parties.

"Miss Elizabeth in Kent! How splendid!"

"Fitzwilliam accompanied me as well."

"Ah yes," Bingley responded. "I am certain he was a welcome addition to your family party."

Darcy hesitated before he went on. He did not often apologise nor admit he had done wrong, so the next, while necessary, was not easy to undertake.

"While in company with Miss Elizabeth—" Darcy cleared his throat, and continued, "I became aware of a misapprehension as it relates to her eldest sister. I—I was made aware of the possibility that my previous advice concerning her affections for a particular gentleman were in fact —inaccurate."

Bingley brushed a speck of dust off of his sleeve and looked up at Darcy with an expression of curiosity. "What are you saying, Darcy? Are you referring to me? Am I the particular gentleman?"

"Miss Elizabeth is of the opinion that there had been a strong attachment."

"She was attached to me," he said blankly. He rose to pour a glass of brandy and once again sat down. He ran his hand over his face.

"This is all very confusing. How can you be certain this information Miss Elizabeth passed on is not a campaign for her sister's own machinations? Caroline would certainly think it was. The match would have benefited Miss Elizabeth as well. It seems rather outrageously forthright of her to enlist your assistance in this business. Besides, Miss Bennet dropped the acquaintance with my sisters—not one letter," Bingley grumbled.

"As to that," Darcy responded, "I know that the lady desired to continue the acquaintance. Miss Bennet—Miss Jane Bennet—has been in London since January. Miss Bingley made me aware of this fact nearly two months ago, and I agreed that seeing her could only be harmful to you. Miss Bennet called at Hurst's town house, and your sisters waited a fortnight to return that call at her relations' home in Cheapside, but only to ensure Miss Bennet understood their acquaintance was at an end."

Bingley straightened; his attention engaged. "Miss Bennet visited in January? That long ago…"

Bingley rose to gaze out of the large window, sipping his drink as he looked out on the city beyond. "It seems I shall never know what her true feelings were. Perhaps that is for the best. You did not want me to align myself with that family. You and Caroline—you cared only for your own repu-tations." This he spoke to the window, but his reflection in the glass revealed his irritation.

"That is not true. And there is still time to find out her feelings, man. Visit her in London. Open Netherfield. Seek her out. Find out the truth."

Bingley swallowed his brandy in one gulp, set the empty glass down on the windowsill and turned back to Darcy. "I find I can barely remember my feelings as they were then. And London has been extremely diverting. Did I not tell you about the lovely young lady Caroline introduced me to?"

"No."

"She is an angel…" Bingley responded with a wistful look

in his eyes. "Long raven-black hair and a substantial estate she will inherit in Surrey."

Darcy was too amazed by his friend's seemingly indifferent sentiments to be polite in his response. "Did you not also call Miss Bennet an angel?"

"I do not know what you want from me," Bingley sputtered, appearing to find the topic exceedingly exasperating. "I do not relish in your meddling—or that of my sister. But I find that I do not have any interest in renewing the acquaintance. I cannot see why you are pressing the issue. You will excuse me. I have another engagement." With that, Bingley quit the room, not bothering to look back.

Darcy sat for a moment in glum astonishment. It had gone very differently than expected. He had hoped to relieve himself of the burden of information and be immediately invited to Netherfield. He had hoped, for once, that Bingley's affection would be more steadfast, more reliable.

He would have understood if Bingley was hurt, but disinterest? Too shocking by half, really. Exceedingly. He never imagined such a result to their discussion. More fool him. In truth, he had been more concerned with how the conversation would benefit his pursual of Elizabeth. Arrogance and selfishness, indeed. He dropped his head back against the soft, leather chair. First Elizabeth, now Bingley. How could he have been so wrong at predicting Bingley's reaction? Darcy was at a loss for what to do next.

The joy of being with her relatives in London did ease some of the unhappiness Elizabeth felt every time she thought of her trip to Kent. Dining with her aunt and uncle allowed for lively and intelligent exchanges that challenged and diverted her, and their children provided many hours of amusement. Gradually, she felt her spirits begin to lift and saw this mirrored in her sister, too.

It produced no little astonishment in Elizabeth and Jane, returning home from a walk with their young cousins one afternoon, to find Sir William Lucas, his daughter, Maria Lucas, and their own youngest sister, Lydia, sitting in their aunt's drawing room.

Their young cousins could not contain their excitement and rushed to greet Lydia, amid shrieks of delight. They were soon hurried off to the nursery while Elizabeth and Jane civilly welcomed the guests.

"Sir William and Maria! Welcome to London! I hope you have left your family in good health?"

"What brings you to town, sir?" Jane asked.

Sir William Lucas stood to greet them, "Oh yes, yes—thank you, ladies. All are in good health—Lady Lucas and of course, John and Harold. We are travelling through town on our way to Kent."

"Kent?" Elizabeth asked, her eyes wide with surprise.

"I have had a capital idea!" Sir William began in his customarily jovial manner. "Lady Lucas is in Dorset visiting her ailing aunt, so Maria and I thought we would visit Charlotte to see how she is getting on. She has been so busy keeping her new home that we have barely heard a word from Hunsford. We thought to surprise her with a short visit —only a month, you see—to attend to Charlotte's contentment, of course, and to enjoy all that Kent has to offer."

If only Elizabeth could find a polite way to discourage any such anticipation!

"We will stay with my sister in town this evening and travel to Kent on the morrow. As you can see, Maria has invited Lydia as her companion for our trip."

"I wanted to travel to Brighton this summer with the regiment as Mrs Forster's special guest," Lydia pronounced with no effort to disguise her peevishness, "but our father imagined my request as a general desire to travel, and so here I am—on my way to spend my summer with our bore of a cousin!"

"Lydia!" Jane scolded and turned to their other guests. "Pray pardon Lydia's manners. I am sure you will all have a lovely trip."

Lydia rolled her eyes and asked her aunt if there were any more lemon biscuits to send along in the carriage.

"You may go and see Cook, Lydia," their aunt responded tersely. Elizabeth, seeing her opportunity to tell someone how things stood, rose to follow her.

"Lydia!" Elizabeth hissed as she followed her sister down the passageway to the kitchens. "Lydia, I *must* speak to you before you depart. Please assure me you will be on your best behaviour while in Kent. Mr Collins will not brook anything but thorough compliance of his expectations."

"Oh Lizzy! What a joke. Who could possibly fear that potato of a man?" Having found a platter of the desired biscuits, Lydia set about noisily and untidily eating them, while also stuffing her pockets with extras.

"I know it is not in your nature and it will not be easy for you, but I have only just left Hunsford. I want to prepare you for his directives."

Lydia laughed heartily and nearly choked. Bits of biscuit shot across the room and down the bodice of her gown. "I would like to see him try!" She patted Elizabeth on the arm, then turned and barrelled back up the stairs to the drawing room.

Their visit was as fleeting as it was turbulent. Just as quickly as the surprise travelling party had arrived, they were taking their leave to board their carriage.

Elizabeth was pleased to hear her father had not allowed Lydia to travel alongside the militia to Brighton, but that Lydia was on her way to visit the Collinses was equally concerning. She tried to imagine the shock that was about to befall the parsonage. She hoped Sir William would ease the tension and provide a buffer for Lydia's outspoken and silly ways.

Elizabeth barely slept that night with worry. Should she have said more to Lydia? At the least, she should have offered to hold anything of a personal nature that her sister carried with her.

CHAPTER 15

Dependable. Useful. Those were the words of affection Charlotte's mother had used to describe her. Those meaningful expressions, though not depictions of beauty nor grace, had meant something to Charlotte. She worked to ensure she was worthy of those descriptions. She had depended on their truth and let the words seep into her entire being; though now she resented her obedience, for her dutiful nature had led her to her present position.

Charlotte pushed the kitchen door open with haste, immediately gaining the attention of Mrs Montgomery and Hayes. "Please, no dawdling. Our guests require sustenance after their journey from London, and we need the rooms prepared as soon as may be."

Hayes hopped down from the table she had been sitting on, shoving the last bit of a biscuit in her mouth before responding, "Yes, ma'am, that is what—"

"No," Charlotte interrupted her maid. "That is not what I found you doing. Please move along." Hayes nodded, curt-seyed, and made a hasty departure.

Charlotte turned her attention to Mrs Montgomery. "Shall we adjust the menu for dinner, or can you make do with three additional mouths to feed?"

"I can make do, ma'am."

Charlotte left as quickly as she had come but stopped on the landing to take a breath. *Why are they come? Why can no one leave me be here?*

Despite her fondness for her father and sister, she could not bear to feign being a happy wife once again. How she would accomplish it, she had no idea. For indeed, another difficult month lay before her. And even harder with Lydia Bennet, no doubt! If Mr Collins thought Elizabeth was a challenge, it would be much worse with her youngest and most untamed sister.

Tears welled in her eyes, and she gripped her skirt in her fists. Nothing in her new life was easy. She just wanted to be left alone. Could not anyone comprehend that in her letters? Was she not allowed the privacy she desired?

"...I shall return forthwith," she heard her husband say, and she could hear his nearing footsteps as he made his way towards her. She wiped her eyes with the back of her hand and stood up straighter before he rounded the corner and discovered her there.

"Mrs Collins, your guests are waiting on the tea cart, and I have just seen Hayes, who informed me that you are unhappy with her?"

"Pardon?"

"Have you no understanding for her position? Your father sprang this visit on the entire household. I am certain preparing three rooms with no notice shall take some time."

"I found her chatting in the kitchen and simply redirected her upstairs to prepare the necessary bedchambers."

Mr Collins leaned towards her, so close that he forced her to tilt her head back in order to look up at him. "I should not have to remind you that Hayes comes from Rosings with only the highest of recommendations."

Charlotte pressed back against the wall. Her husband's malodourous smell made her flinch with reminders of his visit to her bed the night before. If only Lady Catherine would direct him to some regularity in his bathing rituals.

"Of course," she replied and held her peace until he departed to return to their newly arrived guests.

Putting duty once again ahead of her own equanimity, Charlotte blinked away the wetness in her eyes, pinched her cheeks and turned her steps towards the parlour. Her practised smile was set in place just before she crossed the threshold of the room.

At length, the parsonage began to assume a new routine. Charlotte's father enjoyed daily walks to the village, and fortunately, Maria and Lydia relished accompanying him. Her husband's attempts at civility were greater with her father present and watching, but even so, she could feel his last thread of dignity was nearing its end as the days went on.

Lydia especially was wearing on him, and she watched as he painfully held his tongue. She had seen him approach his young cousin in the garden one day, his posture much the same as it was when he spoke a sermon, but Charlotte did not remain to see what Lydia's response was. So far, the girl had been remarkably adept at brushing him aside.

One afternoon found Charlotte mending, attended by two

young ladies who were sprawled out on a nearby settee complaining of boredom, when a knock on the parlour door set the room to rights quickly. "Come in," Charlotte beckoned once the ladies were upright, and a footman from Rosings entered her parlour, offering her a note from Lady Catherine.

"Is it anything of interest, Charlotte? We could certainly do with some diversion," Lydia said.

"Is it from Lady Catherine? Are we being invited to dine?" Maria asked.

"Girls, please," Charlotte scolded them even while she read the note a second time. Lady Catherine requested an audience with her at Rosings Park, immediately, and she was to come alone with all haste. "You will have to excuse me. Lady Catherine has summoned me."

Minutes later Charlotte presented herself at Rosings, having delayed only long enough to change into a more elegant day gown. Though it was an old muslin, it was newly trimmed at the bodice with lace from a discarded gown Maria had carried from home for Charlotte's use.

At the butler's announcement, she entered the morning room to find Lady Catherine sitting with a fierce scowl upon her face. She did not rise to welcome her and simply waved her hand in the direction of a nearby seat, saying only, "Mrs Collins."

To her surprise, Hayes was in the room. Charlotte shot her an uncertain glance as she took a seat and folded her hands primly in her lap; Hayes avoided her gaze.

This was not a social call. Her mind raced at the implications, wondering what this visit could be regarding.

"Hayes, please repeat to Mrs Collins what you have told me," Lady Catherine ordered in her familiar strident tone.

"Yes, your ladyship," Hayes said with a reverence unfamiliar to Charlotte. "As I said before, I witnessed Miss Bennet and Mr Darcy taking private walks together in the mornings."

"Unchaperoned, yes?" Lady Catherine interrupted with theatrical astonishment.

"Yes, your ladyship. They met with regularity, just after sunrise. She would meet him in the woods a far distance from the parsonage, I would say."

Lady Catherine gave Charlotte an accusing glance before returning her attention to Hayes. "Tell me again about their last assignation."

Hayes nodded. "I believe she accepted an *indecent* proposal of sorts, if you take my meaning. At first she was very upset with him, and they argued. He made her cry, but then she was in his arms, and they were very affectionate. I s'pose his offer was a generous one."

Charlotte gasped, her body instinctively heating in response to her humiliation.

"That will be all, Hayes."

Hayes curtseyed and left the room. When she had gone, Lady Catherine looked to Charlotte with raised eyebrows and a question in her expression. "And what do you know of this matter, Mrs Collins?"

Careful to appear composed, Charlotte said, "My apologies, your ladyship, that Hayes has come to you with such gossip and nearly two weeks after Elizabeth has gone home. I cannot imagine why she did not bring her concerns first to me or my husband. It was terribly inappropriate, and it will never happen again. You have my word."

"I cannot but agree with your notion that this information should have been brought to my attention sooner," Lady Catherine responded. "Something of this nature could ruin my dear Anne. What do you have to say for yourself? How could you allow such a woman to reside under your roof while my unsuspecting nephews were visiting?"

"I have to believe that Hayes misunderstood what she saw. I cannot imagine Elizabeth should participate in such a scheme."

"Are you suggesting it would be at the direction of my nephew?"

"Of course not, your ladyship." Charlotte could no longer meet her eyes. How was she back here grovelling to Lady Catherine for another transgression she had not herself committed? In her anxiousness, she felt the balls of her feet begin to tap against the floor and was recalled to her mother's constant oversight of her fidgeting as a young girl. *Calm yourself.* She willed her body to behave.

"What do you know of your friend's arrangement with my nephew?"

"There is no arrangement, madam, of this I am certain." But that was not wholly true, was it? She *did* know of Elizabeth's affection and of a kiss. *But that is not at all the same as agreeing to be a gentleman's mistress! Elizabeth would never consent to that!* She had no reason to degrade herself in such a way.

Her anger rose, however, that Elizabeth had engaged in any of this sort of behaviour at all. What an embarrassment! To have her own guest meeting Mr Darcy in the woods in secret and being spotted kissing him! This was even worse than she had imagined. Her fingernails dug into the palm of her hand.

She did not know what bore better for her—truth or deception. Would Lady Catherine prefer to know Mr Darcy and Elizabeth held each other in affection or would she rather believe Hayes' story? Which version would best benefit Miss de Bourgh?

She supposed it mattered not. Regardless of how she

explained herself, it was likely she and her husband would be held responsible for Eliza's transgressions. But surely her efforts to separate them would be welcome knowledge?

"Do not pretend you know nothing of this," Lady Catherine said, interrupting her thoughts. "You are not witless. Tell me what you know. Now."

CHAPTER 16

Dressed and ready to depart, Darcy was handed a note from his butler merely a moment after calling for his carriage. "Damn," he cursed to himself.

Not only had he not wanted to attend the theatre that night, but now he would be going alone. He had let Fitzwilliam talk him into it, only to find himself staring back at his staircase wondering if he should simply call it a night. Season tickets or no, a glass of brandy in the library sounded much more enticing.

"Sir, the carriage has been brought 'round," his butler informed him.

"Thank you, Ebright."

Darcy hesitated on the front steps, but considered that his cousin, the viscount, could be in attendance, and if not, he would join another friend. It seemed a waste to turn back just then.

Darcy always arrived at the theatre shortly before curtain.

Unlike many who came to see and be seen, he was part of the minority of Londoners who attended the theatre because of a true appreciation of the art. Like most voracious readers, he thoroughly enjoyed seeing a well-known story come to life on the stage.

This night was no different; in fact, he had delayed his arrival to the point where he feared he might miss the opening act. Darcy moved through the vestibule greeting some and avoiding others who he knew might be unduly encouraged by his notice. He had just turned his head to avoid one such young lady when his eyes briefly alit upon a light figure moving in a way he knew well.

His breath hitched. Elizabeth. *My Elizabeth*. It was as if the universe had answered his prayers and dropped her down right in front of his wandering mind.

She was stunning. Her gown stood out in a sea of blatantly garish fashion. Standing in contrast to the crowd of wildly unnatural looking peacock feathers, Elizabeth's muted elegance reminded Darcy why he considered her such a prize. Her beautiful chocolate brown hair was pulled up elegantly, dotted with tiny white flowers that reminded him all too painfully of their walks in Kent.

Moving down, his eyes traced the line of her neck across her shoulders to the capped sleeves which topped her graceful arms. He had never seen this gown before, but it was an immediate favourite. It shimmered as the candlelight danced on the intricate threading nearest to her neck. Her gown was the colour of a soft yellow sunrise, and he reminisced on the mornings spent together with her arched eyebrow and knowing smile. Bathed in sunlight, he remembered accompanying his precious Elizabeth through the meadows in Kent. *It is the east, and Juliet is the sun.*

At once, he was aware that should he continue standing

there gaping, he would miss an opportunity to speak to her. She and her party were attempting to keep up with the bustling crowd which moved in all directions, everyone eager to find their seats before the play began.

His heart began an almost violent staccato as he watched her consider the entire room while being softly guided along by her sister's hand on her back. Darcy could see her expressive eyes curiously observing all the fashion and people. Before he could think, he was moving in her direction.

Eyes widening with surprise, Elizabeth took in Mr Darcy's handsome features and long strides carrying him in her direction. His eyes never left hers, and she held her breath in anticipation. She stood firmly, even when Jane attempted to steer her where their uncle had indicated. She grabbed her sister's hand, guiding her to stay put. By doing so, she also halted the forward motion of her aunt and uncle, who nearly ran into her.

"What is this, Lizzy?" her uncle asked. "We must make haste, or we shall miss the opening."

But move, she did not. She could not. Not when he was merely two strides from her.

When at last he reached her, he opened and closed his mouth twice before Elizabeth took in his clear discomposure and realised it was to her to insert some civility into the meeting. As serenely as she could, she said, "Mr Darcy, good evening."

He bowed, somewhat jerkily, then seemed at a loss for words, so Elizabeth continued, "I hope you left Miss de Bourgh and Lady Catherine in good health? Or have they joined you in London?"

"Um, no, no they have not. Will you introduce me to your friends?"

In spite of her anxiety, this nearly produced a laugh. Mr and Mrs Gardiner did appear people of fashion. She wondered what Mr Darcy would think when she introduced them.

"Sir, may I introduce you to my aunt and uncle, Mr and Mrs Edward Gardiner. Aunt, Uncle, this is Mr Darcy of Pemberley."

Mr Darcy bowed again. His visage was more severe than it had been in Hunsford, but still lighter than during his stay at Netherfield. "I am pleased to find friends among the audience tonight. I would be even more pleased if your party would join me in my box this evening."

Mrs Gardiner was quick to demur, as politeness would dictate, but Mr Darcy was just as quick to insist.

Mr Gardiner said, "Thank you for the kind gesture, Mr Darcy, but we would not wish to put you out, sir."

"I would be honoured to have you," he replied with all civility.

Mr Gardiner looked to the ladies for their approval. "Well then, it is settled. Mr Darcy, we would be delighted to join you. Pray, sir, lead the way for us."

Mr Darcy held out his arm for Elizabeth, who took it quickly, but with an uneasiness she could not name. She laid her gloved hand on his arm so gently she could barely feel his coat underneath. He was not hers and would never be, nor was she certain it was wise to desire his attentions at all.

While she would like to stubbornly continue to hold it against him—to berate him for the liberties shared in a flowered glade in Kent and the unmentioned betrothal—she could not find it within herself to punish him for it. Her feelings for him were so dear, and she knew he was only seeing to his duty. She, who had defied duty, wished he had the power to make the same decision for his own happiness—but alas, he had not.

So, instead of sulking in her defeat, she decided to savour the time in his presence. It was likely the last. Soon, Mr Darcy would be married and off travelling with his new wife to one of his vast estates. But it was her object to be satisfied and her temper to be happy. She would simply enjoy the evening—a moment in time that could belong to only her.

Except, it quickly became clear it was not just her, or the two of them, alone in a moment of time. She could feel the eyes of the crowd as they passed by. She could hear the talk intended to be blocked by their intricately painted fans, "Who is the young lady in yellow?" She could have chosen a more traditional cream colour, but the fabric had been so vibrant and full of life. She could not have envisaged being on display in this way—on the arm of such a man. She turned to take in Jane's countenance. Jane looked serene and lovely as usual, with only a hint of a question in her eyes for Elizabeth. Later. *I must speak to her later.*

She turned her eyes to Mr Darcy, and the satisfied look on his face told her he was planning to enjoy this respite from his duties as well. After years of doing what was expected of him, she imagined he might also enjoy an evening spent only in the present.

The ladies and Uncle Gardiner were shown to the front row, and Elizabeth furtively watched while Mr Darcy chose a seat directly behind her. Jane and Aunt Gardiner were quite taken with the view and exclusivity of the seats. In fact, Jane leaned over to quietly mention the attention they were receiving from the room.

Elizabeth turned back to the large theatre, taking it all in. Tonight's parade of feathers, jewels, and wagging fans was especially diverting. She heard movement behind her, and she could sense him before she felt his breath on her neck, leaning in to speak quietly into her ear. The small space left between them, merely inches, felt overtly intimate for such a public setting. His gloved hand hovered ever so slightly above her shoulder as he leaned in and gently drew her attention to him. She felt it land softly on her capped sleeve, sending shivers throughout her entire body. "Miss Elizabeth, I hope you will enjoy the performance."

Fortifying herself to sound calmer than was her wont, she answered, continuing to keep her eyes on the room rather than his hand, "I am certain we shall all enjoy the performance. Thank you for inviting our party to join you this evening."

He leaned slightly closer, "Of course, Elizabeth. I am exceedingly pleased you are here." She was not even sure if he realised he had spoken her Christian name, but her entire body reacted.

An internal battle of reason versus desire urged Elizabeth first to protect herself by responding blandly and avoiding his attention, while in parallel wanting to let his consideration and kindness seep into her every pore.

Meanwhile, even though the entirety of the theatre did not hear him speak to her so informally, she could feel the eyes and whispers surrounding her increasing.

He seemed entirely oblivious to the growing talk. Perhaps he did not consider this type of attention worthy of his acknowledgment, but this was new for Elizabeth. His friendly gestures and whispers were not going unnoticed.

She knew this type of display would bring undue attention, especially as Mr Darcy's betrothal was undoubtably known among his circle.

Elizabeth was wrong about his attentiveness. Darcy could, in fact, feel the glances and whispers as if they were a tangible, living being—growing and moving as the murmurs about the lovely woman in yellow moved through the throng of people. The crowded room heckled quietly at his display, but Elizabeth meant more to him than the gossip of theatregoers. Their whispers were not untrue. Darcy loved Elizabeth, and he did not care who observed them. Her ease was his priority. He must find a way to ensure she could trust him.

Darcy imagined how fulfilling his future would be with Elizabeth on his arm, holding court with the best of the *ton*. He imagined her soothing his spirit at each required event, and it brought a smile to his face. *How much easier this will all be with her by my side!*

It was during these thoughts that he realised Elizabeth had turned her head just slightly and was speaking to him.

"Pardon me, I was wool-gathering. Are you comfortable?" Darcy asked, pleased she was speaking to him of her own will.

"Certainly, Mr Darcy," she responded. He could hear her smile in the tone of her voice. "These seats are completely pleasing. Your box provides an ideal view of the stage."

She continued, "I am curious when the rest of your party will be joining us?"

He smiled and answered her, "I am quite pleased with the current gathering. I was not expecting anyone else. Colonel Fitzwilliam was supposed to accompany me but was detained at the last minute. I may have joined another friend in their box if I had not the pleasure of encountering your party."

"You came alone tonight, Mr Darcy?" she asked.

"Yes. I enjoy seeing the performances," he whispered. He leaned in a bit farther and lowered his voice. "As you have been a great studier of my character, Elizabeth, I would assume you understand me enough by now to know I do not require a crowd, nor do I enjoy it."

The slow, measured way he said her name reverberated through her. It was clearly said with purpose; but for what purpose, she did not know. Before she thought it was a slip; but not now. She could feel his breath on her shoulder, on her neck, on her ear. Even if he was not engaged to another woman, the implication was intimate. She was unsure how to respond, though her body instinctively leaned in closer. Too close, as it happened—as his lips brushed her earlobe, and she heard a sharp intake of breath.

He moved away from her, but not so quickly as to warrant any additional notice. She wanted to turn around and see his expression—to savour his response to her unplanned movement—but she could sense it affected him when she heard him sigh.

At last, and as if to break up the tension of the moment, the curtain slowly opened, and she heard Mr Darcy adjust his seat.

The performance was all that was lovely and moving. Elizabeth felt her cheeks ache from smiling throughout. It had been two years since she had spent a significant amount of time in London, and the theatre was one aspect of town she missed dearly.

As abruptly as the show ended, she was dropped right back into her present reality. So moving was the performance, that Elizabeth had quite put Mr Darcy out of her mind.

Darcy, on the other hand, had spent the hours with his attention fixed on her neck, her hair, and her reactions to the performance. *She is exquisite*, he thought. He was also brought quickly from his own musings when everyone began to rise.

Formalities and gratitude were shared. The group was a cheerful one leaving the theatre. Darcy was particularly contented to have Elizabeth once again on his arm as they made their way through the crush. He knew their time was to be brief now, so he had only one chance to speak. He leaned in and lowered his voice for Elizabeth only as they moved through the crowd, "Miss Elizabeth, would you do me the honour of allowing me to call on you at your uncle's house?"

Elizabeth froze and looked surprised, "Thank you, Mr Darcy. You are most welcome."

He did not enjoy her shocked expression but thanked her nonetheless. He was eager for the chance to right the past.

She hesitated before saying quietly, "His home is on Gracechurch Street."

Ah, yes—he connected the dots quickly. She was concerned he would not mix with tradesmen after his arrogant behaviour in Meryton. He hoped to reassure her quickly, "Yes, I believe I know the area."

Elizabeth was confused about his request to call on her at Gracechurch Street. It was kind enough to allow her family to join him at the theatre, but there was no need to continue this ruse if he was soon to be married. Besides, it could harm her fragile contentment or perhaps even her reputation. She tried to hush the concern growing inside her and to simply live in the moment, but she had to ask, "Will you be returning to Kent shortly?"

Darcy looked surprised and chuckled, "No, Miss Elizabeth. I believe I have spent quite enough time in that county for the year. I should think even next Easter will come rather too quickly."

She answered quietly, but archly, "I should punish you for being so wicked, Mr Darcy! I could write to my dear cousin, Mr Collins, to request he send you copies of his most recent sermons. He would be grateful to know you have condescended to show interest in furthering your religious studies."

"Minx," he said with a look in his eyes that told her he was not at all displeased with her teasing. His eyes were so intense, she quite lost her ability to breathe for a moment.

Thus they were—smiling and strolling in silence with looks of complete satisfaction—when they reached her uncle's carriage. Mr Gardiner handed in his wife and Jane, nodding to Mr Darcy, who stepped up to hand in Elizabeth.

She was nearly out of breath when she took her seat next to Jane. Ever the example of a refined woman, her aunt would say nothing but would communicate her interest and curiosity with mere glances. Even in the dark, she could read her aunt's teasing expression. She coloured and looked away.

After thanking Mr Darcy for the lovely evening, Mr Gardiner joined the ladies in the carriage. "Well, my dearest ladies, what a charming fellow and what a lovely performance!" He was jolly as usual, and all the ladies offered obliging responses about the evening. Elizabeth provided short answers, distracted as she was. Her mind was reeling. How long would it be until she understood what had just taken place?

CHAPTER 17

The light from the single burning candle danced on the floral pattern papered on the walls of the guest room Elizabeth shared with Jane. Elizabeth lay awake in contemplation as, across the room, her sister plaited her hair to prepare for sleep.

Jane's gentle smile was reflected in the glass and Elizabeth smiled uncomfortably back at her. The dam holding back her emotions was near to breaking, and a single tear ran down her cheek. Jane was adept at reading her expressions and hurried her preparations to join her.

Jane held her as she shed tears for the life she would never have.

"Do you care for him?"

"He is to marry his cousin," Elizabeth answered.

Jane smoothed Elizabeth's hair off her face and continued softly, "I cannot imagine him engaged to his cousin after what I have now witnessed. What honourable man, engaged to one lady, would also openly show preference for another as he did tonight?"

"It is just like you to see only the best in people. You think that if you will, but I cannot allow my mind to travel down that path, no matter how greatly I wish you to be right," Elizabeth confessed.

"I do think him more honourable than you are suggesting. And I believe you know it too, but I understand why you would prefer to guard your heart. I should have protected myself thus," Jane replied.

"Perhaps—or perhaps not. Was it not a lovely season in your life to be wooed by Mr Bingley? I would not trade my time in Kent...even if heartbreak shall be the price."

"It is a special memory—one that will sustain me for some time. I can only hope there shall be another...one day. I have been quite devoted to forgetting Mr Bingley these last months."

Elizabeth mumbled a response and snuggled into Jane, stretching her cold feet into the warmth of her sister's legs. "Lizzy!" Jane stifled her laughter, and she pushed her further away across the bed. Both girls fell into a fit of hushed giggles that took their breath away the longer they tried to restrain their volume.

"I know you are full of uncertainty now, but I assure you, I know what I saw. Mr Darcy cares for you. I only hope he will have the strength Mr Bingley did not—to take action in the direction of his own preferences."

"And how could he make a decision of that nature, dear sister? To go against his family? To break a lengthy betrothal to his own cousin? To choose someone of no connexions who brings no fortune to a marriage? It would be absurd," Elizabeth replied. "And do not placate my vanity, for I am aware I would bring nothing to a marriage with Mr Darcy."

"Perhaps he simply needs *you?*"

If only, Elizabeth thought. "Do you think he will call?"

Jane squeezed her hand and replied, "Nothing could keep him away."

The sound of a carriage followed by a knock on the front door interrupted the ladies' conversation the next afternoon as they enjoyed their individual pursuits in the drawing room. Mrs Gardiner set aside her embroidery and shared a glance with Elizabeth, who closed her book. Anticipation coursed through Elizabeth's veins. *Has he come so soon?*

The ladies awaited the arrival of their visitor's card, and once proffered to their aunt, she rose quickly and responded, "Do show him in, immediately."

The other ladies rose as well, exchanging subtle smiles between them, readying themselves for his entry.

Through the door came not Mr Darcy, but their own father. Mr Bennet looked weary as he greeted them, and Mrs Gardiner was quick to send for some refreshments for him.

"Might you allow me the use of your husband's study? I require an audience with my daughter."

Mr Bennet gave Elizabeth a pointed look, and when her aunt approved his request, he tilted his head in the direction of her uncle's study, an indication that Elizabeth should make haste. Jane and Elizabeth exchanged glances of curiosity as Elizabeth began to follow her father out of the room.

Behind them, Mrs Gardiner said, "I shall send a note to Mr Gardiner to announce your arrival."

"There is no need," Mr Bennet responded curtly. "I shall not remain long. I must return home shortly and will take the girls with me. You might have Jane begin overseeing the packing."

Elizabeth opened her mouth to protest or express her shock but something in her father's air told her she must not. Meekly, she went to the study with him, took a seat, and awaited the tea that was brought to them moments later, fixing her father's cup as she knew he liked it. He cradled the cup in his hands and gave her a hard look. As was his nature, he let the silence curl around the room until she felt nearly squeezed by the words unspoken between them.

He would wait her out, she knew it, so she finally spoke. "Papa?"

"Perhaps you can account for the arrival of a Lady Catherine de Bourgh who appeared on our doorstep just yesterday bringing with her a report of your behaviour while in Kent. Behaviour of a most alarming nature, I believe were her words."

"What?" Elizabeth sputtered. "Indeed, I cannot, sir."

He set his cup aside and levelled a stern glance at her. "I would not have imagined it possible that my second eldest—nay, my most sensible daughter—would be having secret assignations with a gentleman in the woods. With Mr Darcy? You do not even like the gentleman! No. I should never have believed it—not of you. Of my Kitty or Lydia, perhaps I might have expected it, but you? I had thought you better, Lizzy."

Assignations in the woods? Memories of the kiss flooded her. But they had not been seen! Surely, if they had, Lady Catherine would have confronted her immediately.

"My defence of you was absolute," Mr Bennet continued. "I made it clear I would not allow her ladyship, no matter her status and connexions, to speak badly of you. It was not until she produced a letter from my daughter's dearest friend—a letter in Mrs Collins's handwriting—that documented all she knew of these secret meetings."

Charlotte! Elizabeth's stomach dropped and flipped violently, and for a moment, she thought she would be sick. What had Charlotte done? Horrified indignation would not allow her to continue in silence, "It is not—not what it appears."

"Did the gentleman lure you into the woods? Have you been harmed in any way?"

She shook her head, *no.*

"So, you cannot deny it?"

Elizabeth opened her mouth to reply, not knowing what she would say, but Mr Bennet continued, "No. I do not want to hear of it. You have ruined, perhaps, your future and that of your sisters, and have brought scandal upon us all. I have her word that if I bring you home, and you cease all contact with the gentleman, she will hush up this entire business. And you had better hope with every fibre of your being that she can."

Elizabeth could not meet his eyes, blinking rapidly in a pathetic plea for her tears to retreat.

"I am ashamed of you, in a way I thought I never should be. You will join your sister in packing your things. We depart immediately," he said forcefully, and dismissed her with nary a kind glance.

Elizabeth nearly stumbled up the stairs, moving as quickly as possible. Her father rarely stirred himself from his book room and had ever been an idle disciplinarian—and never towards her. She had been under the impression she could do no wrong in his eyes.

When she was punished as a child by her mother for her wild behaviour, he would laugh. When Lydia was too forward with the militia officers, he turned a blind eye. When Bingley left Jane heartbroken, he shut the door to the book room to avoid his wife's complaints. That he had roused himself to travel to London on her behalf was astonishing, and only increased her guilt for her part in the whole affair.

But shame was only some portion of what she was feeling. The betrayal of her former friend was a deep wound. That Charlotte would go to such efforts to harm her and threaten her family's standing in the world was unimaginable, to say nothing of unpardonable. Elizabeth was certain her heart could take no more of such duplicity.

Across town, Darcy was ensconced in his study, trying to focus on a letter from his solicitor, but found his thoughts were filled with only Elizabeth. He was relieved that travel to Hertfordshire would be unnecessary. That she had been somewhat receptive to his attentions at the theatre was encouraging.

While he desired to relish and think on the moments she had seemed most attentive, there was no denying that she treated him more cautiously than she had in Kent. She did not appear put-off, as Mrs Collins had implied; however, he knew there was something. Had it been the crowd? Or her family's presence? Or was it *he* she was uncertain of?

Had his forward behaviour hurt her? Darcy was a tangle of emotions, but no matter the direction of his mind, the result was the same—he would do everything in his power to earn her trust, should she allow it. There was nothing he desired more.

He would call on her. He would introduce her to Georgiana—perhaps even his aunt, Lady Matlock. He would lay a foundation of trust and show her the life he intended to bestow upon her. He hoped one day she might love him as ardently as he loved her.

He attempted to shake off such thoughts and focus on the business at hand when he heard the front door and the sound of footsteps rushing towards his study. He had little time to anticipate his guest's arrival, for only moments later Lady Catherine entered unannounced.

"Lady Catherine de Bourgh," his butler declared, arriving only steps behind her.

Darcy stood and nodded to Ebright that all was well, thankful that the butler was already acquainted with his aunt. He bowed, then motioned for her to take a seat in front of his desk. She declined.

"To what do I owe the pleasure of this visit?" From the high colour on her cheeks and the glitter of anger in her eyes, he had already deduced it was not to be a social call.

"I have been very lenient. I have been patient and under-standing, and I daresay, so has Anne. I shall do everything in my power to ensure the scandal travels no further than Kent, but you must be more cautious, more discerning in your choices. I expected better of you than this."

"I do not have the pleasure of understanding what you are speaking of. May I ring for some tea?"

She shook her finger in his direction, her eyes narrowed. "You understand perfectly. I will not allow Anne to be thrown over by this little dalliance with Miss Bennet. Her father has agreed to bring her home and hush this entire thing up."

"Pardon me?"

"You hear me clearly. Pray, do not feign confusion, Nephew."

Darcy took a step towards his aunt. "When were you in company with Mr Bennet?"

"I travelled to Hertfordshire and spoke to him just yesterday."

The insolence! Keeping his calm was becoming untenable. "What exactly did you say to Miss Bennet's father?"

"I told him everything," she retorted angrily. "The entire county is aware of your secret assignations in the woods. You are the talk of both my household and the parsonage. No doubt the servants have spread the news far and wide! Mrs Collins confirmed the details and has even provided me a written account, which I flatter myself, was helpful when speaking to Mr Bennet."

His shock was so great that he was left frozen in place. "Secret assignations! A written account? By Mrs Collins?"

"Do stop repeating everything I say, Darcy. It is vexing," she replied with a sniff. "I shall tell you what I told her father. I have paid these servants for their loyalty. The scandal must be contained! The written account will never be known beyond myself, Mrs Collins, and Mr Bennet."

"Which is it?" he demanded. "Is it a scandal reaching every corner of the county, or have you contained it by paying off your servants? It cannot be both."

"No matter. In return for my efforts, I shall expect Anne to be married by the end of the year. We will begin plans for an autumn wedding. If not, I shall know what to do." Brandishing a letter in her fist and tapping it upon the table, she added, "I need not remind you that if this letter gets out, your precious Miss Bennet will be ruined."

"You would ruin an innocent young lady to further your desire to join Pemberley and Rosings? You know very well that neither Miss Bennet nor I would—"

She dropped the letter on the table. "Feel free to read the written account yourself. Mrs Collins had it from Miss Bennet herself. I take no joy in exaggeration. It is all here."

She pointed at the letter. "And do not think about burning it. I required she make a second copy which is safely guarded in Kent."

Darcy was disgusted. "I have no need to read Mrs Collins's letter. Whatever it says must be a gross exaggeration to garner this attention. It is nothing but a terrible campaign to ruin an innocent young lady's reputation, and I will not stand for it."

"You will do your duty." Each word was bitten off. "And if you do not, Miss Bennet and her family will suffer."

Darcy began to pace the room. He held his tongue; he was long used to biding his time and choosing his words carefully, and this scene could be no different. An outright refusal to submit to her demands would harm Elizabeth. He would not allow his anger to make the situation any worse than it already was. Every response provided to his aunt could be twisted and misconstrued or could entice her to harm Elizabeth.

If he knew her heart...but no, he did know her heart. She had disliked him, been offended by him, and at length, had fled Kent to get away from him. Even this—clearly she had confided in her friend, but why? He knew enough of her to know that if she considered him as a suitor, she would have kept it to herself. She must have confided in Mrs Collins from distress over his attentions.

He thought of her again, at the theatre. Perhaps it had not been merely reticence, but distaste? The thought pained him.

He glanced at Lady Catherine who seemed visibly swelled with the sense that triumph was near. He would do nothing that would lead his aunt to commit any additional damage; especially since any truth to her claims was entirely his fault. He would protect Elizabeth at all costs, even if it meant stepping back.

He would let her go.

She did not deserve his aunt's derision, nor anyone's. Ruining her reputation would not only hurt her, but it would be like a fire, consuming everyone connected to Elizabeth until they were left smouldering from the heat of it. There would be a pile of ash where sterling reputations had once been. He had no intention of marrying Anne, but his object at that moment must be to placate his aunt and see her on her way back to Rosings Park.

"What say you?" she cut into his wondering thoughts.

"I will not dignify you with an answer to your defamatory accusations."

"Hear me now, Darcy. You will announce your betrothal, or I shall know how to act."

"Your position is understood. Now, I shall have to ask you to leave as I have much business to attend to before travelling to Derbyshire."

"You will not distract me from my purpose."

"Hear *me*, Lady Catherine. I shall not follow Miss Bennet. You may be certain of that. I shall do nothing to give you cause to ruin her reputation. And I shall write to Anne when I reach Pemberley."

The taut outrage left her; Lady Catherine smiled. "You are a good boy, Darcy. I knew you would be prevailed upon to do what was right." With that, she picked up the letter from his desk and departed, contented and smiling.

Darcy rang for Ebright and requested his bags be packed and the carriage be readied for departure. He would leave for Pemberley at first light. There no longer remained a reason for him to stay on in London.

CHAPTER 18

Elizabeth attempted to speak once they were all in the carriage and weaving their way through the busy London streets. "Papa, please, allow me to—"

Mr Bennet held up his hand. "No, I beg you. I shall have silence for the remainder of our journey, if you please."

"If I could only make clear—"

Mr Bennet gave her a sharp glare that stopped her speech short. It was unfamiliar to her, but she could not wonder at its meaning. She was leaving London in disgrace and had lost her father's respect. Jane reached out and took her hand, and she squeezed it back, grateful for her support and care.

The day was warm and the roads dusty. They were required to make a stop to rest and water the horses, whereby Elizabeth was offered both a reprieve from the carriage and the opportunity to tell Jane what had occurred. Her sister was appalled by Charlotte's conduct. It was difficult to speak of with strangers milling about, though both ladies were practised in maintaining appearances.

It was not until they had passed Meryton and approached their home that their father finally spoke, telling Elizabeth that she would be banned from leaving the estate and its surrounding gardens and would not be home to callers —indefinitely.

So, her father planned to hide her away. Her embarrassment was acute. Not only had Lady Catherine accused her of great impropriety, but she had all but confessed to her father that the report was accurate when she did not deny the accusation outright. And her one solace—the comforting and familiar woods beyond the garden—was also removed from her grasp. Her defeat was great. How would she overcome her sorrows being confined to her bedchamber? The impending isolation nearly stole her breath away.

I have exchanged one gaol for another. Disheartened and mortified, Elizabeth kept to her chamber for the first days after returning home to Hertfordshire. Mrs Hill was accommodating, allowing her to take trays in her room. She made a few attempts to speak to her father in his book room, but he only persuaded her to find something to read and return to her room. His disdain of her was painful, and she felt if she had an occasion to apologise, he might forgive her; but alas, she was afforded no such opportunity.

Mary and Kitty were curious about their sudden arrival home. They both visited her chamber with regularity to tell her about their prestigious visitor, Lady Catherine, and about their shock that their father had gone to London to retrieve her and Jane without informing anyone.

"Father said Lady Catherine carried no news of Lydia," Kitty had mentioned, though Elizabeth was none too surprised to hear that no letters had yet arrived home from their youngest sister.

Mary was more concerned about Elizabeth's obvious neglect by their father. "Perhaps if you chose religious texts with more regularity rather than so many novels you would still be in his good graces. I, for one, am pleased to have been allowed entrance to his domain with more frequency."

Jane was making efforts in the drawing room and at the table to hush their sisters' speculations regarding why Elizabeth kept to her chamber. Curiously, they stopped knocking on her door with questions after the first two days.

Their mother was not as easily swayed to disinterest. Though she was happy to see Jane returned to her, her disappointment that Jane had not secured Mr Bingley in town was heard by all. That Elizabeth was to be confined to the estate was news that Mrs Bennet could not comprehend, and it set her aflutter endlessly.

"I am unsurprised to see where your actions have landed you, Lizzy," her mother had said. "Your father tells me nothing, but I daresay, I can guess the substance of it. Oh, I knew the wild ways he always permitted you would come to no good! And now the neighbours will talk, and we will report you ill, which shall be easily enough done as you look rather wan. It must have been a grand ordeal for my brother to order you home. He is always so accommodating of you. Mr Bennet, of course, as I have said, tells me nothing. One day we had news that you and Jane would remain in town for some time and the next my husband is fetching you home. Did I tell you he would not even allow me to serve tea to Lady Catherine de Bourgh? Such an illustrious guest, the daughter of an earl! Our neighbours are still talking of it..."

Elizabeth had simply listened mutely. Her mother only desired to be heard, and she had no intention of acknowledging her suppositions nor telling her the truth. Should her mother hear that she had been traipsing through the woods of Kent with a gentleman worth ten thousand pounds a year, Mrs Bennet would order the carriage readied in the direction of Mr Darcy within the hour. To see a daughter married would be Mrs Bennet's greatest joy, no matter the reason for the marriage, hasty or not. No doubt she would be happy to see Elizabeth removed from Longbourn altogether.

Jane must have been working on their mother as well, for her visits and varied accusations had ceased. And at length, the entire neighbourhood was taken up with a new diversion.

The servants at Netherfield Park were reporting that they were preparing the estate for a new family. The neighbourhood was humming with the news of Mr Bingley breaking his lease before the year was complete. It was rarely done, and Elizabeth was certain the news pained Jane.

"Every caller looks at me with pity when they mention it," Jane told her one night as they lay in bed.

Neither sister was especially excited about the arrival of a new family at Netherfield. The last family to take the lease had only brought them both loss and heartbreak.

Elizabeth had not the heart to tell Jane that it was not pity that they looked on her with. They were all jealous when Mr Bingley singled her out rather than their own daughters. Jane's loss raised their self-importance, and they were making their rounds now, eager to see the spectacle of the broken-hearted lass he left behind.

"Do not let the gossiping matrons bother you, Jane."

"I shall do my best. And how are you? I wish Papa would relent on these restrictions."

"I find myself lost in my reflections most of the day. I

considered writing to our aunt this morning, curious whether Mr Darcy had called as he requested, but I thought the better of it. I should not like to hear the answer just now. If he did *not* call, it merely supports the rumours of his betrothal. If he *did*, I think my heart shall break further. What would he think of my swift departure from town?"

Jane did not respond, only sighed into the quiet of the night.

"And Charlotte."

"Yes?"

"I have not the words to explain my anguish for her betrayal."

"No one would, my dear."

Elizabeth had treated her first week as if she were in mourning—and perhaps, in some sense, she was. One morning, Elizabeth woke with an itch to move her feet and decided to resume her usual routines. While she was not at home to callers, it did not follow that she could not take the air in the morning while her mother and father and sisters remained in bed. She rose with the sun and quietly slipped on an old day dress and her half boots. She wrapped her long, plaited hair in a simple style that did not require assistance nor many hairpins.

She picked up the letter she had finally finished writing to her aunt. She had apologised for their abrupt departure and gave a vague summary of why they had left in such haste. It would not do if the letter contained incriminating details and was misplaced, so she provided enough information to soothe her aunt's worries but not enough to add to her aunt's concerns.

She stepped lightly down the staircase to place the sealed letter in the silver salver by the front door with the outgoing post. She took a moment to pick up the stack of letters that had arrived the day before. Hill had clearly not yet distributed the correspondence to the household. She searched the pile for Lydia's handwriting—eager for news that her worries for her youngest sister were misplaced. Instead, she was arrested by the sight of a strong, masculine hand—a letter addressed to her father—from an 'F. Darcy,' sent from a Mayfair direction in London.

Mr Darcy had written to her father? She wanted to tear into the note immediately, but instead ran her fingers gingerly over the writing, trying to memorise the way he looped the D in Darcy—distinctly him, she imagined.

She set it down, adding it back to the pile and prayed she would garner her father's attention enough in the coming days so as to be allowed to know the contents. One could hope—though, she doubted it. With another long glance at the letter, she exited the house quietly.

The morning air filled her senses with the scent of new roses. It had been many years since she had contained her walks to their gardens, and so she was seeing them with new eyes. The well-kept gravel paths weaved through a neat and tidy garden filled with the various species of flowers her mother preferred.

After meandering for some time, Elizabeth eventually sat on a bench on the edge of the garden, staring off towards the great oak trees that lined the path she had frequented over the years. She longed to take a lengthy, brisk walk—the kind that heated her face and burned in her legs—the kind that punished her body, while brightening her mind and decreasing her worries.

When she returned to the house, the family was breaking

their fast. It was difficult to set aside her own thoughts and focus on the conversation, but she must—especially if she desired *not* to be the subject of their discussions any longer.

"Papa visited our new neighbours," Kitty announced to Elizabeth as she joined her sisters and their mother at the table.

She chose some items for her plate. "Yes, I have heard of our new neighbours."

"That call was returned yesterday morning by a Mr and Mrs Raleigh and their guest—a cousin, Mr Baldwin, who is visiting for the summer before he returns to his *own* estate in Staffordshire. That is where they all hail from." Their mother shared this information with a gleam in her eye.

"What did you think of them?" Elizabeth asked, not really caring but glad to hear her mother speak on something besides her own disgrace.

"I have been invited to tea with Mrs Raleigh on the morrow," Jane offered. "She is eager to introduce me to her two young daughters, aged two and four."

"It is a shame that Mr Raleigh has already chosen a wife when he could have had his choice of ladies from the area, though it is hopeful they brought Mr Baldwin who is in possession of a fine estate, as I understand it. He is nothing to Mr Bingley, of course, but he might do very well."

"Do you think they will remain?" Elizabeth asked, ignoring the last.

"Why would they not, Lizzy?" her mother responded. "The Raleighs are of an older, more genteel family than the Bingleys. They wish to return Netherfield to its former glory, and I am sure they recognise quality society when they see it. If only Lydia were here, I am sure Mr Baldwin would favour her high spirits. He merely wants for some liveliness, I think."

"They are a lovely addition to the neighbourhood and appear to enjoy the society we can offer," Jane volunteered. "Mrs Raleigh indicated to me that they intend to purchase an estate and enjoy the prospect of Netherfield's nearness to town. I look forward to furthering the acquaintance and believe you will enjoy our new neighbours as well, Lizzy."

"If her father ever allows her to meet the neighbours. How I shall continue to explain her absence, I shall never know. But Mr Bennet will not explain to me what has happened," Mrs Bennet said to Jane, then resumed eating her sausages.

When the ladies of the house left to call on their neighbours, Elizabeth took Jane's work basket from the drawing room up to their room. She had not the patience, nor the equanimity, to read and lately preferred employing her time at more significant tasks. She had never been considered a talent with needle and thread, but the many hours keeping her hands busy in Kent had improved her sewing skills. It was encouraging to know that her efforts would benefit their tenants come winter.

She would rather be useful than spend all her time thinking on Mr Darcy's letter or his upcoming marriage or Charlotte's deceit or her father's disappointment—and certainly not her worries for Lydia's visit to Hunsford. The days where she succumbed to her long list of concerns did her no favours, only sinking her more deeply into melancholy.

Lydia Bennet had had her fill of Mr Collins. Her indignation soared as she grabbed a morning gown out of the wardrobe and pulled it over her nightdress. She had become adept at fastening her own gowns ever since she had found that wicked maid, Hayes, going through her trunk. That Mr Collins had been more upset that Lydia had reported this action to him than the bad behaviour of the maid itself was abominable. The nerve of that man!

He reminded her nothing of the simpering fool from the autumn before. When her cousin began to follow her throughout the day, she started a habit of staying as near to Sir William Lucas as possible, but now even Sir William's constant presence had become irksome.

She wondered why her mother had never responded to her letters. The first should have reached her weeks ago, when she had first recognised how strange the goings on at Hunsford Parsonage were. For a moment the idea that Mr Collins might have prevented it being sent crossed her mind —but surely not?

And now her dreadful cousin had had the audacity to confine her to her bedchamber. Her mother would be livid when she learned of her treatment.

She pulled a small valise out of her trunk and set it upon the window seat. She began pulling gowns out of the wardrobe as quickly as she could manage and shoving them into the bag. Wrinkles, she could endure—leaving her pretty gowns behind, she could not. She looked desperately at her beloved, beautiful bonnets and wondered which would be left. Perhaps she could carry some by the ribbons? She dearly hoped Mr Collins would not destroy her creations once he discovered her missing.

Dusk was long gone, and the cloudless night allowed her to see just beyond the hedge that lined the garden below. Lydia opened the window to hear any approaching horses more easily. She imagined the wait would not be long.

In the distance, she eventually heard the soft nickering

and blowing of impatient horses. The excitement of her now inevitable escape coursed through her and nearly brought her to a fit of giggles as she pitched her bag out the window. It was all so romantic!

At the last moment, Lydia looked longingly at a newly remade bonnet, then snatched it up and secured it atop the other already on her head. It mattered not what she looked like.

Lydia stuck her head out of the window and took a deep breath of the cool night air before swinging her legs over the edge and finding her footing on the trellis. Heaving herself out of the window was not an option and scaling the trellis, after all, appeared more difficult in her skirts than she had originally imagined, but she did eventually prevail.

"Goodbye, Mr Collins," she whispered brightly as she slipped out into the night.

CHAPTER 19

A great oak stood on the edge of the garden, and beneath it, Elizabeth found she could shelter herself from the sun and also from her father's watchful eye. She saw when he paced in his book room intermittently throughout each morning, following her movements around the garden, and she resented him. He had no understanding of her experiences in Kent, with regards to Mr Collins's imperious standards and the isolation he forced upon her.

Could her father not comprehend the treachery Charlotte had committed? To have her most vulnerable and private whisperings to a friend recorded—tangible evidence of her misguided affection and foolishness—preserved, and shared with others was unforgivable. Two weeks had passed since her return home, and still her father paced, book in hand, to keep watch of her through the window. What deviousness did he imagine her capable of? Hiding from him was childish, she knew, but she could not enjoy his oversight when he would not also favour her with some concern or a listening ear.

It was from this vantage point that Elizabeth saw the lone rider arrive at Longbourn. The man swiftly dismounted and approached the house. It was not long before she saw her father turn from his perch at the window and attend to whatever news had arrived.

At length, she heard the sound of her mother wailing and spied Jane leaving the house and walking briskly in her direction. "Lizzy, dear. Something has happened in Kent."

Elizabeth's stomach dropped. "What has happened?"

"It appears Lydia has left the protection of the parsonage. No one knows where she has gone. They discovered her empty room yesterday. They believe she left sometime in the night. Our father will travel to London at first light on the morrow before journeying on to Kent to try and find her."

"Left in the night?"

"Their cook sent a dinner tray, which was consumed, but she was not in her room when they brought her morning meal."

Elizabeth felt her world bend and an uneasiness settle in her stomach. *Taking trays in her room.* She understood that preference all too well. She had made the same choice in Kent after a time. Of course, knowing Lydia and her cousin as she did, it was entirely likely Mr Collins had enforced a sequestration for Lydia's behaviour.

Would that she knew more! It had been a foolish notion to expect that Sir William's presence would protect Lydia. Of course Mr Collins would not allow for Lydia's sharp tongue and childish opinions.

"I need to speak to our father," Elizabeth said quickly, and began moving towards the house.

"Lizzy," Jane breathed while she tried to keep up with her sister's pace. "Our father has begged to be left alone."

"I cannot leave this be. She is our sister. I am familiar with Mr and Mrs Collins. I can provide pertinent information. He must hear me now—he must."

Jane stopped, out of breath, and allowed Elizabeth to continue on her way.

Elizabeth went straight to her father's book room, stopping only to knock quickly before entering. "I must speak to you," she said, even while she was still opening the door.

"And I must have silence, Lizzy. Leave me be." He did not lift his eyes to meet hers, keeping his focused on the open book resting on his desk.

"I beg you to listen to me. I have just heard that Lydia has disappeared in Kent."

"Just so."

"You must allow me to tell you about Mr Collins—about his ridiculous demands. Each week that I stayed under their roof, I found myself under new restrictions."

"I daresay we might have found ourselves in different circumstances if I, too, had only put restrictions on my daughters."

"Papa, *please*. You must take me with you to recover Lydia. I can help find her. I am certain I can."

He ignored this, turning his head away.

"Sir, he read my letters!"

"Perhaps I should have been reading your letters! Maybe then I would better understand you, my child," he roared, suddenly enraged. "I will not take you to town so you can find your young gentleman once again. We have not received word of whether your scandal has been contained in Kent. You are to remain at home. I shall not be moved on this point."

"You cannot comprehend what Mr Collins put me through! And what he likely put Lydia through as well!"

Her father rolled his eyes and waved his hand in the direction of the door. "If I must rouse myself to travel to Kent on the morrow, I demand privacy today."

She was wholly shocked by his disinterest, but it still stung. "As you please," she muttered as she left the room.

Elizabeth found Kitty and Mary in the drawing room. Kitty was horrified and scared, while Mary mused that their youngest sister had likely brought it upon herself.

"Jane is attending our mother," Kitty said between sobs. "She believes Lydia was stolen from her bed in the night. What if she is hurt or lost?"

She could be lost to them forever, that was certain, but Elizabeth's mind was moving too rapidly to develop an explanation for where her youngest sister might have gone and under whose protection she might have landed. She could imagine no one in Kent who might have harmed Lydia, but it was likely her sister may have put her trust in the first person who would pay her any little attention, just as Elizabeth had. If only she knew who Lydia had been introduced to!

"Have you received any letters from Kent?" Elizabeth asked Kitty, hoping for more information.

"No," Kitty whimpered, wiping her tears away with a handkerchief. "Lydia was never much for letter writing, I suppose."

Elizabeth patted Kitty on the shoulder and stood, agitated to the point where she was unable to sit still. Abandoning Kitty in her time of need was certainly unkind, but she had to *do* something—anything. Sitting by and watching this play out in front of her was impossible.

She slipped quietly into her chamber, took a seat at her

escritoire, and pulled out a clean sheet of paper. Her father had not meant to introduce the notion, but Elizabeth was certain Mr Darcy *would* help if he knew of Lydia's disappearance.

She felt it was her fault that Lydia had disappeared. If she had only warned Lydia more vehemently or had convinced her father to listen to the dangers of her sister being placed under the authority of a man too willing to abuse it—if she had made Mr Bennet understand. Even with his general wish to disregard his daughters, surely he had been made aware enough of Lydia's youthful and silly manner to understand the gravity of the situation. Perhaps she could have persuaded him to retrieve Lydia from Kent before this damage was done.

Taking a deep breath to steel her courage, Elizabeth smoothed the already stiff paper and took out her quill pen and ink. Hands shaking, she dipped the pen and began making another foolish decision.

May 25, 1812
Longbourn, Hertfordshire

Mr Darcy,

Be not alarmed, sir, on receiving this letter. My apprehension in penning it is likely greater than yours in receiving it. There was a time this spring when you told me that should I require assistance, you would be willing to offer it, and I write asking for aid now.

My youngest sister, Lydia, has been lately visiting the Collinses in Kent. She accompanied Sir William Lucas and his daughter, Miss Maria Lucas. An express arrived today at Longbourn informing us that Lydia has left the protection of the parsonage and her friends. She is missing, and I feel powerless to assist in her recovery. There is no evidence for where she may have gone.

I hope you will forgive my forward speech forthwith when I tell you that my father is unwilling to listen to any report I can provide about Kent. I have many suppositions about her experience staying with the Collinses, and I know you will share my concern, as you were such a kind, listening ear during my own visit. These explanations might offer some insight into any possible distress she suffered. My understanding of the area alone could be helpful. But my father will not favour discourse with me at this time.

On the morrow, he will depart Hertfordshire to assist in recovering my sister. I know not precisely what I ask you to accomplish, but I feel I must do something before she is lost to us forever. Though I cannot say why, I feel with certainty that you will not blame me for writing to you with haste. I shall finish now, so that this may reach you more quickly.

I will only add, God bless you.
EB

Elizabeth folded and sanded the letter before she could talk herself out of her daring act. She then cautiously penned the illustrious direction of Mr Darcy's London home on the front, careful to emulate her father's masculine writing. It did not surprise her that his direction was etched into the fabric of her mind, and she prayed he would forgive her this lapse in judgment.

Down in the hall, she quietly slipped the letter among those already collected for the outgoing post. If nothing came of her indiscretion, she would be in the same condition as she was presently—full of worry and relying on her father's consideration alone. But if Mr Darcy took some little action to help, perhaps her recklessness would be worth it in the end.

It was a strange thing to look for someone who was determined not to be found. Charlotte was certain that Lydia had left the house on her own. She could understand the notion, frankly. But her father and sister were concerned about what mischief could have taken place, and so an organised search had commenced. She begged her father to hold off on sending the express to Hertfordshire, but Sir William stood his ground. Mr Bennet did have a right to know about his daughter's disappearance, but Charlotte was not eager for the continued upheaval of her home. *Blast that Lydia!*

They had engaged the local magistrate to assist with the search, but there was an understanding that should the news of Lydia's disappearance reach the entire parish and be shared beyond it, Lydia could be ruined. Young ladies did not leave in the night and survive it with their reputation intact.

Curiously, Mr Collins did not want to involve Lady Catherine. He was deeply mortified by his cousin's actions and felt the scandal reflected negatively on his household. He had been most clear with the magistrate that her ladyship was not to be involved.

His long-winded speech at dinner about the evils of temptation to those of the female persuasion had been unrelenting. Even her loquacious father had found it hard to join in the one-sided conversation. It was no surprise that the entire household retired early that night.

Though she was unable to conjure the weather, when the rain had fallen persistently in the night, she had a fleeting thought that it reflected her own unrelenting suffering and distress. She had woken the next morning feeling uneasy—going through the motions of the morning but having to remind herself to speak and nod and smile. She felt beyond herself—*unlike* herself—as if she was watching her person from the outside but was not within her own power.

That morning, Charlotte once again spent her day making calls to the neighbours in order to gather any pertinent, related news. Her father felt calling on the neighbours would suit their purposes two-fold—in the first place, it would appear as if nothing was amiss. In the second, she could mention Lydia and watch and listen for any information that could be useful. She felt it was unimportant to the task at hand to mention to her father that calling on their neighbours would not be considered typical behaviour. She disliked the idea of upsetting him and hoped their impending departure would come before he noticed she had not one friend in Kent.

Charlotte trudged up a hill that would take her to a few small estates that lay to the south of the parish. She did not favour being out of doors, nor did she feel she was designed for walks of this length, but she would do her part to end this ridiculous situation Lydia had imposed upon them.

One could immediately know when they had left Lady Catherine's realm, for the road conditions deteriorated significantly. The narrow lane she travelled was not well maintained, and she felt with a certainty that her half boots were nearly ruined by the mud. She attempted to step carefully, but it was no use.

Finally, she rounded a bend and saw the home of Mrs Jacobson come into view and let out a sigh of relief that she was nearing her first destination. She glanced down at the dirty hem of her favourite morning dress and grimaced. *When will the Bennet family stop wreaking havoc upon my life?*

There was little sleep to be had at Longbourn that night. Mrs Bennet had required laudanum to finally quiet her anxieties, and Jane, in her invariable kindness, had stayed by her side until she knew their mother found rest. Elizabeth felt Jane toss and turn in the night, and knew that she too was sleeping little.

Thoughts of Lydia alone in the world, coupled with an acute embarrassment for having brazenly sent off a letter to Mr Darcy, whirled in her head. If she thought her father was unhappy with her previous actions, the results of writing to an unmarried gentleman would carry much more weight, should he become aware of it.

She had spent most of the night unable to quiet her mind but tried to lie still, for Jane's sake. Her thoughts ranged from desperation to an almost fitful giddiness when she imagined Mr Darcy opening her letter and finding her feminine handwriting within. What would he think of her boldness? And would he help them to find Lydia, unattached to them as he was?

When the first light of the early morning flickered into the room, Elizabeth quietly rose and escaped the house. Once in the comforting shadow of the oak tree on the edge of the garden, she released her concerns to the world and begged God to give her the strength and wisdom to be of some help to her family.

As the sun began to rise in the sky, Elizabeth watched as their carriage was readied and her father's trunk was carried from the house. Elizabeth leant back against the tree and closed her eyes. The tightness in her chest unwavering, she had to force herself to regulate her breaths as guilt and fear and worry washed over her in equal measures.

She startled when she heard her father speak her name and straightened immediately.

His eyes brushed over her face, unconcealed concern in his eyes. She was certain she looked as weary as she felt.

"You are leaving for town?"

"Yes." And after one more moment of hesitation, and a sigh conveying his acquiescence, he asked, "What more should I know before I leave?"

A sense of relief shuddered through her at his invitation. She stood immediately, and the words began pouring out of her in rapid succession, "Mr Collins is not the man who stayed in our home last autumn. He was demanding and overbearing—self-important. He went through my things. He read a letter I was penning to you, and when he was not pleased with what I wrote, he forbade me from leaving the house. That is why I never wrote to you. He also read my incoming correspondence—a letter from you was deemed inappropriate reading material! A letter from my own father! He also required daily religious study from me. Can you imagine? Charlotte, too, is miserable, and I am certain he has made Lydia wretched. I am convinced he has a part in Lydia's disappearance. Did you not see in the express that she was taking trays in her room? Does that sound like your youngest daughter to hide away from society?"

His eyes grew wider and wider during her speech.

"Papa, I know I have shamed you. Indeed I have shamed myself! I cannot be proud of what indiscretions were committed and can only excuse myself by saying that I...I thought Mr Darcy held me in affection, and I thought...I think I love him, too. It matters not, not now, but only...it was not merely imprudence, or the desire for flirtation which drove me. I could not have done any such thing if I had not truly believed I loved him, and he loved me. If I have been a fool, then so I am, but I am not some libertine."

A faint smile touched his lips when she said 'libertine', but Mr Bennet took a moment before he spoke to consider all that had spilled out from her.

"Pray find Mrs Hill. Tell her to assist you in packing a bag —quickly, if you please. We leave within the hour," he responded and turned towards the stables.

CHAPTER 20

Elizabeth was relieved that her father had favoured her company and had let her speak of her concerns, though it did not follow that the carriage ride was congenial. For the majority of the trip, Mr Bennet feigned sleep, for Elizabeth occasionally saw one eyelid lift in her direction.

She wondered at his thoughts. What he must think of her! To speak of Mr Collins's controlling manner and her love for Mr Darcy in one breath—she must appear a great fool. She had not owned her feelings for the gentleman to herself, yet had poured out her heart to her father.

How mortifying! What folly! To be in love with a gentleman who could never be hers! But love him, she did.

Their entrance into London brought with it much distraction, allowing Elizabeth to forget her concerns, and enjoy the sights they saw, and the people they passed. Relief flooded her being when she saw they had arrived at Gracechurch

Street and would soon be in the company of her dearest family.

When Elizabeth and her father's arrival was announced to the drawing room, it was with great shock that they found Charlotte and Lydia sitting with Mrs Gardiner.

"Lydia!" Elizabeth exclaimed and moved forward to embrace her sister.

Mr Bennet did not conceal his frustration, sighing loudly and wiping his palm down his face. "Lydia, a private word, if you please. Now," he said without allowing for any proper greetings to be had. He waved his hand in the direction of the passageway, and Lydia immediately obeyed, following with an unusual reverence.

Elizabeth watched them exit the room and found herself confused as to what she should do. She had no interest in entertaining Charlotte—seeing her made every inch of her being seize with anger and shake with nerves, but she did not want to embarrass her aunt.

Charlotte, too, looked uncomfortable. She had been smiling when Elizabeth entered the room, but since seeing the new arrivals, had not raised her eyes from her folded hands in her lap.

Mrs Gardiner looked curiously at Elizabeth, nodding in the direction of Charlotte, as if to ask her to acknowledge the guest. She could not be obtuse—the ladies had not even greeted one another and had favoured each other with nary a glance.

Elizabeth had no interest in speaking to her old friend. She chose to sit in a large chair nearest to the window to avoid any feigned intimacy. Charlotte had wrought pain enough for Elizabeth, and she desired no more.

Mrs Gardiner gave her a hard look, narrowing her eyes, and announced she would leave to check on her children.

Elizabeth pursed her lips in response but felt she would be unmoved.

Only the ticking of the clock could be heard for some time. And at length, uncomfortable with the silence, she finally spoke in a forced, polite manner, "I am happy to find Lydia is safe. She was discovered after the express was sent?"

"I found her yesterday afternoon. She was with our neighbour, Mrs Jacobson, whom you met while in Kent. The lady was kind enough to offer her carriage so that I could return Lydia to her family."

Elizabeth nodded her understanding. "She left on her own?"

"Yes."

"And I suppose you will feign confusion as to why a young lady would wish to escape your home?"

"I beg your pardon?" Charlotte finally raised her eyes to meet Elizabeth's.

"Pardon you, I shall not," Elizabeth retorted. "I am certain you found my sister's company as dreadful as you found mine."

No answer came from Charlotte. Elizabeth stared at her former friend who merely lowered her eyes to focus on her primly folded hands. Only a slight blush gave Elizabeth the impression that Charlotte felt anything at all.

"And why are you here? Why did you not take her back to the parsonage and send word that she was found safe? Were not your guests to travel home within the week?"

When Charlotte remained silent, Elizabeth continued, saying, "Perhaps she was no longer welcome in your home?"

Something suddenly broke in Charlotte's cool, disconnected demeanour. "Of course she was not welcome. Mr Collins had already restricted her to her rooms, all while telling my father that she was ill. How was I going to explain to my father and Maria that I found her—escaped of her own volition? Or was I to tell them that my husband had locked her in her room?! First, your secret dalliances with Mr Darcy, and now a runaway—I have never been so utterly embarrassed!"

"Embarrassed?" Elizabeth raised her voice slightly and sent a hard look to Charlotte. "If anyone should know embarrassment, it shall be me! Your betrayal nearly ruined me! Maybe not yet in the eyes of society, but certainly in those of my father—and society may decide upon me yet! What did you think would happen when you composed an account of my most private and personal thoughts—shared with you in confidence—and then delivered them to Lady Catherine? You left it to her to decide my fate!"

"Perhaps you should have thought of that before you went traipsing through the woods with Mr Darcy and left little consideration for propriety!"

Anger burned through Elizabeth, flushing her hot. "You must think very little of me and our history together to threaten my entire future."

Charlotte turned away from her.

"Perhaps you should have cared more for Lydia's comfort —or for my reputation—than that of your husband and his *beloved* patroness!"

"He was never supposed to be *my* husband! He was supposed to be *yours*," Charlotte said with feeling. "It was *you* who was supposed to live with him and carry his children, not me! If not for your infinite selfishness—" She stopped at that and rubbed her hand over her growing midsection. Elizabeth had not noticed it until she saw the simple, maternal gesture. The thought of Charlotte carrying a child stunted Elizabeth's anger.

She answered calmly, "You had the same power to choose

as I, Mrs Collins, and if you regret that choice, the blame cannot be mine. It was you who accepted him with such haste, knowing I had only just declined him the day prior!"

"I did not have any good choice, and you know it," Charlotte whispered wistfully into the room. "Should I have remained a burden to my parents and then later prayed one of my brothers would take me on as well?"

"Would that not have been better?"

"Anything would be better," she said very quietly, but something clearly roused within her, and she turned more confident eyes back on Elizabeth. "You must know—that his true measure was understood by no one. And now the entire neighbourhood will hear stories from Mrs Jacobson, and all will know that I had a guest who detested my husband enough that she was willing to throw herself from a window into the night rather than remain under our roof." She looked defeated, a smaller version of herself than Elizabeth had ever seen, but Elizabeth could not so easily feel compassion for her.

"Why are you here in London? Why not simply send her to town on her own?"

"I had to see to Lydia's removal from the area. She had created damage enough."

It was then that Mr Bennet joined them in the drawing room. "Mrs Collins, thank you for returning Lydia to her family. Mr Gardiner has graciously agreed to take Elizabeth and Lydia to Longbourn in the morning. I shall escort you home to Kent. I am certain your family will be relieved to see you too are safe and well."

Though she had initially seemed somewhat subdued, unrepentant would have been an apt description of Lydia's attitude at dinner. She appeared greatly diverted to be in town and only wished she could stay in London longer than one night.

"Could I not stay and attend the theatre, Aunt?" Lydia begged once the ladies were settled in the drawing room after the meal. "We could host dinner parties or attend an assembly, could we not?"

Their father answered from the doorway as he and their uncle joined the ladies, "Your uncle has been gracious enough to offer to return you home, and that is where you will go. Your mother will be relieved to see you are well and safe. I shall not hear another word about it."

Elizabeth put a restraining hand on Lydia's and responded politely, "Thank you for your generosity, Uncle."

It was all she could do not to ask for the carriage to be readied to return home immediately. Sitting in the drawing room with Charlotte was excruciating, and it appeared it was a strain for Charlotte as well, for she remained still and silent all evening, only responding when it was required.

Elizabeth eventually announced to the room that she and Lydia would retire early. Her sister attempted to protest, but their aunt stood to bid them both a good night.

The eldest of Elizabeth's young cousins had returned to the nursery so that Mr Bennet and Charlotte could use the two readied guest rooms. Elizabeth led her sister upstairs to the small chamber they would share for the night, and once assured privacy, she enquired about Lydia's experiences in Kent.

"A monstrous man that Mr Collins! I have never seen the like. As you can no doubt imagine, I told him my father would have words with him when he learnt of my treatment!

He followed me about all day—watching me, glaring at me—it was amusing at first. I enjoyed trying to put him off and set about distracting him or confusing him regarding my whereabouts. But lately, I began to be frightened of him."

Lydia's explanation only increased her concern. She had never felt frightened of their cousin. "Did he attempt to harm you in any way?"

"No—only he eventually locked me in my room because I called him a worm! That dreadful maid would deliver my meals and then lock the door again with him keeping watch each time from the corridor. He was so pleased with himself, and it made my blood boil."

"How did you find yourself with Mrs Jacobson?"

"Oh, one morning Cook brought my morning meal instead of Hayes, so I asked her to get a note to Mrs Jacobson. I found a response from my friend hidden in my dinner tray. Did you meet Mrs Jacobson, Lizzy? Oh, what a lovely lady, and with the most creatively decorated bonnets! We became fast friends after I met her at the milliner, and we would meet regularly while shopping in the village."

Elizabeth stifled a laugh. Yes, she was familiar with those bonnets. "Yes, I was acquainted with Mrs Jacobson."

"So," Lydia went on, "you see, I climbed out of my window and down the trellis that night. Mrs Jacobson was waiting for me on the nearby lane. I was never truly in danger."

Lydia flopped down on the bed, "I wish I were a young, beautiful widow like Mrs Jacobson. She has no one to answer to and such a lovely home!"

"Lydia!" Elizabeth scolded quietly from her stance by the window.

"No, Lizzy," Lydia insisted. "She is perfectly within her own power! She has two young children and a nanny to raise them. She gets to make her own decisions as well. I rather think it a dreamy way to live. One cannot predict becoming a widow, though, so I believe I should rather not marry at all. I could not imagine finding myself married to someone like our cousin. To think we all thought him a foolish and spineless type of a man!"

"What about your devotion to all the fine, red-coated men in fair England?" Elizabeth teased as she joined her in bed.

"No, Lizzy," she responded seriously. "I do not believe I shall marry."

"Nor I," Elizabeth responded honestly. She turned over and stared into the dark of the room, breathing a sigh of relief that Lydia was well, and finding some solace in their shared disillusionment of marriage.

But of love—that pure and elevating passion—she was not disillusioned; she was only sad it would never be hers.

CHAPTER 21

M r Bennet rode ahead of the carriage for the last leg of their journey, apparently anxious to be done with this business of returning Charlotte to Kent. Charlotte felt a strange kinship with the older man. She too would like to be left to herself. Knowing she was returning to Hunsford—to her husband—was no comfort to her. She could not return home and simply order trays to her room. There would be menus to plan, accounts to balance, mending to be completed—and of course, a husband to pacify. Not to mention that any shred of contentment would be tied to Lady Catherine's whims and pleasures.

Little tempests of dirt kicked up behind Mr Bennet and his horse, sending dust swirling in the air and clouding her view. Charlotte leaned her head back against the seat as familiar vantage points began signalling that they were nearing home. Her chest felt tight at the thought, and she found herself humming a familiar tune from her childhood to ease the tension in her breast.

When they turned down the lane that would take her to the parsonage, Charlotte watched as Mr Bennet sped his horse around the bend in anticipation of their arrival. She imagined herself knocking on the carriage roof to gain the driver's attention and asking him to turn around. It was a lovely thought.

She closed her eyes and hummed a little louder, focusing on the sway of the carriage and the feel of the road that lay beneath the wheels. She could do this. She could go home, see her family off to Hertfordshire soon, and ease back into the life she had vowed to live.

Life would settle for a time, until her husband came to notice her growing midsection, and then who could guess at his reaction to that. Perchance he would finally be proud of her—approve of her. She had done her duty and even now conceivably carried the heir to Longbourn in her womb. She hoped with every fibre of her being that it was a male child. She would keep her secret a while longer—at least until the quickening. She had no interest yet in hearing Lady Catherine's recommendations for carrying a child.

Raised voices awakened her mind, and she opened one eye to see that the carriage was stopping just short of the cottage. The manservant did not come to open the door, and suddenly, the voice of her husband grabbed her attention. She lifted the latch on the carriage door to let herself down.

Charlotte froze at the sight before her. Mr Bennet's horse, which still carried the gentleman, was moving in strange, spirited patterns just beyond the hedge that lined the lane. Mr Collins could be seen darting to and fro, speaking sternly to Mr Bennet, and waving one finger in the air.

She was only able to catch pieces of his speech, "the

behaviour of your daughters," and "if only you would bother to rein them in." Charlotte's hand flew to her mouth at hearing another comment he sputtered at Mr Bennet, "…advise you to leave her to reap the fruits of her own heinous offence!"

Mr Bennet's voice carried much more easily, responding to her husband's lecture by saying, "Desist, Collins."

In awe of the confrontation she was witnessing, Charlotte held her breath, moving more closely but not wanting to alert her husband to her presence just yet. She was familiar with her husband's anger, but she hardly recognised the man in this fit of fury.

She caught movement out of the corner of her eye and saw her father coming out of the parsonage, waving his arms and speaking loudly, "Collins, let the man be. He has travelled a long way."

But Mr Collins, spittle running down his chin as he continued to harangue Mr Bennet, did not back down. "Is this the thanks I shall receive for taking your ungrateful daughters into my humble abode?"

The horse was skiting around in an attempt to avoid her bulky husband's ungraceful movements, though the agitated horse did not deter Mr Collins in his eagerness to gain Mr Bennet's full attention.

"Collins, you are upsetting my long-tired horse. I will see you inside shortly. Lydia has gone to Longbourn, and I have brought your wife home to you," Mr Bennet said.

Charlotte froze and instinctively wanted to hide at the thought of her presence being brought to her husband's attention. But Mr Collins was not easily distracted from his point. He took not a moment to look for his wife, who had been missing for three days, but only continued his evidently practised speech for his cousin.

"Charlotte!" she heard called from across the garden, coming from her sister who stood near the front door. "Charlotte, you are home!"

Taking in the fractious scene, Sir William bellowed towards the cottage, "Return to the house, Maria." He was making his way down the path to join the others.

"Now, now, gentlemen," she heard her father say as he approached the others gathered in the lane.

"I shall not desist, Bennet," she heard Mr Collins shout, and returned her attention to him. "As my dear patroness, the honourable Lady Catherine de–"

The resolution of their heated exchange came swiftly—too rapidly. The horse reared, nearly throwing Mr Bennet, before setting his front legs back down. Then the great beast kicked his hind legs back—a strong, swift hoof making contact with Mr Collins's face.

Charlotte watched in horror as her husband's body was pitched into the nearby hedge. She heard screaming in the distance and wondered at the sound before realising it was coming from her.

What followed was a blur. Mr Bennet settled his horse and dismounted. Her father came forward more quickly, yelling for assistance. She watched as the two older gentlemen pulled her husband's limp body from the hedge and laid him on the dirt. Servants came from the carriage and the cottage to assist, but Charlotte was frozen in shock. There was so much blood. She felt hot and faint, and her stomach contracted at the sight. She turned away from the scene, and at a run, made her way around the side of the garden to cast up her accounts into the newly planted rose bushes.

Early June brought with it much distraction for Darcy as he oversaw many projects and improvements at Pemberley. There was much to do, and he found that when he threw himself into the work, he would keep her from his thoughts —though it was often impossible. Elizabeth was always with him.

Licking his wounds in Derbyshire over the last month had been a trying time. The scandal appeared contained. No word reached the papers, and his aunt's threats had ceased, but it did not follow that he was ready to abandon all consideration for a potential future with her; he was biding his time. He felt confident that if he kept up the correspondence he had begun with his cousin Anne, perhaps her ladyship would not even notice as summer turned to autumn and no wedding occurred.

A response from Bingley about his annual visit to Pemberley had finally arrived in late May. Darcy had read the missive so many times he had nearly memorised it.

I reflected upon our last conversation and realised that I could not condone Caroline's conduct towards Miss Bennet. After a severe scolding and threats to set her up in her own establishment, Caroline went willingly to Cheapside to call on Miss Bennet. I told her she must visit to apologise for her previous behaviour. Miss Bennet did not deserve my sister's uncivil treatment. Unfortunately, the Bennets were no longer in London. That was weeks ago now, and I had nearly forgotten until I sat down to write to you.

Caroline and the lovely Miss Asher keep me busy with engage-

ments each night—balls, the theatre, dinners. I find myself the happiest gentleman in all of London, squiring around such a charming lady. I hope that I have the pleasure of introducing her to you one day. Just last week, I was afforded an opportunity to hear her exhibit, and she has the most angelic voice. If only you could hear her.

But that is neither here nor there; I am writing to let you know that we are unable to travel to Pemberley this summer as we have recently accepted an invitation to spend two months at Miss Asher's estate in Surrey...

Darcy was discouraged, for he felt certain he had brought about the end of Miss Bennet's hopes—even if it was at the hand of his capricious friend. He would never again provide advice about love or marriage—what did he know of it anyway? He had made a grand muddle of his efforts to woo Elizabeth, and now it seemed she despised him at worst, or was merely frightened of him at best.

At least Georgiana was happy, seeming particularly relieved that she would not have to entertain Miss Bingley for a month.

Georgiana's recent confidence and returned happiness brought Darcy some joy. She was pleased to have their cousin, Colonel Fitzwilliam, staying with them. Together with her companion, Mrs Annesley, they made a merry party.

To see Georgiana smiling upon her horse after a long morning ride or singing along when she played the pianoforte brought to mind the days before Wickham's attempted elopement. She was thriving once again, and Darcy wondered if they could remain at Pemberley always.

One morning found Darcy breaking his fast when his butler brought in his newly arrived letters, including one from Anne. While their combined intention was to pacify Lady Catherine, he had been surprised by her quiet wit and ability to make him laugh out loud when her first letter had arrived. Where had this version of his cousin been all this time?

Settled in his study later that morning, he tore open the letter with anticipation.

Rosings Park, Kent
May 28, 1812

Cousin Darcy,

I have informed my mother that I shall spend my day writing a letter to you, of which she is particularly approving—so I shall thank you in advance for the quiet you have provided me today. I shall paint a picture with words of the moment I asked for not one but two sheets of paper necessary for my efforts. There was a cry of joy from my mother (shocking, I know), and Mrs Jenkinson nearly leapt out of her seat with a kind smile to hasten the arrival of the required writing implements.

Mrs Jenkinson is practising the pianoforte, so I find myself without encouragement for subjects to include in this corre-spondence. I am pleased to hear that you enjoyed my letter detailing the flowers in the gardens at Rosings and have passed on your thanks to Mrs Jenkinson for her suggestion.

Shall I tell you of the weather or report on neighbourhood news this time? I think not. If I am to fill two pages complete by the end of today, I shall need some inspiration. Ah, I have it! If it is the most significant news from Rosings that you desire, I shall share that of most importance—my mother.

Lady Catherine took butter on toast and sausages for her morning meal, followed by a lengthy meeting with Mrs Jonas regarding the menus for the day. Apparently, she cannot abide the recent tarts coming from the kitchen. The berries were much too ripe. She proposes a meeting with the head gardener on the morrow to discuss the horticultural methods he is imposing upon us all, to our apparent detriment.

Darcy laughed out loud as he read on, enjoying the literal accounting of Lady Catherine's day. He mused that her ladyship very certainly relished seeing Anne's devotion to the letter-writing and hoped that their continued ruse would keep her efforts to see them married by the end of the year at bay.

"Darcy, are you hiding away in here?" Fitzwilliam interrupted his thoughts as he entered the study. "I thought we were to ride to the western fields today."

"Yes, that was my object, but it will have to wait I have spent the last two hours complete dealing with letters from my solicitor."

Fitzwilliam leaned over Darcy's desk with an amused expression, "Not just business letters, it appears. What have you there, Cousin?"

He reached for Anne's letter and took it to a comfortable chair by the fireplace. He leaned at an angle into the large chair and kicked his legs over the arm of the other side. A big smile crossed his face as he read. "Ah! Our Anne has done it again!" he exclaimed. "Another ridiculously mundane letter, and another week's appeasement of her mother, I am sure."

Darcy waited for him to finish the letter.

"I am of a mind to start writing to Anne as well," Fitzwilliam added. "I should like to see Lady Catherine squirm while wondering at all of her daughter's suitors."

Darcy chuckled, "As you know, our agreed-upon corre-spondence is meant to keep Lady Catherine distracted from her purpose, not increase her ire."

"Yes, well, please do go on—I enjoy Anne's letters immensely."

Fitzwilliam stood from the chair to lay the letter on Darcy's desk and then moved to the sideboard to partake of his cousin's French brandy. He lifted the vessel in Darcy's direction so as to offer him some as well, but Darcy shook his head.

Fitzwilliam grabbed a newspaper from the edge of Darcy's desk and settled back into his chosen chair. Appar-ently he meant to stay. So, Darcy chose another missive from the pile of incoming post. The next letter had evidently gone to his London house before being forwarded by his servants to Pemberley.

Hertfordshire? The return address made his stomach drop. The script was too precise to be Bingley's, so he quickly tore open the letter. Could it be that Mr Bennet had finally responded to his letter? But no—the light, feminine hand-writing found within seized him, and he held his breath as he scanned quickly to the bottom of the letter to find it signed, "EB."

Wide eyed and shocked, Darcy looked up to see that Fitzwilliam was thankfully distracted, and ran a hand through his hair. *She has written!*

He swept his fingers reverently over her handwriting. The letter was read no less than four times and then tucked into the inside pocket of his jacket, directly beside his thudding, elated heart.

She *trusted* him. It was in him she put her faith. She was in distress and wrote to *him*. In equal measures, he felt anger that she was distressed and completely overjoyed that she sought him out. The impropriety of it did not matter to him at all—he could not imagine a token that would bring him more clarity—she loved him. She had been run home by Lady Catherine, had seemingly lost her father's favour, and still, she had reached out to him. She must care for him, at least a little, to have risked it. Of course, he would go to Kent. He would move mountains for her. If it were within his power, it would be done.

That her relationship with her father was fractured appeared an understatement. From what he knew of Elizabeth and her father, theirs was a close relationship, and Darcy felt a pang of sadness knowing that it was likely his own actions in Kent that had brought about this change. Not only would he help recover Lydia, but he would do what he could to fix what he had broken between Elizabeth and her father.

Darcy knew that the Bennets could hardly rely on Collins to help recover Lydia. He was a spineless coward. No, he would go, and he would bring Fitzwilliam, whose military experience could prove useful in the search.

Darcy cleared his throat to get Fitzwilliam's attention.

"Yes?" His cousin responded without looking up from the paper he was reading.

"I have some news. After we left Kent, Mr and Mrs Collins received some new houseguests from Hertfordshire, and one has gone missing—Miss Lydia Bennet—Miss Elizabeth's youngest sister."

"What is being done to recover her?" He now had his cousin's attention.

"I am not entirely certain. The letter was sent first to London and then forwarded here, so the news is some days behind."

"Surely Collins has engaged the magistrate. I am sure

Lady Catherine is offering assistance as well. Perhaps the young lady has already been found. What did she say?"

"Who?"

"Lady Catherine."

"Hmm?"

"In her letter...I am assuming Lady Catherine wrote to you? Perhaps it is a trap, Darcy—an object to drive you back to Kent?" he said while moving his eyebrow up and down exaggeratedly.

Darcy chuckled, "Nevertheless, I plan to help in the search, and I would be pleased if you accompanied me. Georgiana can stay with Mrs Annesley. If I can be of some help—"

"Go to Kent? Now?"

"Yes."

"Darcy, as you say the news is old, and can only grow older in the time required to travel to Kent. Could you not send some of your men to Kent to assist?"

Darcy sighed and gripped the back of his neck. Of course, Fitzwilliam would not want to leave Pemberley and go back to Rosings. It was the last place Darcy wanted to be as well.

"Out with it, Darcy. Why do you want to go?"

Darcy sighed, "I need to ensure that Elizabeth is well... err, her sister, Miss Lydia, I mean."

"It is *Elizabeth*, is it?" Colonel Fitzwilliam nearly spat out his large gulp of brandy. Darcy thought it served him right to have that burning liquid smouldering his insides for the outburst. He rolled his eyes at his cousin's theatrics and then levelled him with a stern gaze.

Fitzwilliam let out a long whistle and laughed heartily. "Dash it, Darcy! I knew you were taken with Miss Bennet, but this! I am shocked! Am I to wish you joy?"

"My intentions are honourable," Darcy said tentatively.

"Lady Catherine caught wind of my interest in her while we were in Kent and sought to threaten her with ruination in response. She was sent home in disgrace. I have no idea if the lady will have me—if she cares for me at all—or if she blames me for our aunt's interference—but if she needs my help..."

"What lady would not have you, Darcy?"

Darcy levelled a serious look at his cousin, "Elizabeth Bennet, that is who."

"You truly are besotted! How did I not see it? I had a mind to question you regarding all your moping about lately," Fitzwilliam said between laughter. "Well, why are you here? Let us go to Kent or wherever your lady-love is!"

Darcy cleared his throat, "As I was saying, her sister has gone missing..."

Darcy and Fitzwilliam arrived four days later, late in the evening, having barely stopped to sleep and rest their horses. Darcy's valet had followed them in the carriage at a more sedate pace, and both men were eager to bathe and retire early.

"Darcy! Fitzwilliam!" Lady Catherine exclaimed when they were announced to the drawing room, "You are such good boys; I knew you would be back soon. I was just telling Mrs Collins that you were both so excessively sorry to leave Kent."

Both gentlemen greeted their aunt with politeness and informed the lady that they were in need of refreshing themselves and asked to have food sent to their rooms.

"Of course," their aunt responded. "Your rooms are always ready for you, and I shall see that hot water and a light repast are sent to you immediately. Anne will be exceedingly happy to see you."

The last she said with a particular gleam in her eye, meant only for Darcy. It was all he could do to refrain from sighing or rolling his eyes.

"We shall be pleased to see Anne as well," Darcy responded, but he was in need of information from the parsonage before he could simply retire to a guest room. He had come all this way and needed the latest information regarding Miss Lydia's disappearance.

"How is Mrs Collins?" Fitzwilliam said, as if he read Darcy's mind.

"She will make do, I suppose. She is a useful sort. It is a tragic thing, what happened to my parson. Mr Collins shall never regain his speech, my physician says. But the curate is come down and will be taking up his duties."

"Pardon me, Aunt. What has happened to Mr Collins?" Darcy asked.

"An accident with a horse. He was kicked in the throat," she responded lightly, as if these things happened every day. "Though it was the fever that nearly took him. Seems he shall make a full recovery, well, with the exception of speaking, that is."

Both men exchanged looks of shock and curiosity. "And the guests at the parsonage?" Darcy asked carefully.

"Yes, well, Mrs Collins has much help. Her father, sister, and Mr Bennet have been very obliging."

"What of Miss Lydia Bennet?" Fitzwilliam asked, sharing a glance with Darcy. "Anne mentioned she was visiting in a letter to Georgiana."

"Oh, that unfortunate girl. No, no—she was sent home to Hertfordshire. She never even came to take her leave of me… I should have known after her sister's disgraceful behaviour that I could not expect much more from that family. Five daughters out at once! I have never heard of such a thing, and here are the fruits of such carelessness."

Darcy and Fitzwilliam both seemed to question the information and exchanged meaningful glances between them with nary a word. Was she still missing, or had she actually returned home? It was natural for families to keep such things quiet.

With that, Lady Catherine announced she would speak to her housekeeper, and left the gentlemen alone.

"What do you think?" Darcy asked Fitzwilliam.

He could see Fitzwilliam's mind was turning the information around and around, attempting to reach an opinion. "Time will tell," was his only response.

"Perhaps I can shed some light," a gentle voice spoke up, and both men turned quickly towards the fireplace where their cousin Anne sat in the shadows, tucked into the corner of a chair with a shawl covering every inch of her from the neck down. "Do close your mouths. My mother was so overcome with excitement that she forgot I sat nearby. It is to my advantage at times to remain quiet," she said with a giggle.

Both gentlemen bowed and greeted their cousin properly.

"Lydia was recovered nearly a week ago and sent home. My mother is still unaware that the lady went missing at all. Perhaps it is best if you do not tell her. She is distressed enough with her parson going and getting himself injured."

Fitzwilliam stepped closer, an eyebrow lifted, "And how did you come to know about her disappearance?"

"I could ask the same of you," she said, raising her own eyebrow at her cousin. "Though I have my suppositions. I overheard some of the servants speaking. They were unaware of my presence, and I was not about to announce myself when I could instead learn of what they were discussing."

"Perhaps the army should recruit you! You would make a good spy, Cousin." Fitzwilliam laughed and took a seat next to her.

She blushed and averted her eyes.

Darcy felt awash with relief that Miss Lydia had been recovered. He could sleep well that night knowing Elizabeth's sister was well and whole and home. Now, if only he could find a way to insist Elizabeth make *her* home with him.

CHAPTER 22

Each time Darcy had woken in the same guest chamber at Rosings just two months prior had held the promise of possibly seeing Elizabeth. Waking to find the first rays of sunlight slip into his room brought with it the sadness that she was not there—he would not find her on the familiar paths or in the glade.

He found himself at the stables at dawn, needing a long ride, though he had spent the last four days riding hard towards Kent. His body did not desire more time in the saddle, but his mind craved motion—and so he found himself winding his way through the woods of Kent and stopping in the glade that held precious memories for him.

The early summer had changed its appearance, but he could almost see and feel the moments shared with Elizabeth—her hair peeking out from under her bonnet, her face tipped towards the sun. Being there was as painful as it was reinvigorating. His purpose was clear and simple: he must find a way back to her, back to the way it felt to be with her in Kent. Back to the smiles shared only with him. And, God help him, back to holding her in his arms.

Possessed by his memories, he found himself walking away from the glade and towards the parsonage, with his horse following closely behind. When the fork in the path came, he kept on, walking farther from Rosings. It was on those paths that they had shared so much of themselves. Amongst those trees, with her by his side, he had begun to hope for something different for his future than he had previously allowed himself to believe was possible—a partnership, a love match. The grip she had on him had only grown every day, and eventually, it was on these paths that he had found himself deeply and ardently in love with her.

The sun had risen further in the sky as he approached the parsonage. There was movement in the garden, yet it was too early for visitors, so Darcy turned quietly to take the lane back to Rosings.

He rounded a bend and at once found himself standing face to face with Mr Bennet. Both men remained quiet as they took the measure of one another, and finally Darcy found his voice and greeted the gentleman.

"Mr Bennet."

The older man raised his eyebrows and did not favour Darcy with a bow, only a terse and slowly enunciated, "Mr Darcy."

It was clear to Darcy that he was the last gentleman in the world that Mr Bennet would favour meeting unexpectedly. What could he say to Elizabeth's father to improve his opinion of him? Had Mr Bennet read his letter of apology? His claim that his intentions were honourable? He did not want to upset the man further, for he knew Mr Bennet could either help or hinder his future with Elizabeth.

"Good morning, sir," Darcy finally began, "I hope your family is well."

Mr Bennet cocked his head to the side and narrowed his eyes. "I find it hard to believe that you have any consideration for my family."

"I must apologise for my behaviour this past April, sir—as well as that of my aunt, for her threats and interference. I am sure it does appear that I have given little consideration to your family, though that would be furthest from the truth."

"Do you and your friend travel the country with the intention of breaking young ladies' hearts or is it a natural consequence of your wealth and status?"

"I apologise for any consequences your family has suffered for being acquainted with Mr Bingley and myself. Perhaps when he returns to Netherfield—"

"He broke the lease; a Mr Raleigh has moved into Netherfield and thankfully brought a wife with him."

Bingley broke the lease? That was a shock. While Darcy had understood that Bingley had made a choice not to pursue Miss Bennet, the breaking of the lease felt more final than Darcy had imagined. So, his friend would not be returning to Hertfordshire—ever.

Suddenly, Darcy remembered to reply, "Mr Harold Raleigh?"

"Wonderful," Mr Bennet said slowly, his expression revealing he found the news nothing of the sort. "I should have known you would be acquainted with the man. Should I expect your visit to our fair county soon?"

"My plans are not fixed, sir."

"With all due respect, Mr Darcy, I should like to know if you plan to visit, for the protection of my daughter."

"Sir, your daughter has no reason to fear my presence."

"Has she not?"

"My intentions were honourable; they still are. Lady Catherine is under the impression—"

"That you are betrothed to her daughter?"

Darcy cleared his throat and responded, "Yes, sir. She is. Though it is not the truth. I am engaged to no one. My cousin and I have no intention of marrying. I assure you."

Mr Bennet only pursed his lips and dragged his hand across his brow.

Darcy was tempted to leave the man be and to save this conversation for another day, but he steeled himself to his purpose. He sent a silent prayer up to God that the truth could remedy what had been broken.

"I love your daughter, Mr Bennet. If she would agree to be my wife, I would be the happiest man in the world."

Some sentiment registered in the man's eyes, but Darcy was too unfamiliar with him to recognise it. Mr Bennet excelled at keeping his emotions under regulation. Elizabeth shared his intelligence, but of her feelings, he felt certain he could recognise them at only a glance. Her expressive eyes left him with few questions regarding her state of mind. Mr Bennet was another species altogether. He was all indifference and control.

When Darcy thought Elizabeth's father would say no more, the man surprised him by smirking and responding, "I was under the impression that my daughter thought very little of you. I would wager half of Hertfordshire was aware of her disdain last autumn."

Darcy nodded. "I would like to imagine I have subsequently changed her mind."

Mr Bennet raised his eyebrows and responded lightly, "I suppose time will tell." He tipped his hat to Darcy and walked the way from which he had come.

Jaw clenched and heels dug in roughly, Darcy rode hard back to Rosings. To say that the conversation had frustrated him was a vast understatement. It was rare that he let anyone see his temper, nor such vulnerability. Attempting to avoid his aunt, he made his way to the library once he had changed out of his riding clothes.

To his surprise, Darcy found both of his cousins within, their heads bent over a piece of paper laid on a table on the far side of the room.

"Darcy!" Anne called. "Come and see."

"What are you two up to?"

Anne surprised him with her energy and genuine smile, giggling as he drew near to see what it was that brought them both such amusement.

"Are you really such a romantic, Cousin?" Anne asked him as he approached.

Fitzwilliam clapped him on the back and handed him a letter. It was an unfamiliar handwriting, but feminine to be sure. It did not take long to figure out what he was holding. It was Mrs Collins's account of Darcy and Elizabeth's time together in Kent, followed by a distinctly untrained handwriting—written sloppily with inaccurate spelling. The second writer included specifics from someone who had watched them in the woods, including far more details than Darcy had before expected to find his aunt in possession of. Darcy flushed with embarrassment and took in his cousins' pleased smirks.

"Where did you find this?" Darcy asked.

Fitzwilliam responded, "Anne was shocked to learn about her mother's blackmail, and she offered to lend me her most excellent skills in espionage today to ensure a clear path to happiness is made available to you."

Darcy shot Fitzwilliam a curious glance. Had he really spoken so freely of the matter to *Anne* of all people? It had taken two days on the road before even Darcy had divulged the entirety to Fitzwilliam. Long days of travel favour confessions when you are in the presence of a career military man.

"I found it in my mother's safe," Anne replied.

"But where is the other? Lady Catherine claimed a copy was made."

"Oh, she always says there are copies, but she only has one safe," Anne said confidently. "This was all I found."

"Always? Are you saying her ladyship frequently threatens family members with humiliating documents meant to ruin them?" Darcy asked.

With an impertinent grin, Anne said, "You are not the first, I assure you."

The sounds of a carriage roused Elizabeth from her reading. She turned her face to the window to see that it was her father returned home. Uncertainty prevailed, and she remained in the drawing room, unsure of his welcome. He had been gone nearly a fortnight, and Elizabeth's concerns about what he found in Kent had grown daily. Perhaps the gossip of her liaisons with Mr Darcy truly had spread throughout the area? Her father surely would not remain in Lady Catherine's realm by choice.

It was not long before Mrs Hill sought her out and informed her that her father desired an audience with her in his book room.

Elizabeth opened the door and entered, showing a quiet

deference to her father in her greeting. Keeping her eyes averted, she curtseyed and took the seat before his desk.

"Where are your mother and your sisters?"

"They are shopping, sir. The Raleighs have announced that they will host a ball at the end of the month."

Her father sighed, "And you, my only sensible daughter, stays behind? Should you not desire new lace and ribbons as well?"

"I was unaware that I was allowed out of the house. I have continued to obey your restrictions."

He sighed. "Oh those." He waved his hand in the air. "I believe we can safely say your restrictions are lifted. Can I trust you, Elizabeth?"

"Of course you can, Papa." She released her own sigh, but of relief.

He nodded. "I am certain your mother can be roused to organise another shopping trip for ribbons and lace for you as well."

"I have a new gown from London."

Mr Bennet nodded, having lost interest in the subject of gowns, and pulled a letter from his jacket.

"Mrs Collins asked that I carry this note for you."

He held out the missive, and Elizabeth took it by rote. A message from Charlotte might once have brought her joy, but now? She set the letter upon her lap and stared at the hand-writing that had once been so familiar—a sign of home and comfort and the deepest friendship. She looked at her father curiously, hoping he might divulge what had kept him so long on his travels.

At length, her father cleared his throat and simply said, "Take your letter and go, my dear."

Elizabeth smiled at the affectionate language and nodded

in response. It was definitely an improvement upon their recent exchanges.

Desirous of privacy, Elizabeth took the letter out into the garden to a bench nestled amongst the rose bushes.

Hunsford Parsonage, Kent
June 7, 1812

Dear Elizabeth,

I hope this letter finds you and your family in good health. Please thank your father once again for his assistance in returning me to Kent and for his aid in the aftermath of that arrival. As you may have already heard, Mr Collins was recently the victim of an accident with a horse. He was kicked rather violently, and I do believe it is a miracle that he still lives. Far be it from me to understand what plans God still has for my husband, as they are yet unknown to me.

Mr Collins is still abed and will be for some time. Mr Bennet, along with my father and Maria, were kind enough to stay through the worst of it. A fever nearly took him in the first few days.

Lady Catherine generously sent her own personal physician to see to Mr Collins, and the gentleman has reported that my husband will recover but may never regain his ability to speak. The doctor says we are fortunate he was kicked in the throat and not in the head. Should my husband be able to voice his opinion, I am unsure whether he would agree.

A curate has stepped in, taking up my husband's duties to the parish. Lady Catherine has already indicated that she will give over the parsonage to the gentleman permanently once Mr

Collins is able to be moved. The physician advises we shall be able to leave the parsonage in four weeks' time.

Mr Collins and I will enjoy a small cottage among her ladyship's tenants. His position will be in name only until we one day return to Hertfordshire. I confess I am greatly relieved by her generosity. Lady Catherine also tells me there is much a parson's wife can do for the poor but worthy parishioners, and I shall endeavour to do so.

My father and Maria will remain in Kent for some time to help oversee the care of my husband and our removal to a new home. My mother has sent lengthy letters with healthful instructions and has even offered to leave my great aunt's bedside to assist me, but I have told her to stay. I have it all in hand.

And now I shall come to my point. My dear friend, this is the first letter I have written since my marriage that was not dictated by my husband but written in my own hand and containing my own words. I feel at once saddened by our circumstances and also encouraged by little matters such as this opportunity to tell you how sorry I am for the last time we spoke.

I hope you will accept my most sincere apologies for my words and actions of late. I have been outside myself, a stranger to my own thoughts, feelings, and deeds. I cannot explain it, and I shall not excuse it. I was wrong, and I beg you to forgive me one day. Just this morning, I was fortunate enough to have an opportunity to apologise to Mr Darcy when he came to call at the parsonage, and it brought me hope.

The best I can think to explain it is to say that I was resentful of your bravery and good fortune, and now I find I am only ashamed of myself. I will do better, Eliza.

I will understand if you do not write. But I do hope you will.

Your humble friend,
Charlotte Collins

The letter was more alarming than Elizabeth could have ever imagined. Mr Collins permanently injured, Mr Darcy's presence in Kent, and Charlotte apologising—it was all too much. How could so much shocking news be found in one letter?

First and foremost on her mind was Mr Darcy. He was there! Elizabeth's heart leapt at the notion that Mr Darcy may have received her letter and gone to Kent. She closed her eyes and breathed in deeply at the thought of the constancy of his affection, though she could think of no reason to imagine their paths would cross again. Either way, she was grateful and comforted to know that he may have been there on her behalf. Of course, he could have already been there, visiting Miss de Bourgh. What a tangled muddle her heart was, vacillating from pleasure to disappointment in rapid succession.

Mr Darcy being in Kent also meant that her father may have seen him. She suddenly turned her eyes towards the house, looking to her father's book room. She winced, imagining how badly that meeting might have gone. Could Mr Darcy have mentioned her letter to her father? Surely not. But there was a possibility the two gentlemen met, and she wondered if her father would divulge it to her.

And Charlotte—she was unsure what to think of her old

friend. Sorrow for her provoked Elizabeth's compassion, but it did not reduce the pain Charlotte had inflicted upon her life so callously, even eagerly. Charlotte would be in significantly reduced circumstances, living off the charity of a woman who could as easily deny it as approve it, yet Elizabeth could feel the hopefulness in her friend's letter. Perhaps she would find some peace now.

Could she forgive her? She had no notion whether it was possible. Her anger towards Charlotte had not yet abated, and certainly not her resentment towards Mr Collins. Though, what did it signify? The man held less power than he ever had before and would never speak ill to her again, nor anyone for that matter.

Tears began to well in her eyes as she wrestled with all the emotions the letter had wrought. She flushed with embarrassment and quickly wiped her eyes with her handkerchief when she noticed Lydia's approach.

"Are you well?" Lydia asked kindly as she joined her on the bench.

"Yes, thank you. Only a little overwhelmed. I have had a letter from Charlotte."

"Oh, la! Do not tell me you are weeping over Mr Collins's injuries! That gentleman got his just deserts, if you ask me!"

"Lydia!" Elizabeth scolded, all while subduing her own laughter.

"Charlotte will be much happier now; do you not think?"

Elizabeth felt certain her sister was right but was not interested in discussing Charlotte. "How did you know about his injuries?"

"I have had it in letters from both Mrs Jacobson and Miss de Bourgh."

"And you did not think to share the news?"

"And add to our mother's anxieties?" Lydia asked with

wide eyed surprise. "What if he died from his injuries, and we had to search for another heir? I would rather not see our mother take to her bed and instead keep her focused on the upcoming ball. Do you think it will be as grand as Mr Bingley's ball?"

Elizabeth was amused by her sister's quick leaps from one topic to another, so casual in her responses, though exhibiting an astute intuition as it pertained to their mother. "Surely grander," Elizabeth responded. She wrapped her arm around her sister's elbow and pulled her up from the bench to return to the house. Surely her sister had more news from Kent within these letters, and she would do her best to wrestle the information from her.

"I return to London tomorrow," Darcy announced to the breakfast room, both cousins dining with him looking up at his announcement. He had stayed three days, for appearances only, and had no interest in remaining when he was not required. With all his aunt's requests and estate needs tended to a short few months prior, there were only so many days he could bear to sit with her ladyship at meals listening to her wedding plans for him.

"Such a short visit. My mother will be sad to hear it," Anne said.

"But not you, Anne?" Fitzwilliam responded lightly.

"Of course, I shall be sad to see you both go. Though I shall find solace in my letter writing, shall I not?" she said with a gleam in her eye.

Darcy chuckled and returned his attention to his plate. "I shall look forward to it," he replied evenly.

"I think I am of a mind to stay," Fitzwilliam said casually, and Darcy returned his attention to him.

"Stay in Kent?"

Fitzwilliam leaned back in his chair and sighed, "I have a letter to return to my barracks in a month's time. If you will not go to Pemberley, I think I should rather remain in the country for these last weeks of freedom, if you do not mind."

Darcy nodded in agreement, though surprised that his cousin would choose to remain at Rosings.

"Perhaps I may help Anne compose her next letter? Surely her ladyship would not object to my interference."

Darcy smiled but turned a serious look on Anne. "Are you certain you do not want me to speak to your mother about our intentions before I leave? I would feel infinitely better about leaving—"

Anne waved his offer away, "I would rather she should remain in the dark for now. She will know soon enough. Leave it be. She has been rather cheerful as of late, with our regular correspondence and your quick return to Rosings. I should not rejoice to see her reaction when you tell her that her plans will not come to fruition."

"Just so," Fitzwilliam added. "I shall like to be an ocean away when she receives the news."

"As you wish," Darcy responded before rising from his chair.

He was free to tell Lady Catherine to stand down now that the letter was turned to ash. He had enjoyed watching the incriminating document burn. For one, it was humiliating. He had burned red with embarrassment reading it even alone in his chamber. The manner in which their interactions had been written on paper had cheapened what he knew to be meaningful and affectionate exchanges. In addition to freeing him from his humiliation, he knew now that Elizabeth was safe—from it and any repercussions it would have wrought.

He turned his head over his shoulder as he was leaving. He saw Anne shiver and Fitzwilliam responded attentively, "Are you cold? Shall I call for Mrs Jenkinson to bring you a shawl?"

"Thank you, no. I shall only require another cup of tea, if you please." And Fitzwilliam obliged her.

Darcy shook his head at their antics and kindness. He too felt a strange pull to remain at Rosings, shocking though the notion was. It had been his most pleasing visit to date, thanks to Anne's helpful interference. But remain, he could not. He had responsibilities elsewhere.

CHAPTER 23

A particular melancholy overcame Elizabeth as she watched the maid bring in the yellow gown that she had worn to the theatre in London, pressed and ready for the ball to take place that evening at Netherfield Park. The day was a far cry from the last time she and Jane had readied themselves for a ball at the grand estate. There were few expectations of them this time, merely that they both intended to find pleasure in the company of one another. There were no gentlemen to concern themselves with, particularly as their mother was pointedly throwing the entire household's efforts into Lydia's appearance in order to impress Mr Benjamin Baldwin. He was their last hope, according to her.

Elizabeth put her hand on Jane's shoulder to keep her still while she placed flowers throughout her hair.

"Save a few for your hair, Lizzy," her sister protested.

"I should rather leave my hair as it is, thank you."

Elizabeth looked at herself in the mirror and wondered at her future. How many more balls and assemblies would she attend as a young, marriageable-aged lady? Would anyone ever turn her head again?

Later that night, Elizabeth watched as Mr Baldwin led Jane to the centre of the room where all the young couples lined up to dance the first set. Her mother was likely having a fit seeing the man lead her eldest daughter into the dance rather than her youngest. She had to stifle a laugh at the thought of her mother's hopes and plans being dashed.

Jane's face had lit with pleasure when the young man had approached to invite her to dance, and though Elizabeth was happy to see her sister receive attention, it did not follow that she was unaffected by the sting of jealousy—which made her feel like a wretched sister. Jane would never resent Elizabeth's happiness.

Elizabeth was not engaged for the first set—and rather than continue to watch over the many happy dancers, she decided to take in some air. She exited the doors at the back of the ballroom, and found herself on the stone terrace that lined the back of Netherfield Park. The terrace boasted three sets of steps that would take one down into the formal gardens, which she happily toured daily during her stay last autumn—though that felt a lifetime ago.

Elizabeth rested her hands on the railing and took in the view of the night. The length of the terrace was alight with lanterns, and the cool night air was refreshing. A full moon hung low in the sky, illuminating the gardens below. She closed her eyes and breathed deeply.

"You are as lovely as the last time I saw you in that gown."

The sound of the voice—so warm and familiar—made her gasp. Had she imagined him there? She turned in an instant and took in the tall, handsome form of Mr Darcy stepping out of the shadows and approaching her.

"Mr Darcy!"

"Miss Elizabeth," was all he said, though his eyes said more. Even in the dark she could see the intent gaze she had come to imagine existed only in her dreams.

"How have you come to be here?"

"Raleigh invited me. I am pleased to see *you* here," he responded. It was said with all appropriate propriety, but she heard more in his enunciation of that phrase—more than what he said—and it stirred her insides and brought a blush to her face. Her heart was hammering wildly, and she leaned back on the railing for support.

She looked down at her feet, her mouth dry with anticipation and nerves. "I am pleased to see you as well."

"Your father was in Kent when I arrived. He mentioned that Raleigh had taken over the lease, and being that he is an acquaintance of long standing, I enquired whether he might be willing to host me while I saw to business in the area."

"And what business is that, sir?"

"I am seeing to it—just now," he breathed in his familiar, comforting tone, never taking his eyes from her. The richness of his voice cradled her very heart. A heart that had felt fragile and hopeless only moments ago but now felt as if it would leap out of her chest and right into his arms.

"Did my aunt's meddling harm you?" he asked.

"Not in the way she intended."

He looked at her intently, a question in his eyes, "And are you much recovered? Did the rumours follow you?"

"Yes." She took a deep breath to steady herself. "And no."

"Dance with me," he said, stepping closer to her. He was so near she fancied she could hear the beating of his heart, pounding in rhythm with her own.

"What about your cousin?"

"Which cousin?"

"Your betrothed, of course."

"Anne and I are not betrothed. We never were. I am, neither by honour nor by inclination, bound to her, nor shall I ever be."

Elizabeth nodded in response, unable to take her eyes from his. Her heart was beating fast, and her breath sped up. He was not engaged—he never was. It had been real—everything she thought had transpired between them in Kent had been true. It had not been merely a dreadfully foolish rendezvous, but something based in real feeling, for them both. She had not imagined it.

She feared what would come out if she attempted to speak. It was difficult—the moments of longing in conflict with her deeply rooted understanding of propriety—every expectation for gently-bred ladies was combating her current desires.

"Did you receive my letter?" she asked very quietly.

"Yes."

"And you were not upset with my presumption?"

"Of course not. I would do anything to please you. I left for Kent at first light, ready to do all I could for you, for your family."

The strength of her power over him and his over her, combined with his frank answers and close proximity, made her lightheaded. Mr Darcy reached out to her shoulder and squeezed it gently. His thumb made small circles along the curve of her neck. He breathed a sigh and then ran his hand down the length of her arm, eventually grasping her hand lightly.

"I thought you must despise me for...for that day, in the woods," he said.

"No," she said, looking up at him. "Not at all, ever."

There was a long moment of silent understanding between them, the hurt and misunderstandings fading away as the truth of their hearts was made plain. "Dance with me," he whispered this time, a quiet petition for her acquiescence.

It was beyond her abilities to deny him. She merely squeezed his hand, nodded and followed him into the ballroom, where partners were lining up for the second set.

Taking their places, he held her hand for a moment longer than was necessary and finally released it. Her body was alert to his every movement and gesture as well as to the loss of his touch.

Looking into his eyes as they waited for the music to begin, it was as if all movement in the ballroom stopped— the music pitched—and the breath left her lungs. It was exhilarating looking at him and knowing he was there for her. The rest of the room dissolved from her vision—it was only him, and her. The two of them—together—as if time stood still.

The dance was memorable, though little was said. It took all of her power to stay focused enough on the dance steps that she would not make a fool of herself in front of the entire neighbourhood. All of her doubts were pouring from her as she kept her eyes on him, intently watching her too. That moment—it was all she had wanted and dreamed of and desired.

When the dance ended, he led her to the side of the room and offered to find them both some refreshment. Her body thrummed with excitement as much as it was grieving the loss of his nearness.

Elizabeth's mother appeared almost as quickly as Mr Darcy excused himself, leaning in conspiratorially, saying rather too loudly, "I am quite sorry, Lizzy, that you should be forced to have that disagreeable man all to yourself for the set. But I hope you will not mind it; it is all for Jane's sake, you know, if Mr Darcy is friends with Mr Baldwin. I told you that they would make a lovely match, did I not?"

Elizabeth smiled at her mother's antics. "I am perfectly well, Mother. And as you see, he is returning to me just now."

Her mother turned to see him walking in their direction, both of his hands carrying punch.

"Mr Darcy." Mrs Bennet curtseyed, then looked at Elizabeth pointedly and departed.

Mr Darcy handed her a glass and leaned in to ask, "Have I done something to upset your mother?"

Elizabeth smiled, pushing down a laugh, "She is merely sorry that I should be forced to spend so much time with the disagreeable Mr Darcy."

He cleared his throat, hand placed across his heart, "Well, I am sorry to hear it. It appears your mother has taken my measure, and she has found me wanting, much like your father."

"My father?"

"We had words in Kent."

She suddenly realised they were no longer teasing. "And?"

"And I had determined that there would be a great distance to cross in order to convince your father that I am worthy of you."

She blushed and averted her eyes.

"Until his letter arrived in London last week," he said quietly.

She turned to take in his smug expression. "Pardon?"

"I assumed your father wrote in response to a letter I sent

him in April—or perhaps in response to our conversation in Kent. But, he merely wrote to tell me of a ball planned at Netherfield. Strange letter, that. But I decided to accept it as an invitation. Would you not agree with my deduction?"

Elizabeth laughed outright. "My father is the reason you are here?"

"Something I said in Kent must have moved him to act."

It was shocking indeed to imagine her father had any part in Mr Darcy's arrival. It warmed her heart to know that he was endorsing Mr Darcy's suit in his quiet, apathetic way.

"Your mother is not the only person in your family with whom I need to make amends."

Elizabeth raised her eyebrows in response. "Who else?"

"Your elder sister." He sighed and forged on, "I talked to Bingley when I arrived in London in April. I attempted to right my insult to your sister, to tell Bingley the truth, but I only made a bigger muddle of it. Bingley now seems resigned to adhere to his sister's wishes for his future, but it could have been different—I could have handled things better."

He could have, but Elizabeth could not bring herself to begrudge his interference. Not now. Elizabeth waited for him to look her in the eye and then responded with sincerity, "Mr Darcy, there is no one to blame for Mr Bingley's decisions other than Mr Bingley himself. Jane will endure. She is strong."

As soon as she said the words, she knew them to be true. It was Mr Bingley who broke her sister's heart—no one else. No one had forced the gentleman to stay away. And Jane *had* seemed happier of late. Especially now, as she spied her sister in a cheerful conversation with Mr Baldwin across the ballroom. Jane laughed at something the gentleman said to her, and a soft, pink blush tinted her cheeks.

Elizabeth gestured to the other side of the room. "See

there," she said quietly. "She is enjoying her time speaking to our hosts and their cousin."

He smiled down at her and said only, "Thank you."

Then he leaned in, very quietly, to ask, "Do you walk in the early mornings in Hertfordshire as you did in Kent?"

She blushed, "At sunrise tomorrow I shall likely still be here or only returning home, sir; however, I may walk to Oakham Mount once I wake. It is a nice long walk, and I do not believe you have ever visited."

He nodded and smiled at her, "I shall look forward to seeing the view from the Mount."

Elizabeth and Jane crawled into bed as the first light of dawn began seeping into their room. Though the night air was cool, the bedclothes felt stifling, and Elizabeth found herself tossing and turning in anticipation for the morning—or better yet, later that morning.

Jane softly reached out, "Are you well?"

"Yes," Elizabeth murmured. "Only I cannot find a comfortable position to sleep."

"Are you happy he is here?"

Elizabeth stopped her fidgeting and sighed. "Yes, I am happy."

"That is all that matters. Find rest, dear sister. He will call, you will see. I am sure of it."

Elizabeth grinned into the darkened room, wondering what her sister would think of her making plans already to meet him.

"And what of Mr Baldwin? The first *and* the supper set?"

Jane giggled into her pillow. "I could tease you all the same for your own two sets with Mr Darcy."

Elizabeth wriggled into the bed and plumped her pillow to support her neck more fully. "Yes, I suppose you could."

The quiet seemed to overtake her, and just as she was on the brink of sleep, she heard Jane once more, "How long do you suppose we have together here? I am happy for you, but I cannot help but wish for time to slow down."

"Mmm," Elizabeth responded sleepily and wished something of time as well, but not for it to slow. She wished to fall asleep quickly and speed the time until she saw Mr Darcy again.

Elizabeth was the first to wake, and she quietly changed into a favourite morning gown and pulled on her half boots. Food was laid out in the dining room, and she quickly grabbed a roll and poured herself some tea. She was tempted to forgo the meal entirely, but she knew she must calm herself before departing.

Once satisfied, she quietly exited the house and began walking briskly in the direction of her future. Her springtime daydreams of Mr Darcy's potential affection had been replaced by a deep longing to become his wife. She wished to lift the burdens from his shoulders—to tease, to hold, to love him—to bring him joy. She had seen many sides of him, but her favourite version was the one she was coming to understand belonged to her alone—the tender man, the man who loved to laugh, the man with eyes only for her. She imagined their life together, a life filled with joy, constancy, and contentedness, and she walked more energetically towards her destination.

A thrum of excitement shot through her when she saw his tall form atop a horse, crossing a nearby field, moving towards the woods. She stepped out from the line of trees so that he might see her more clearly. Even at a distance, she noticed the moment he saw her, for a wide smile crossed his face and he turned his horse in her direction.

His smile never left his face as he approached and dismounted. The horse was not to follow them that morning but was tied to a tree conveniently located near a stream.

After giving the great beast a pat, Mr Darcy turned to her. "Good morning."

Elizabeth waved in the direction of the path, "Shall we?"

He nodded and offered his arm. She felt awash with joy to be once again walking on his arm in the privacy of a quiet, country morning. She felt as if she had come home. She breathed deeply, taking in his presence and the beauty and promise of the day.

They walked in companionable silence towards the Mount, and once they arrived, she began to point out the various locations that could be seen from that vantage point.

"...and over there, you can see the chimneys from Long-bourn peeking from amongst the trees."

"Beautiful," he whispered, and she turned to see that he watched her and not the view beyond.

Discomfited by his attentions, she turned her gaze back over the small village she had called home her entire life. She felt his hand on her hand, his fingers lightly moving in and out of hers in an effort to gain her attention, which she gave him by turning to face him and grasping his other hand.

"Elizabeth, I want to apologise for my behaviour in the glade. If I had not kissed you that day, my aunt would have had no justification for her threats—no reason to visit your father—and certainly no reason for your father to have thought less of you—"

"Please do not apologise. I am not sorry for it," Elizabeth

whispered back as she squeezed his hands, hoping to calm his nerves.

Recognition of her statement rang through him, and a smile crossed his beautiful, strong features.

"Almost from the earliest moments of our acquaintance, I have come to feel for you a passionate admiration and regard, Elizabeth. You are perpetually on my mind and in my heart—as constant as the sun's rising and setting—and I cannot imagine living a life without you by my side. I beg you, most fervently, to relieve my suffering and consent to be my wife."

She bit her lip. Something in his eyes compelled her entire body to shiver with anticipation and pleasure. Her future lay before her, and she squeezed his hands again, attempting to gain the courage needed to respond.

Before she could quiet her desire to tease him, the words were leaving her lips, "This request comes at a precarious time. I recently vowed that I was not to ever marry."

"Not to marry?" His eyes narrowed, and he flashed a flicker of a smile. "Whyever not?"

"I was certain there was only one man who was best suited to me, and I had been told he was betrothed to another. Besides, I was unsure whether he wanted to marry me as I wanted to marry him. It was quite the dilemma."

"All you had to do was beckon," he said. "Any indication that you cared for me—that you would have welcomed my suit—would have carried me to your door in an instant, on my knees. Pray forgive me for not making my intentions clearer from the beginning. I did not know if you would welcome my attentions after my aunt's interference."

"I hoped I understood your intentions rightly. It appears I was correct."

"And, what say you?" Mr Darcy asked her, "Will you not marry me, my dearest, loveliest Elizabeth?"

"Yes. I will marry you."

Mr Darcy dropped her hands and held his arms open to her. She stepped closer to him without hesitation. He wrapped his arms around her waist and lifted her off the ground to kiss her forehead and her cheeks, which set off her happy laughter. When he placed her on her feet, his eyes were dark with desire.

He pulled her back from the edge of the Mount, under the cover of trees, allowing for some privacy away from the path. "Thank you, Elizabeth. I shall never give you reason to regret it," he said reverently.

He laid his forehead against hers. Her breaths, quick and shallow, were a reflection of his own. She hoped he would kiss her and did not have to wait long. A brilliant smile preceded his kiss and commanded her entire body into elation.

Unlike their first shared kiss, she was more inquisitive and insistent—this kiss was less shock and more desire than the first. She had imagined this moment a million times—ever since the first in the glade. If she had another opportunity—if she had another chance to enjoy his embrace—she would give herself over to him more fully. She pressed herself closer to him. His strong arms felt like home—like sanctuary and solace—like a refuge for her pounding heart.

He broke the kiss, placing his hand under her chin, tipping her head back to look into her eyes. His lips hovered over her own as he sought her full attention, his familiar gaze boring into her soul.

Then, playfully, his lips sought hers in slow movements, all while his eyes were on hers. She watched each whisper-soft kiss and could feel his breath coming and going in the space their lips shared. "I love you, Elizabeth."

"And I love you." She heard his quick intake of air. What

followed would not be called delicate. Mr Darcy kissed her with a determination she did not know he could possess. He deepened the kiss, leaning her against the trunk of a nearby tree, leaving her with no uncertainty as to the depth of his feelings.

She could sense he longed to make up for lost time, and she gave over control to him with reckless abandon, allowing her behaviour to reflect her shared desire.

The grip around her waist tightened, forcing her body to arch against his. A low moan escaped her mouth, causing Mr Darcy to gasp and pull back slightly. "Good heavens!" he said between breaths, "Elizabeth, forgive me."

He hugged her then, laying her face against his chest. He held her there for some time, resting his chin on the top of her head. She fit him so well. His strong, substantial body pressed against hers managed to both thrill and comfort her. She listened as the pounding of his heartbeat began to slow.

"You do realise," he said while he stroked her back, "we shall have to inform your father and mother of our decision."

Elizabeth sighed at the remembrance of reality. "And if I said I did not want to return to face them?"

He leaned his forehead against hers and whispered, "I could have the carriage readied to carry us to Gretna Green. Just say the word."

What a pretty picture he illustrated—and she was tempted to ask if it were possible, though she scolded him properly, "For shame, sir. I shall not run off as if we have done something untoward, though I do wish we could be married as soon as possible."

"I could ride for London and secure a licence," he said with a smirk on his face.

"My mother would enjoy that distinction, I am sure, but please say you will not leave for London. If you do, I shall miss you greatly and wonder if this is all real. Stay here. Marry me here. We can call the first of the banns in three short days and marry as soon as the last is called, could we not?"

"As you wish, my dear."

She knew he would not concede their privacy just yet, and she was not about to release him either. Her hands moved from their place on his chest to weave through his hair. He seemed to relish her interest, closing his eyes and enjoying the sensation as she brushed her fingers lightly across his cheek and jaw. He was as exquisite as their shared moment.

He responded by pulling her closer once again—showering sweet, soft kisses on her forehead and cheeks and then lower to the side of her neck.

At length, Elizabeth finally relented and said, "It is time, my dear. Let us go to them and share our joy."

CHAPTER 24

"Sleep well," Charlotte whispered to her husband before shutting their chamber door and quietly descending the stairs.

Charlotte took a seat in her small drawing room and poured herself a steaming cup of tea from the pot the maid had left her. Perhaps it did not require the distinction of being named the drawing room, as it was the *only* room in their new cottage for a person to sit; however, Charlotte found it felt a good measure more like home than the parsonage ever had.

Nursing her convalescing husband had had its challenges, but she had lately discovered within herself a new conviction to live her life as she pleased. They had even less help than they had before, but Charlotte was not unfamiliar with a kitchen nor a stranger to hard work. In fact, she found the employment boosted her energy and made her feel more like herself than she had since the beginning of her short marriage.

She had spent so many months full of resentment and anger that she had come to barely recognise herself. She had been no more important in their lives than the furnishings Lady Catherine had selected for the parsonage—present but inconsequential, in attendance but not valuable.

Now settled in their new home, and with the quickening of the babe growing within her, she was feeling more comfortable with her future. It would not be what she had expected—it would be harder, but she rather preferred it to the numb existence she had been living before.

Even Mr Collins seemed further resolved to his new reality. In the first weeks, he was hard to manage and distraught, especially as he was unable to express himself. But he had calmed more in the last week and had begun to write notes to Charlotte, expressing his joy over the coming birth of their child and his plans for a new garden once he was able to move about more freely.

Charlotte did not see the babe as the olive branch that her husband perceived it as, but as a second chance—a chance to do better and love better. She was resolved to accept that her own decisions had led her to the present, and she was determined to ensure future choices were taken with more care.

She pulled a letter out of her apron that had arrived from Elizabeth earlier in the day and opened it once again. Though she had read it thrice, she longed to revisit one part in particular once more.

I find myself feeling rather pensive and optimistic as my wedding day approaches, and with that comes a deep longing to extend my forgiveness to you—my oldest friend. It is true that I may have harboured anger and resentment towards you for some time had not my own happiness come riding into Hertfordshire merely two weeks ago. But now that he is here and we are to be wed and gone from this place I have always called home, I find I want to start my new life on a foundation of compassion and hope——and that includes extending as much towards you. I will only look upon our past together as it brings me pleasure——and there were many years where you brought me joy. Perhaps our friendship will never be what it once was, but I will say that I wish you nothing but the best.

God bless you,
Elizabeth Bennet

Charlotte held the letter to her breast and released tears of joy that Elizabeth would extend such grace to her—especially as her own vindictive efforts had been to ensure her friend's happy marriage would never be. It was a kindness, indeed, as Charlotte doubted she would ever forgive herself for her treachery.

Charlotte tucked the letter into the drawer of a nearby table, banked the fire and blew out all but one of the remaining candles. Once upstairs, she looked in on her sleeping husband, thankful that he had found rest, and then crept into the room across the corridor. For now, it was a quiet place for Charlotte to sleep, but one day soon, it would be the nursery, and her entire life would be changed. Within those four walls, she could imagine herself redefined—Charlotte Collins: mother, helper, friend.

The sun rose as it always did, but Elizabeth was of a mind to acknowledge its arrival in a new and profound way. Mr Darcy had told her his love was as constant as the sun's coming and going, and ever since he spoke those words, she was reminded of his faithfulness every day.

This day's sunrise marked the day Elizabeth would vow before all to be his wife. She was acutely aware of how close they had come to never marrying at all. With shaking hands and trepidation, Elizabeth had penned her first letter to Charlotte the week before. Though Charlotte had requested forgiveness, it was for herself that she had granted it. She wanted to move forward with hope.

After a long examination of the prior months, it had become clear to her that Charlotte's anger and deceit had little to do with her. Charlotte was upset with herself, not Elizabeth. But as Charlotte must continue on the path she had chosen, Elizabeth wanted not to be a hindrance to any possible happiness she might discover. And on this, the day of her wedding, she was pleased to find the burden of her own resentment departed.

Everything Elizabeth would take with her into her married life was packed into two trunks stacked in the corner of her bedchamber. A small case rested on top, open, awaiting any last items she would need to take. A strange thing, marriage—a lady was meant to leave all she knew behind her, even her name, in exchange for a new one. *Elizabeth Darcy*.

Much to the chagrin of Lady Catherine, married they would be. A laugh bubbled within her as Elizabeth remembered Mr Darcy writing to his aunt to announce their marriage but later deciding not to send the missive until the day prior to the wedding. It would be too late once she knew.

Colonel Fitzwilliam and Anne de Bourgh were informed almost immediately, but there was no concern that interference would come from those quarters.

A visit to Oakham Mount was not on the schedule the morning of the wedding, though it had been nearly every day since their engagement. But not this day—this last morning as a Bennet, Elizabeth wanted only to curl into the soft leather chair in her father's book room and relish the last moments of quiet together before the entire household awoke.

"I shall go distracted!" Elizabeth heard her mother yell from down the corridor, and set her book aside, sharing a knowing glance with her father.

"And so, they have awoken," he said with a chuckle. "Take the book with you, Lizzy. You have not finished it."

Elizabeth laughed. "You certainly know I have read this book before."

"Nevertheless," he responded and waved her comment away, "let your old papa send you off with something."

It warmed Elizabeth's heart to see him so affected by her leaving. Their relationship had been slowly improving over the last month, but he had been extremely attentive since the announcement of her betrothal. They had been both keenly aware that their days together had been numbered.

"Lizzy!" Her mother sprung into the room. "I have been looking for you! Hurry now, we must have you ready in time."

With one last wistful look at her father and the room they often shared, she turned to leave. Her father rose from his chair, picked up the book she had been reading, and pressed it into her hands. She held the old tome tight to her breast and thanked him—for the book, and hopefully he knew, also for his love and affection over the years.

"Your Mr Darcy is likely to have three copies of his own, but I shall find comfort knowing you shall finish the tale." He hugged her tightly and scooted her out of the room.

The pitter patter of slippered feet and giggles made her stop at the foot of the stairs to breathe it all in—home, her last morning at Longbourn. Even her mother's strident tones above stairs made her feel a longing to bottle up the moment and keep it with her always.

But it was Jane's gentle greeting when she arrived in their bedchamber that nearly did her in.

"Do not cry!" Jane cooed. "You do not want red eyes today. Come and sit. I will start on your hair."

Jane guided her into a chair, and Elizabeth pressed her sister's hand on her shoulder, "Nothing too extravagant."

Jane nodded, "As you say, Elizabeth Bennet."

"With this ring, I thee wed. With my body, I thee worship. And with all my worldly goods, I thee endow. In the name of the Father, and of the Son, and of the Holy Ghost. Amen."

It was done. A thrill of emotion ran through Darcy as he surveyed his wife's joy when they exited the church together. His wife!

The wedding breakfast that followed was sumptuous and attended by countless neighbours and some family. Mrs Bennet was very vocal in her pleasure over her own efforts. Darcy was forced to summon all his patience for their conversations, although she was easier to endure than the flood of well-wishing strangers.

Darcy had been surprised to see his cousin Anne among the guests in the church, and took his first opportunity to lead Elizabeth in her direction once all their appropriate greetings had been executed. Anne was seated with Fitzwilliam in the Bennets' drawing room, and his cousins both rose when the couple approached.

"It is lovely to see you, Miss de Bourgh," Elizabeth said to Anne, reaching out a hand in greeting. "We had not heard you would be attending the wedding. What a delightful surprise."

Fitzwilliam responded, "I had to stand up with Darcy and could not very well leave Anne behind to face her mother alone when the news arrived. It was work enough that we have been forced to feign misplacing your correspondence for weeks now to avoid her interest in what news you had to share." To this he added a wink for Anne.

Anne added, "One morning my mother nearly caught me dropping your letter into the fire, and I had to pretend a chill to explain my position in the room. She had me sent to bed for two full days!"

"And where does your mother think you are now?" Darcy asked.

Fitzwilliam responded again, "I had to tell Lady Catherine that we had been summoned to Darcy House. She was delighted. Mrs Jenkinson accompanied us and was not happy when our travels were met with an empty Darcy House and plans to continue on to Hertfordshire this morning."

Anne grinned at Darcy. "I had to come. Not only to support you both but to ensure I was miles away when my mother learned of your marriage."

The foursome could not contain their laughter. Though it was not long before Darcy leaned over to whisper to his lovely bride that he would be ever so happy to have the carriage readied for their own departure. Immediately, if it would please her.

Elizabeth squeezed his elbow and laughed, leaning in to provide her response quietly, "I will go and change into my travelling dress, and bid my family farewell."

Before departing, Elizabeth found a quick moment to pull Anne aside and enquire about Mrs Collins.

"She is well," Anne responded kindly. "Her cottage is so quiet you would not even know her husband is at home."

"You have called on her?"

"Fitzwilliam has been encouraging me out of the house. He suggests I should use my phaeton to visit tenants rather than only for pleasure rides. Mrs Jenkinson and I have been preparing baskets and delivering them. They have been met with great pleasure. I think one day I shall enjoy being mistress of Rosings."

"You are already mistress of Rosings," the colonel said, appearing at her side to interrupt her speech. "Only your mother would not like you to consider it."

Elizabeth smiled at the pair of them and excused herself to ready for their departure. After changing into travelling clothes, Elizabeth stepped out of her chamber and gave one final nostalgic glance down the long corridor. Lydia appeared at that moment, wrapping an arm around Elizabeth's waist and sighing.

"I shall miss you," Lydia said quietly.

Elizabeth leaned back to look her sister in the eye. "You know, I should thank you for jumping out of that window in Kent. In a roundabout way, I would not be married today if you had not."

Lydia laughed outright. "Perchance you should thank Mr Collins, because in a very *direct* way, he was the reason I left. And do not dissemble, Lizzy. I will have you know that I never jumped! I climbed out."

Elizabeth squeezed her youngest sister, told her to write, and gave her a kiss on the cheek.

After the breakfast, the newly wedded couple travelled to London and arrived by late afternoon. They spent their time upon arrival reading and resting in the library. A more thorough tour of the house was planned for the next morning.

Elizabeth was overwhelmed with the collection of books, eventually selecting a short stack of tomes which she directed be sent up to her private sitting room. That the indulgence of the collection would always be at her disposal was overwhelming.

Even with all her choices that evening, she decided to continue reading the book her father had told her to bring to London, but could not focus on the words. Simply having the opportunity to sit near her new husband with no one else about was a distraction, and she eventually excused herself to dress for dinner.

Mr Darcy led her up a grand staircase to her chambers. She was reluctant to release his hand when he said goodbye at her door, holding tightly as he attempted to move down the corridor to his own room. She smiled teasingly and pulled him back to her.

He seemed pleasantly surprised at her playfulness, pressing her back against the wall and asking quietly, "Can I help you with something, Mrs Darcy?" He arched his eyebrow in a suggestive way that rendered her unable to contain her laughter.

She placed her hand on his cheek, running it slowly back through his hair and twisting her fingers into his curls. "It is not help I require."

His eyes darkened, and he placed a finger over her mouth to illustrate his desire for her to 'shh'. Pressing his body against hers, he kissed his wife in a manner that made all of her teasing melt away, and she was left with only yearning. Heat poured through her body, and her knees became weak. When he released her, satiated and smug, he backed away slowly and whispered, "I shall see you at dinner."

Left in the corridor, out of breath and flushed with anticipation, Elizabeth leaned her head back against the wall and counted her many blessings—her husband's spontaneity being one of them.

She entered her room and rang for Jones, her newly appointed lady's maid, who ordered her into a hot bath that smelled of citrus. After helping her dress and towelling her hair dry, Jones laid a gown on her bed for dinner before being dismissed. Yes, she would enjoy the luxuries of being Mrs Darcy.

Dressed in only a shift and a new, silk dressing gown, Elizabeth curled up in an armchair near the fire with her hair fanned out on the back of the chair to help it finish drying more quickly. Observing the spacious and tastefully decorated room, she could not but feel grateful for the path her life had taken; nevertheless, she remained a little uneasy surrounded by such elegant, expensive things, which now belonged to her. This part of accepting Mr Darcy's hand was still a bit shocking.

While musing on the lovely, comfortable room, she heard a soft knock. Elizabeth turned to face each of the four doors in rapid succession. The knock had not come from the door to the corridor, nor the door that led to her private sitting room. Perhaps her dressing room? But no. This knock came from the door that adjoined her husband's chambers. Her eyes went wide with anticipation.

"Come," she called quietly while pulling her dressing gown more tightly over her shoulders.

An immensely pleased looking Darcy entered her room.

"I think you mean to intimidate me, entering my rooms before I have dressed for dinner!" She wrapped her arms around her waist as she stood.

He looked at her with hunger in his eyes. His intent was clear, and her heart began beating quickly. Thankfully, she was reminded of her aunt Gardiner's kind and thoughtful explanation for the night to come. *Calm yourself.*

He approached slowly. "There is no reason to dress. I have just asked Cook to send our meal up to my sitting room. I have no plans to depart these rooms for many hours, my love. I hope you will not be too disappointed."

Elizabeth laughed uneasily at his boldness. "What will your servants think of me! Not attending my first meal at Darcy House?"

"I think we can consider it your second meal. You did take refreshments when we arrived, did you not?"

His impatience was enjoyable to see so displayed. She smiled and responded, "You missed me already?"

His eyes softened at the question, and he pulled her into a warm embrace. Cupping her face in his hand, he said with loving sincerity, "Elizabeth, my dearest, I believe I missed you long before I met you."

Elizabeth already knew she loved her husband. He was a complicated man, but she enjoyed studying new aspects of his personality—especially the surprisingly eager gentleman that stood before her. She looked forward to learning all she could about this wonderful man over the years.

She still felt some little shame knowing she had questioned his character so frequently in their earliest acquaintance and even later in Kent. She had been surrounded by others who, in their cruelty and deception, made her second guess his nature. Their duplicitous behaviour had made her uncertain what was up and what was down. And she had learned that duplicity can come in many shapes and forms—a broken friend, a controlling aunt, or a cruel parson. Their changing ways and deceit were the very opposite of Mr Darcy, who was simply hard to know—a private man who preferred to show his truest self only to those he trusted and loved.

Studying Mr Darcy was to be the joy of her life—the charitable landowner of Pemberley, the generous brother, the giving husband and, hopefully, the playful father; and perhaps, if she was exceedingly blessed, even the doting grandfather.

Elizabeth wrapped her arms tightly around his waist as a flood of sudden self-awareness rushed through her. She searched her husband's eyes for the answers to her uncertainties. When she found only acceptance and approval and devotion in their depths, she relaxed into his comforting embrace. She was home.

EPILOGUE

April 1830

"Mother, they are come!" Henry Collins, now a nearly grown young gentleman of seventeen years, called into the parlour.

"Who is come, my dear?" Charlotte looked up from her mending to respond to her son.

"The entire Easter party. I saw their carriages proceeding through the village on my way home!"

Charlotte set her mending down on the table beside her and quietly responded, "Let us not inform your father just yet."

Her son leaned down to place a kiss on her cheek and nodded his acquiescence. "Of course. I shall change now. I long to see Bennet."

Charlotte looked wistfully at her son and remembered the joy of spending time with her friends during her formative years. Henry had long developed a friendship with Bennet Darcy, the eldest of Elizabeth's five children, and she was relieved for it. The connexion alone would benefit her son's future, but thankfully, the family had many times invited Henry to visit Pemberley for long periods in the summer, where Mr Darcy spent countless hours with both his own son and Henry, preparing them to be landowners as their futures dictated. As long as Mr Bennet still lived, this was the only first-hand experience Henry would attain, and she was grateful for it.

Charlotte had no desire to bring their arrival to her husband's attention, though they visited each Easter, and her husband was well acquainted with the church calendar. She dreaded the particular agitation which afflicted her husband when the Darcys were near; one might have believed the passing of the years would have dimmed his fury, but somehow it had not.

This time of year found him prone to violent outbursts, which included the throwing of objects at the wall or spending hours scribbling down his discontent in his journals. He still claimed that his deceitful cousin had usurped Anne de Bourgh's place in the world—though Anne's happiness in her own marriage seemed pleasing enough to the lady herself.

Mrs Anne Fitzwilliam, née de Bourgh, married her husband some two months after the Darcys were wed. Once called Colonel Fitzwilliam, Mr Fitzwilliam was now simply their landlord, and a friendly one at that. The Fitzwilliams had two sons who were of an age with Henry, named Paul and Owen. The three boys had grown up together, and the Fitzwilliams allowed for a close relationship, as they were aware that Henry's inheritance would raise his position in society one day.

Also presumably in the entourage of carriages that rolled into Kent that day would be the Baldwins, Jane Bennet's large brood. If she recollected correctly, Charlotte would say the Baldwins married in early 1813, but she was never good with dates—and of course, she had not been in attendance for their nuptials. Charlotte allowed herself a small smile, imagining that her son would be eager to see Beth Baldwin, Jane's eldest and most beautiful daughter. *Henry is much too young to think of marriage, and I should not be thinking of matchmaking!*

A thud in the next room chased Charlotte's brief smile away. Was it her husband? Had Mr Collins heard the news already? Though the man had not spoken in eighteen years, he had found other ways in which to communicate, mostly through his extensive collection of journals. Charlotte found that living with him and enduring his vile temper was best met by turning her attention to other employment, pretending she did not feel the bruises he inflicted upon her, and adding a few drops of laudanum to his tea.

This had kept his anger at bay for some years, but his growing desire for the sluggish effects of the bitter-tasting medicine had taken hold of her husband some time ago, and now the tincture was kept under lock and key, administered only by Charlotte. Of course, this too had its challenges, as he would write abusive notes demanding laudanum, notes which decried her stupidity and emphasised her worth-lessness.

The last occasion that necessitated he be medically subdued were the weeks that followed the death of Lady Catherine. Had he a voice, his mourning wails would have been heard by all and sundry, likely two counties over.

She rose and went to the window, spotting her husband in their modest garden; she decided to make herself scarce above stairs. Sheets of paper and journals littered the corner of their bedchamber that Mr Collins called his 'study' and signalled to Charlotte that the impending arrival of guests at Rosings was not lost on her husband.

Bending to pick up the crumpled papers and place some of his old journals back onto his desk, Charlotte could not help but feel pulled to glance at his recent journal entry, laid open for anyone to find.

April 6, 1830

My cousins from the North will soon enter our fair county once again, bringing with them their shame and disgrace. If Lady Catherine were still living it would be a burden to her as well, I am certain. The dower house now sits empty of her authority and good sense, and I find myself once again mourning our society's great loss.

If I were still installed in the pulpit, I would rejoice in providing much-needed guidance to our esteemed visitors—for direction, they certainly all require, I am sure. But God has deemed me unfit for that position, halting my tongue for all time.

I am certain God removed my ability to speak as a small penance for my not preventing Elizabeth's treachery. As I see it now, I should have been struck down just then, but God showed me mercy, and I shall rely on the senses he has allowed me to retain to properly atone for my sins.

He that committeth sin is of the devil, and I believe God will call in my cousin for her sins in due time—her first: denying me her hand. Perhaps He shall use me as an instrument to bring

*about her punishment. I shall be watchful in the coming days
for a sign to make good on God's promises.*

Wide eyed, Charlotte dropped the journal where she had
found it, as if it had been a snake come up through the grass
to bite her. She had known their visit would make him rest-
less, but she had not comprehended the depth of his resentment and obsession. The serpent in the grass was certainly
not Elizabeth, and she felt it was to her to ensure her friend
had a safe visit to Kent.

Charlotte rushed downstairs and called for some fresh
tea, while she quietly retrieved the last of the laudanum from
her stores. Patting the small phial in her pocket, Charlotte
felt certain God would forgive her for helping her husband
rest.

By dinner, the tea was finding its purpose, making her
husband lethargic and crippling his motor skills. Henry
called out with concern when his father dropped his spoon of
soup into his lap due to nodding off at the table.

Charlotte ushered him up to bed and came back to the
table, where she found her distraught son.

"I do not understand what comes over him each year
when the Darcys and Baldwins visit," Henry murmured with
concern. "He is not fit to be seen!"

"Yes, I know. Let him find some rest, and perhaps he will
feel more fit tomorrow," Charlotte answered gently.

"I have turned the other cheek for many years, Mother,
but this year I believe I shall say something. They accept me
but snub my own father—and it pains him deeply! And for
what? A defect that was derived from a riding accident?
Would they snub me as well if I too were injured by a horse?"

Charlotte smiled. He was a good boy, even if he did try to

defend a monster. "There is more to it than that, Henry—and you know it."

"I know our place in society is a fickle one, but my father shall be the master of Longbourn one day—a gentleman—a landowner. Is he not their own cousin?"

"He is their cousin, but it is a complicated history. It is not by accident that you are summoned to Rosings alone during their visits."

"And what of the history?"

Charlotte felt unprepared to share such an account with her son. It did not paint her in the best light, and she sought, above all, to ensure that her part in their shared history did not affect her son's prospects.

"I had imagined we would be settled at Longbourn by the time you came of age. I—I imagined you entering university the son of a landowner. That will likely not be. Mr Bennet is as hale as ever and—never mind, I only mean that you will encounter many people in society who will judge you for your parentage, so you must prepare yourself for that truth; however, this is not one of those times. You have ever been accepted by the Fitzwilliams, Darcys, and Baldwins. And I am thankful for it—more grateful than I can express. The ill will towards your father is not because of our place in society. You can be certain of that."

"You are not answering my question." Henry stood from the table and began to pace the room.

"You have seen how close Marjorie and Margaret Darcy are to their cousin, Beth Baldwin?"

"Of course."

"That is how close I once was to Mrs Darcy and Mrs Baldwin, although we were not separated by twenty miles as they are. We could walk to one anothers' houses every day. We could send notes and expect a response within the hour," she said wistfully. "They were my closest friends."

Henry sat down, his eyebrows raised in question. "But you never call on them when they visit."

"No. I do not. Though, I do occasionally exchange letters with Mrs Darcy."

Henry was deep in thought, the wheels turning in his mind. With Elizabeth, Charlotte was able to be frank and honest in a way she was unable to be with any other living being. Their correspondence had often felt an escape to Charlotte. Elizabeth knew enough of Mr Collins and their lives that Charlotte was not required to hide the truth nor embellish it. It was by design that they kept their letter writing private. Charlotte did not mind that their friendship was not publicly recognised.

Charlotte could not resist the pleading look of curiosity in her child's eyes and sighed her acquiescence. "Before your father offered for me, he first offered for his cousin, Mrs Darcy. He was humiliated by her refusal, even after our marriage. In the spring of 1812, just before you were born, Mrs Darcy came to stay with us in the parsonage, while your father was still rector. While she was visiting, she and Mr Darcy began to fall in love, and they would sometimes meet secretly for walks in the groves. Your father and I were unhappy when we discovered it, because Lady Catherine was convinced that Mr Darcy should marry her daughter, Mrs Fitzwilliam. And we greatly believed that her happiness, and that of her daughter, was tied to our own contentment."

Charlotte trailed off, and her son nudged her to go on. "Your father and I—we made her miserable. He, because he was still humiliated by her very public rejection, and myself, because I thought her usurping the heiress of Rosings would bring shame upon our household. Not to mention—well, I was terribly envious of the attentions she was receiving from such a wealthy man after her rejection of the man I accepted. Does that make sense?"

Henry nodded in response.

"For your father, I believe his hatred runs even deeper. I think it best we not mention this conversation to him. Their very presence in Kent is upsetting to him, as you saw for yourself."

Henry nodded in agreement and responded quietly, "Why do they accept me?"

"Well, Henry, I believe that has more to do with Longbourn," she said with a smile. "And I am grateful for the attention and education they have provided you over the years. I am truly undeserving of their kindness—but you, my boy, you are." Charlotte smiled and, kissing her dear son on his head, excused herself to retire early.

At sunrise, Charlotte was startled awake by the sound of approaching horses and the voices of shouting men. Turning over to see if the noise had woken her husband, she was surprised to find him missing from their bed. She quickly donned a simple morning dress and pulled a heavy shawl around her shoulders before making her way outside.

"Mrs Collins!" She opened the door to find Mr Fitzwilliam astride a large, black stallion, nearly upon her doorstep. The gentleman dismounted, tipped his hat to her, and gestured something to the men behind him. Mr Darcy and some servants began to approach.

"Mrs Collins," Mr Darcy said, removing his hat and nodding politely. His expression was grave, and Charlotte felt her stomach spin in anticipation of the news they carried.

"Good morning," Charlotte began hesitantly. "I hope all is well—"

Mr Fitzwilliam stepped forward. "Pardon me, madam. We bring sad tidings to you this morning."

Charlotte's fear began to creep up from her stomach to her throat, squeezing off her ability to breathe. *Was it Henry?*

"Your husband has been in an accident," Mr Fitzwilliam said gently, reaching out to take her shaking hand.

"George here," he gestured to a young servant in Rosings livery who had stepped forward, "was doing his morning rounds and discovered your husband in the bushes that line the south wing. We are yet uncertain what he was doing there, but at first glance, we think your husband took a fall into the hedge...and we summoned a physician, but he did not arrive in time. I am sorry to tell you, Mrs Collins, that you husband is dead."

The breath she was holding released like a strong current, unravelling through her and forcibly making her sway on her feet. She strengthened her grip on Mr Fitzwilliam's hand to gain her composure.

"We have laid him out at Rosings, and we would be more than happy to have him brought here today—or to have a physician examine him— whatever you wish."

"He fell? Into the bushes?" Charlotte was unable to exert energy into a more thoughtful question.

Mr Fitzwilliam looked warily at Mr Darcy before responding. "Yes, ma'am. We believe he might have been attempting to gain entry to the house—to reach one of the lower balconies of the guest wing. We are not certain why he did not approach one of the doors. It was likely dark. No one saw anything. It was not the fall that harmed him, but a large kitchen knife he carried in his jacket. It was unsheathed. We believe it cut his leg when he fell. The gash was deep."

Perhaps He shall use me as an instrument to bring about her punishment. I shall be watchful in the coming days for a sign to make good on God's promises. Charlotte remembered her husband's dreadful remarks in his journal and lost command of her balance. Relief and fear poured through her in rapid succession. Had he attempted to harm Elizabeth?

Charlotte had to be helped into the house while the gentlemen went to wake Henry. Her maid of all work, Rosie, arrived some time later and put a kettle on, providing refreshment for the gentlemen who were gathered with Henry, making arrangements for her husband.

Charlotte sat in a haze of disbelief before she finally rose to make herself a cup of tea, allowing herself a few drops of laudanum. And while the morning had only just begun, she took her bitter beverage to her bedchamber and retired for the day.

Not two weeks later found Charlotte alone in the churchyard, wearing black from head to toe, staring at the heap of dirt that lay above the remains of her husband.

She knew a tumult of feelings when she thought of their life together and his impact on her own. She knelt to lay down a cutting of roses and stood quickly, tears blurring the edge of her eyesight. She was being such a ninny! Why was she weeping? Theirs had been a hard and complicated marriage, but he was still her husband—the only one she would ever know, and now she was alone in the world.

Suddenly, a small, dainty, gloved hand grasped hers and held tight, causing a gasp to escape Charlotte's lips. She turned to take in the form of Elizabeth Darcy. Lips puckered in her frustration for her outburst and unrelenting tears, she merely nodded at her friend, who responded by squeezing her hand.

Charlotte looked over her shoulder and saw two carriages with the Darcy crest stopped just past the hedge.

"We were on our way to London, and I saw you here. I could not leave before expressing my condolences for your loss once again," Elizabeth told her gently, and wiped a tear from Charlotte's cheek with her handkerchief.

"Thank you, Mrs Darcy."

Charlotte watched as Elizabeth turned to look at her husband, who seemed a bit overrun by their youngest boys who had exited the carriages and were now running about in the churchyard. A glance passed between them, and Charlotte saw a hint of a smile on the man's usually grave face. The exchange, wordless as it was, had clearly communicated much between the two and pulled at Charlotte's heart. What would it have been like to have a marriage of such understanding? To perceive another's thoughts as they had in a mere glance?

"Do not worry for yourself or Henry." Elizabeth turned back to her, looking her in the eye. "I have spoken to the Fitzwilliams, and they would be pleased if you kept on as a tenant until Henry has completed university. Should you not wish to remove to Lucas Lodge—"

"Thank you, but it is all arranged. We leave for Hertfordshire at the end of the month. John and Mary have been very obliging. Besides, it will be good for Henry to spend some time in Meryton society." Charlotte hoped her voice did not betray her nerves about the changes soon to occur in her life. She turned back to view the newly placed marker at her husband's grave. Mr William Collins. She hoped that he would appreciate that his final resting place was so near to Lady Catherine's.

Squeezing her hand once again to gain her attention, Elizabeth added, "I am happy to hear it. And I will look forward to your letters."

"Of course," Charlotte responded. "Always."

Elizabeth nodded and once again looked back to her husband and gave a nod. He was soon ushering their children and nannies back into their carriages.

Charlotte watched as Elizabeth approached her husband. Mr Darcy's hand came to rest softly at the small of her back, guiding her to the road. He bent to say something to her, and was rewarded by Elizabeth shifting to lean herself into his shoulder, as they approached their carriage. Elizabeth turned to wave at Charlotte, Mr Darcy tipped his hat to her, and they were off.

Watching the dust cloud that followed their carriages down the lane, Charlotte found herself overwhelmed by the feeling that she was ending a season of her life—once again finding herself standing on the precipice of what was before and what would come after. The unknown provided her some apprehension, but she felt hopeful all the same. She had completed her task as a wife, and what stood before her held the promise of being a life of her own.

Elizabeth leaned into her husband, grateful they had a conveyance to themselves. Bennet and Marjorie rode on horseback alongside the carriages, and Margaret would assist the nannies with the younger boys in the carriage that followed.

"Is it strange that I am relieved now that Mr Collins is gone?" Elizabeth asked quietly.

"No, my dear. He brought naught but chaos over the

years. Besides, now we can look forward to Henry's keen oversight of Longbourn. We no longer require all the legal documentation we put in place to protect the estate from your cousin's destruction. Henry will be an ideal custodian of the land and of your childhood home."

Elizabeth squeezed his hand. "I know it is too soon, but I would wager that Beth will one day be mistress of Longbourn."

"Come, Elizabeth! Beth will not be out for at least three years. And you know better than to be the meddling aunt." He offered her a sly grin that told her he did not exactly disagree with her presumption.

She laughed, and he kissed her forehead.

She snuggled in a bit closer, and at length, he asked her, "Would Ben and Jane approve of the match?"

"Of course! Henry is nothing like his father...besides which, we must start thinking about the prospects of *all* of Jane's daughters, or she will turn into my mother, despairing of their futures and calling for her salts to calm her nerves."

"Surely between all your sisters and my own, we can find enough strapping and industrious sons to take on each of the Baldwin girls," he said with a chuckle.

She smiled, imagining their progeny all lined up in a row. Besides Jane's four daughters, the Bennet sisters had proudly produced far more sons than they ever thought possible, though none of them feared an entailment tied to their homes.

All of the Bennet sisters had married, with the exception of Lydia. True to her promise those many years ago, she spent her time travelling between Longbourn and the homes of her sisters. She spoiled her many nephews and nieces and spent much of her time writing. She had dreams of being an author—always writing fanciful, romantic stories that Mr

Collins would never have approved of, but Elizabeth had copied a scene or two into letters for Charlotte over the years.

She had recently written a tale with a vain, red-headed villainess named Caroline Bington that had brought tears of laughter to even Jane's eyes. Though so many years had passed, Elizabeth was relieved that the reminder did not bring pain to her elder sister.

She should not have been surprised. The Bingleys were of a different time—a time *before* Mrs Darcy and Mrs Baldwin— and both sisters would agree that the best of their lives had come decidedly *after*. Jane was happy in her marriage, and Elizabeth could not imagine their lives otherwise. It did pain her to know that Darcy's old friend did not enjoy the same happiness. His wife and sister devoted most of their time to entertaining in town, while he spent his time alone at his estate in Surrey. Elizabeth was happy that her husband continued the acquaintance when time allowed, though it was never what it had been before their marriage.

Darcy released another chuckle, and Elizabeth was brought back to the present, looking at him curiously. "And what, pray, has you so amused, my dear?" she asked.

He leaned in to whisper in her ear, "I was thinking of this morning."

She blushed at the memory, and he smiled smugly, continuing to chuckle.

Elizabeth reached for his hand and wound her fingers in his grasp, enjoying her own recollection of their morning. It was long a tradition of theirs to sneak off into the forest and revisit the glade from their courtship during their visits to Kent. But this particular morning had felt wildly reminiscent of their first, tortuous kisses shared in that space—needy and longing and fervent kisses that had left her speechless and her appearance in a state of disarray. Even after nearly eighteen years, her husband could make her heart pound and her breath quicken with anticipation.

"I never would have thought I would long for visits to Rosings," she whispered back, arching an eyebrow in his direction. She too could be smug.

He laughed, "That is the truth."

"Mmm. I shall look forward to our return." Elizabeth pulled the curtains to assure their privacy and settled more deeply against her husband.

"As shall I."

Theirs had not always been an easy life, but their shared affection was steady and constant and sound. And if one were to peel back the layers of all they had learned and accomplished together, they would find at the centre, an unexpected but beautiful friendship that began in the early morning hours of a shared springtime in Kent.

ACKNOWLEDGMENTS

To my mother, Vicky—Without you, this book would never have been written. Thank you for encouraging me to write this story, for being my beta reader, and especially for listening during long, rambling phone calls when I needed guidance to complete this project. I only hope I can show Ben the same kind of confidence in his abilities throughout his whole life.

To Amy D'Orazio—Your brilliant storytelling skills pushed me to tell a stronger story and made me a better writer. I will be forever grateful for what this story evolved into because of you.

To Jennifer Altman—Your keen eye and thoughtful recommendations were a gift to this story. Thank you for identifying the loose ends and encouraging me to resolve every 'why' to the benefit of all of our beloved characters.

And thank you to everyone at Quills & Quartos Publishing for their faith in this story.

To my husband, John, and son, Benjamin—You two are my world. Thank you for giving me the encouragement (and let's be real, the *time*) to achieve this goal. I love you most of most.

To my Book Club girls—I will never be described as an obstinate, headstrong girl, like our dear heroine, but I am thankful that I've surrounded myself with so many smart, hilarious, and fearless ladies who inspire me to be my best self but also love me for exactly who I am. Thank you for keeping me reading all these years. But, let's be honest, we don't meet for the books.

Special thanks also to my sister and cousins for keeping me afloat these last two years. Where would I be without your support? I love you all.

ABOUT THE AUTHOR

Paige Badgett lives in the Kansas City area with her husband and son. By day, she is a communications professional for a technology corporation. In her free time, she can be often found reading historical romance novels and stories inspired by Jane Austen—as many as she can get her hands on.

Paige is a lifelong storyteller who credits her love of reading to her mother and her long-standing book club. *Against Every Expectation* is Paige's first novel.

facebook.com/paige.badgettauthor

twitter.com/paigebadgett

goodreads.com/paigebadgett

linkedin.com/in/paigebadgett

Made in United States
North Haven, CT
16 July 2023

39136937R00189